MAGGIE UNDEFEATED

"We're all here, Maggie," Maiden Hell said. "The Warriors are ready to roll. What's the word?"

Maggie took out a mascara pencil. Glancing in a tiny mirror, she ran the pencil once over her eyes where her eyebrows used to be. Blinked to make sure her artificial eyelashes were still in place. She passed her steady sloe-eyed gaze over her Warriors. While the others strapped on elbow pads, she pulled on a helmet with a single stripe.

"Is the Thunderbird popped?" Maggie asked.

The Warriors nodded. "For the victory celebration."

"The Anthrax Pack is stupid. *Let's roll.*"

"Roberts' [Adventures of Maggie, the Radiated Lesbian Nun] is a fast paced narrative filled with...sarcasm, quirkiness and screwball circumstance... Happy to recommend for those not easily dismayed, repulsed or dazed." —*Authorsden.com*

"Nuts!" —*SiriusReviews.com*

Dedicated to

Wild Bill Walker

The Warriors

by
Glenn Lazar Roberts

Dark Lotus Books

www.equuspublishing.com

This work is speculative fiction intended for entertainment only. All characters and events are fictional and any resemblance to any actual persons is coincidental.

ISBN: 978-0-9675809-7-5

THE WARRIORS

or

THE RADIATED LESBIAN NUN MEETS EVIL MIMES

'HOW THE HOLY POLKA & NON-PATRIARCHAL FAIR TRADE ASTRONOMY SAVED MAGGIE FROM SIRIUS TIMES IN GRIFFITH PARK'

Book 3

ADVENTURES OF MAGGIE, THE RADIATED LESBIAN NUN

Episode 1

"*Not fair.*"

The voice penetrated a wall of smoke hanging over the entrance to the Pollo Ranchero Casino & Bowlarama, briefly obscuring the neon nun on the façade above, whose exposed derriere flashed blue and red. The smiling nun winked, enticing new bowlers to compete for the Casino's 'Special Reward'.

An olive-skinned juggernaut burst from the smoke. Skating down a wheelchair ramp, the figure rolled to the sidewalk.

From inside the casino rang a voice. "Bitch. I'll get you where the sun don't shine."

"You wish you could," the skater called back.

Madam G-Spot exited waving away the smoke with a large fan which she kept by the front entrance for such occasions and watched as Maggie's derriere dwindled in the bright morning. Madam G-Spot sighed and turned her preternaturally spherical body around and her little stick-legs hobbled back into the Casino where she joined the other nuns in putting out the fire with extinguishers.

Sloe eyes, the inner edges of which reflected the merest hint of oriental origin, combined with expanses of dark-hued skin that evoked leaden seas and overcast skies, matched indigo-dyed hair descending midway between ears and shoulders, the curled fringe bobbing with each rhythmic impulse.

Sweet pokelicious
Likes her nopalitos
No sinful water man
Will touch her little piggy toes

Up ahead—two cholos with red bandanas sauntered up one part of the walk, leaving most of the way clear. They paused.

"Manigua, *coge* some juice for me, dog."

"*Coge* yourself, Manuel. You got your own."

Kicking a rock, Manuel pulled a drink out of a parachute

pocket. Hand in air, he paused. A muscled figure was barreling upon them. His first flush was to hurl a lewd invitation but this was quickly displaced by a mental image of a flashing red light. The figure swelled; its almond eyes stared intently into his.

He managed one step—a shoulder slammed him, crashing Manuel into his friend. Their drinks hurled into the air, and as the two cholos tumbled, the drinks exploded like bombs on the concrete.

"Hey, puta! Come back. I'm gonna kick your gringo ass!"

Manigua put a hand on Manuel's arm. "Don' do that, fool. Don you know who that is?"

Staring harder, Manuel grew quiet. "Why didn you tell me, dog? I don need that kind of trouble."

Life was good.

Minutes passed and the Juggernaut entered Venice Boulevard, and nearing Venice Beach, arrived beneath a large sign displaying another neon nun on the marquee: Holy Rollers Derby Club.

Maggie rolled inside.

A derby-girl elbowed two companions. "She's here." Quickly they finished strapping on elbow and wrist pads and grabbed acrylic helmets.

With a dull squeak, Maggie braked to a full stop.

"The Anthrax Pack is already in the rink," said a roller derby girl with red shoulder-length bushy pigtails, pink corset, and pleated skirt, sporting blue over black leather.

"We'll get em, Bloody Mary," a derby girl added, one side of her head shaved. "They don't call me Maiden Hell for nothing." She flexed one arm with a tattoo of a medieval coffin, a white skull encased within, and inspected the star on her helmet, designating her as jammer.

A third finished strapping her pads and checked her own pink corset and dark blue skirt. She perched on wheels. “Vexinator and Pussy Kicker have one skate in the rink. They’re ready to roll.”

Maiden Hell passed an urgent glance over the Holy Roller Rink where several more roller derby teams were putting the finishing touches on battle equipment and preparing to claim the field from whoever won the current match. “Here comes Thrill Killa, Queen Cobra, and Hatecrime Hattie.” Several more pink corsets rolled up to join. “And Nite Shade, Suki Vicious, and Crybaby Baiter.” All wore pink corsets with blue flaps over black leather skirts that lifted with every roll to reveal tight buns.

“We’re all here, Maggie,” Maiden Hell said. “The Warriors are ready to roll. What’s the word?”

Maggie took out a mascara pencil. Glancing in a tiny mirror, she ran the pencil once over her eyes where her eyebrows used to be. Blinked to make sure her artificial eyelashes were still in place. She passed her steady sloe-eyed gaze over her Warriors. While the others strapped on elbow pads, she pulled on a helmet with a single stripe.

“Is the Thunderbird popped?” Maggie asked.

The Warriors nodded. “For the victory celebration.”

“The Anthrax Pack is stupid. Let’s roll.”

“Yeah!” Bursting with energy, the Warriors tore up the ground and the first five exploded onto the rink, Maggie not bothering with elbow pads or the mewling protests of the water-loving referees. Frantic not to be ignored, one referee uselessly blew a whistle just as Maggie and three other Warriors blew past the pivot line, Maiden Hell blasting from behind as Jammer.

In seconds, the first lap was done. Shoulders collided. With Maggie body-slamming Anthrax skaters, the Warriors soon cleared a path for Maiden Hell—the Anthrax pivot Primal Fear slid into Maiden Hell, the pivot's zombie makeup a perfect match for Maiden's tattoo coffin. Maiden glanced at Maggie, who nodded. Maiden thrust an elbow into Primal's neck and sent her rival tumbling under two Anthrax blockers, both of whom joined their teammate face-down on the track, leaving teeth and gore.

Angry referees swooshed Maiden to the penalty box. Nite Shade took her place, and as no Lead Jammer was yet designated, Maggie seized the lead, bludgeoning the Anthrax Jammer with hips and shoulder till the Warriors' own blockers owned the track.

Point after point scored.

The Anthrax Pack strove to reverse the inevitable by pitching over Pussy Kicker, jabbing her from behind, and by tripping up Nite Shade—which only sent the Anthrax rollers to the Box and triggered the entry of Crybaby Baiter and Suki Vicious into the Jam.

Nothing could stop the Warriors. Two minutes gone in seconds, Maggie rolled over the finish line, sealing the Jam and leading her Warriors to victory once again.

Undefeated.

Rolling to their "bivouac"—as Maggie insisted on calling it—they popped the bottles of Thunderbird wine and drenched their faces and necks in its life-giving essence.

"Happy inoculation," laughed Bloody Mary at the bruised and bleeding Anthrax bunch across the rink where they sat, staring back moodily. "You should know better than to challenge the Warriors."

"Go blind and skate in traffic," drifted the reply.

"That's the only way you'll ever win, crybabies," yelled Crybaby Baiter, re-tying her fishnet hose to her blue flaps.

Maiden laughed. "Never trust eight wheels and a smile."

Thrill Killa drained her Thunderbird and flung it behind, almost hitting a referee before it landed in a trash can. The rest of the Warriors guffawed at the referee's protests and shot the finger at Trash Can, who rolled past with her own finger extended, and true to her name, holding a trash can.

"I've got rink rash again," spewed Hatecrime Hattie. She glanced at the flat track where blood was still being cleaned. "Leave it, Pedro. Some of that's mine. It's a sacrament."

"Hey, Hatecrime. Don't you ever get tired of insulting people?" asked Suki Vicious.

Hatecrime snorted and wiped her nose. "Worried about your yellow ass, Suki? I'll make it red any day you like."

"You'll never whip this black ass, Hatecrime," said Queen Cobra, rattling her reggae braids. She adjusted the metal bands on her brassiere and covertly removed the brass strips from her elbows. Wouldn't do to be caught in clear violation, red-faced referees or no.

"Not unless you let your guard down."

"Nobody could ever accuse you of niceness," said Vexinator.

"I'm an equal-opportunity hater. If you can't take it, get off the rink." She rinsed the cuts on her arms with Thunderbird, arousing a look of frustration from Pedro as the high-octane liquid splashed on the changing area floor mixed with blood. Thunderbird wine drenched the tattoos of all of Hatecrime's Exes, each woman's face carefully tattooed over with the universal red ban of a slash inside a circle.

Maggie circled clockwise.

"Queer bait," taunted someone from the Anthrax Pack.

"You wish you could," Maggie purred, bending over with a backward wink. That silenced them.

"Stupid fucks," Maggie said. She slopped wine over her ample breasts with a sly glance at the Anthrax bunch who she knew were staring. "Don't they know? *Nobody* messes with the Squatch." The Warriors all looked at their team leader with admiration as she flexed her rock-hard biceps, gliding around her crew with as little effort as a seagull.

And her crew it was. None equaled the Squatch in pivoting a path or blocking foolishly ambitious rivals unfamiliar with her reputation for jamming through to victory over ranks of mangled derby girls. And few could keep their eyes off her chiseled features, Arnold derriere, and bulldog buxom northern exposure. "Pop the Thunderbird" was all they needed to hear to whoop them up for another successful Jam that would sweep the rink, led by their Leader, Maggie.

The whoops raised. No one had ever beat The Warriors.

"Gotta roll now," dropped Queer Bait. "It's class time for kiddies."

The Warriors leveled more admiring stares at the Juggernaut, even more impressed with their leader for the fact that she was rumored to be a 'perfessor'. If not for their allergy to mortarboards and enclosed spaces, her crew might have followed her. As it was, Maggie accepted her usual ride from the UCLA minority recruitment vehicle that pulled smoothly in front of the Holy Roller Rink—a black limo stretched to the max, complete with uniformed driver who rushed to open the back door for Maggie, with a "Thang ya very much, ma'am."

Inside she found mini bottles of red Thunderbird Wine, her favorite food group. And yet another envelope of those puzzling slips of paper called 'cash' from the College. Minutes later she was skating across the UCLA campus.

Maggie entered a classroom and deftly rolled down carpeted steps to where a podium was set up for her, two smiling scarecrow-thin woman professors instructing the students to rise and clap.

"Students," said one of the professors by way of introduction, "please welcome our school's resident Hairy S. Truman Memorial Chair for Non-Earth Raping Gay Feminist Sasquatch Studies, former Roads Scholar, Professor Magdalene P. Squatch, here to enlighten us on her latest research in the new and exciting field of Sasquatch Feminist Studies." The students clapped and hooted as Maggie took the podium.

Putting the podium back down, Maggie stared at the paper that the other professors had provided with topic suggestions. She turned it sideways. Upside-down. She tossed it on the floor amid instant admiring exclamations from the students.

She paused, letting the tension build. Stared up at the coffered ceiling.

Finally she looked down.

"They. . .them. . .the *stupid* ones. . ."

The students' eyes grew big.

"They don't know my struggle."

The audience grew rapt.

Maggie nodded her head knowingly—pointed the big finger.

"My struggle has been long and hard. . ."

Yes, agreed the eager listeners, the professors too watching rapturously.

"I roll *from* nowhere. . . *to* nowhere. . ." Maggie folded her arms.

Yes, yes! the eyes said.

"They don't know my pain. . .my tears. . .I cry for The Planet. . .but I keep rolling. I don't let *them* stop me. . .we know who they are: the *bad* ones. We know what they do—evil sinful men trying to drown the world in water—the Global Warmers." She raised a clenched fist. "*Not fair!*"

The students stood.

She raised her other fist. "Let the water-lovers drown in their poison. They're stupid!"

The audience cheered. Chants of "Ban Water Now!" "Stop Global Warming!" and "Up with Maggie!" resounded through the hall. Several slid skates on and tore up the carpet while popping open bottles of Thunderbird wine and cans of nopalitos in imitation of their idol, Maggie.

Making as if to skate to the door, Maggie muttered to her professor colleagues, "They passed."

One of the professors put a hand on her arm.

Maggie paused.

"Students," called the professor. "We have a special announcement today." Turning to Maggie, the professor beamed approval. "I know this is only your second lecture here at our renowned school, Professor Squatch, but our very own 'Department of Film For Smashing Nazi Earth-Rapers with English Accents', in coordination with the 'Fuck in the Backside Institute for Piece & Just Us'—recently advanced Professor Squatch's name, as our school's most outstanding scholar, to a very *special* organization. I now have the honor of announcing that. . ." She let the tension build as eyes grew bigger.

". . .that Professor Squatch has been awarded the *Nobel Peace Prize* for her exciting contributions to world peace and her outstanding standout scholarship in the field of Feminist Sasquatch Studies."

"*Gay* Feminist Sasquatch Studies," corrected Maggie.

"*Gay* Feminist Sasquatch Studies," confirmed the professor.

Everyone stood and clapped, shouting encouragement. Maggie eyed the prize. She rolled to the podium.

The hall grew quiet.

"And—My Struggle?" she inquired innocently. "What about the plight of Sasquatches everywhere? How does a prize make up for what the Bad Ones did to me and my kind?" She directed an expression of indignation and outrage at the audience. "This Mr. *No-Bull*," Maggie stumbled over the unfamiliar syllables, "What does *he* know about My Struggle? What could an evil sinful man ever know? Why should we listen to him? He's just another dead white Global Warmer." The clenched fist raised again. "Not fair. He's stupid. I say: fuck you, water-lover! You can keep your No-Bull Peace Prize—*and stuff it!*" Maggie tossed the Prize through the nearest window, shattering the glass.

The crowd went wild. Restraint thrown aside, they flung their bottles of Thunderbird wine and pickled nopalitos through the other windows and hugged each other.

Snapping up yet another fat envelope of cash ("reparations" whispered one of the professors), Maggie skipped up the carpeted steps and rolled out of the building, ignoring repeated calls for encores. Skating outside the room, she paused below a smashed window to retrieve the No-Bull Prize and stuff it into her fanny pack.

Enough playtime. She had an appointment.

Skating down Wilshire Boulevard, Maggie popped into her favorite coffee chain. The line was short. One look at Maggie and the line parted like the Red Sea. A single customer remained in front, a young man in sandals and Mohawk, silver chains hanging off his faded jeans and jacket. A quick eight-wheeled roll over his sandaled toes sent him howling to the sidelines.

Maggie had been surprised to learn that she could get an endless supply of energy served to her in paper cups by complete strangers—and for mere slips of paper. A young woman with boringly unadorned mid-length hair leveled a blank stare at Maggie.

"A regular coffee," Maggie said. She plopped down the first slip of paper that emerged from her pocket.

"Regular?"

"Yeah. Regular. As in Not Big. And Not Small."

"Big? Small?" The blank stare continued.

Maggie looked equally puzzled. "Regular, as in in-between."

Comprehension dawned. "Oh, you mean 'Tall'."

"That'll do. I'll take that."

"Coming right up." The barista hesitated. Held up the slip. "Hey. This is a hundred-dollar bill."

"Is that enough?"

"I should say so, Ma'am. Luckily I can break this today. Here's your change." The barista dumped a slew of bills and coins into Maggie's waiting hands and for a moment Maggie stood, unsure what to do with it all. The barista got busy. As Maggie stuffed the change into her fanny pack, the barista turned around and stared blankly again.

"Room for cream?"

Maggie shook her head. "Never touch it. Too white."

The dull stare continued. "Do you want room for cream?"

"I don't drink cream. I don't like it. It's stupid."

Still the barista stared uncomprehendingly, not preparing anything. "Room? Do you want room?"

"No. Just give me the coffee."

"Okay. So that's a 'no' on Room," the barista repeated. "Coming right up—no Room for Cream." A minute later and the coffee was ready.

Maggie snapped it up and rolled out, catching one toe of another slow water-lover beneath her wheels. He yelped even louder than the Mohawk.

Life was good.

In Santa Monica the Juggernaut arrived at her destination. Maggie glanced up at the sign: 'Law Firm of Gloria Warbler & Ass.' Rolling inside, she caught a glimpse of a hairy arm and a man in a suit with briefcase, quickly obscured by closing elevator doors. When the elevator came back down, Maggie rolled inside.

It opened on a suite constructed mostly of glass, a spacious view of Santa Monica Boulevard and its environs visible through the transparent windows.

Ms. Warbler met her at the door. "Right this way, my dear." She leaned close to Maggie, her red formal jacket almost touching Maggie's bulging pink corset. "And remember what I told you. Let me do the talking. No one else in this State has my experience in semi-pre-nups. I can stop palimony before it happens."

Maggie shrugged and wheeled into the conference room.

Already seated were the man in the suit with his briefcase open on the wide table before him, and a seven-foot Sasquatch draped in tailored white silk that was open down the back, showing an expanse of furry cleavage, her face shielded by a wide, elegant white hat. Maggie noted the Sasquatch's lack of facial hair—since their days together at Mount St. Helens, Gilda, her Ex-, had taken up shaving.

"My client," Gilda's lawyer said, his bald head gleaming, "in accordance with the recent law issued by the State of California, in its wisdom requiring persons to agree affirmatively in writing before engaging in any risky personal relationship, would like it clearly spelled out what exactly is to be involved in her relationship with Ms. Squatch—"

"*Professor* Squatch," Ms. Warbler corrected sharply. "Don't think you can denigrate my client, Snippet, by just barging into my offices and dropping insults. We won't stand for it."

"Nobody intended to denigrate your client, Warbler."

"That's *Ms*. Warbler, thank you Snippet," yelled Gloria.

"Well, that's *Mr.* Snippet, thank you *Ms*. Warbler."

Warbler leaned forward on her elbows and raised her

voice higher. "You wanna go to the mat already, Snippet? Just say the word!"

"Whine all you want, Gloria. It won't get you a thing."

Both lawyers growled, inching forward on their elbows, noses almost touching.

A clerk walked in with coffee and donuts.

"Oh, look at this, Bill," Gloria announced. "You like jelly-filled, don't you?"

"Yes, I do. How nice of you to remember, Gloria." Arm in arm, Snippet and Warbler sampled the donuts and downed them with fresh coffee.

Wiping his fingers, Snippet returned to the task at hand. "But don't think that stuffing me with donuts, Warbler, will gain you a damned thing in negotiations."

"Only what we're entitled to, Snippet. And I assure you we'll get every damned thing we have a right to."

Gilda looked at Snippet and grunted. He leaned forward so Gilda could whisper in his ear. A moment later, he smiled and returned to Gloria.

"My client wants to make clear that the contract she is prepared to execute with Ms. Maggie P. Squatch will include not just the routine sex to be expected between consenting Sasquatches, but covers other eventualities as well."

Gloria leaned to Maggie and they whispered together.

"My client agrees to that, Mr. Snippet. How do you propose that we cover these. . .uh, eventualities?"

"Certainly by the general, Gloria."

"And don't forget by the particular, Bill."

"Agreed," said Snippet. "Can we agree then on the following: Party of the first part proposes to include in their relationship not only tactile, but embracing contact, with long walks in conifer forests."

Warbler looked at Maggie. Maggie nodded.

"My client," Warbler added, "consents to embracing contact—otherwise known as 'hugs'—with long walks in conifer forests. And party of the second part, my client, Professor Squatch, proposes to add mammary contact with torsion."

Gilda looked puzzled. Snippet looked back to Warbler.

"Titty-twisting," Warbler explained.

Snippet nodded and whispered with Gilda. He turned. "Party of the first part accepts party of the second part's proposal—on condition that the parties add thigh-to-thigh wrestling."

Maggie and Gloria whispered together. "Thigh-to-thigh wrestling accepted—on condition that kissing and wine-bathing in my client's hot tub of Thunderbird wine be included. And on condition that party of the first part does not interfere with party of the second part's exercise routine at the Holy Rollers Derby Club."

Gilda and Snippet again conferred. "My client agrees to kissing and hot tub wine-bathing, and agrees not to interfere with your client's exercise routine." Snippet fingered his tie, then ventured, "And party of the first part—my client—proposes," he risked a sidelong glance at Gilda, who stared out the window under her fashionable white hat, "that party of the second part pay for my client's exclusive residence at the Hotel d'Ivoire overlooking Malibu Beach."

Maggie frowned. She whispered with Warbler, who sniffed. "My client has an issue with that, Snippet. She resides at the Pollo Ranchero Casino & Bowlarama and has no wish to take up residence with party of the first part separately from my client's residence at the Casino."

Again Snippet fingered his tie while Gilda stared out the window. "Uh, my client, however. . .Ms. Warbler. . .is not entirely married to the idea of exclusive residence anywhere with party of the second part. My client proposes that they test out the relationship—sort of drive it around the block—before enacting that particular part of this semi-pre-nup."

Maggie's frown deepened.

Gloria conferred with her client in whispers. She turned to Snippet. "Party of the second part sees no reason why their engagement should be delayed given their long prior association in the forests of Washington State. My client was pleasantly surprised that your client decided to relocate to Southern California, but my client did not invite her and has no intent of financially supporting what appears to my client to be an extravagant lifestyle."

Again the nervous tic. Snippet swallowed and resumed, "My client reminds party of the second part that since taking up residence in Southern California, other parties have expressed an interest in my client, and that she is under no compulsion to accept your client's offer."

Gloria laid a sidelong glance at Maggie. Maggie stared out the window. "I will have to confer with my client in private over your proposals, Mr. Snippet. I think this may require some time to resolve."

Snippet blinked. Shutting his briefcase, he stood. Gilda also stood. Turning on their heels, they strode out of the conference room together. In another moment, the elevator rang and they left the building.

Descending the elevator in turn, Maggie reached the street just in time to see Gilda drive away in a spanking new white Tesla Model X. Maggie tapped the sidewalk with one skate: *How does one spell 'trouble in paradise'*?

Episode 2

"It is time to light the candles, Habiba. The sun has gone down and soon no one will be able to read our signs." The deep-voiced speaker adjusted her full-length black abayah that covered all skin except her face, and one hand scratched stubble that she had not had time to shave. Below the stubble glinted a gold chain on a bed of black chest hair, clashing garishly with her purple eyeliner.

"Hold the signs higher, Amina. Our duty is clear. We must maintain our vigil until we stop the evil ones, whatever the sacrifice." Aliyah ceased speaking and peered over a wooden railing that separated the Santa Monica pizza restaurant's outdoor patio from the sandy beach that met lapping waves a short distance away. Adjusting her chair, Aliyah glanced wistfully at their table, which was empty but for glasses of tea.

"I wasn't talking to you, Aliyah. I was talking to Habiba." Amina sniffed and turned her nose up.

Wearing her own full-length black gown, Aliyah thrust out her lower lip, a week's stubble on her own chin, another gold chain peeking from amid a rug of chest-hair. "No need to get snarky with me, girlfriend," she said. "It's not my fault the Halal Mall didn't have anything in your size. After all," Aliyah smiled with a hint of schadenfreude, "you are not their. . .*usual* customer."

Amina's jaw dropped. "Don't go there, girlfriend. Just look who chose a purse and shoes that clash with her black gown."

Aliyah sniffed back a tear. "I can't help it. I don't have the money for anything better."

"And why not?" Amina continued. "Your father's hotel finally got four stars—after he took my advice and started spelunking the maids."

Aliyah puffed out her flat chest. "Don't talk about my family, Amina."

"Then shut your mouth, harlot." Amina jumped up.

"Make me, tramp." Aliyah stood.

"Whore."

"Strumpet."

"Slut."

"Shish kabob on heels."

"Allahu akbar!" Amina raised nail-scissors over her head for a downward thrust.

"Allahu akbar!" Aliyah raised both arms and a leg to deliver karate blows.

Habiba choked up and bit her knuckle. "At least you two are not stuck with a dull brown pantsuit from the 1940s with hideous shoulder pads." She sighed.

"Girls—we've dropped our signs again."

Habiba helped Aliyah and Amina lift two poles at either end of a wide expanse of white cloth on which were painted large black letters: 'Join our *Stop Global Warming* vigil'. They propped it next to Habiba's sign which read: 'Ban Water Now!' Habiba sat and stroked her own unshaven chin until at length Amina and Aliyah calmed and took their seats by the table.

"Humph," snorted Amina. "Anyway, Aliyah, you missed the morning prayer again."

Aliyah caught her breath. "Not true. I was in the back. You could not see me."

"You may fool others, Aliyah, but I know you are not a good Muslim."

"I was just late. I was at the mosque this time. I swear it."

A waitress loomed over Aliyah holding a large platter. "One bacon, ham, sausage, and pepperoni pizza. Hold the pepperoni."

Amina turned to stare down her nose at an embarrassed Aliyah.

"Ha, ha." Aliyah looked at Amina, forcing a bright laugh. "Why that order cannot be mine, dear lady. Ham is against my religion. You have made a mistake."

The waitress took a deep breath. "*One Canadian bacon, ham, and pepperoni. Size: large. Hold the pepperoni. Signed—*"

"No, dear lady!"

"*—Aliyah.*"

Amina folded her arms in disgust and looked away.

"Ah ha ha ha—that is impossible." Aliyah cast a nervous glance at Amina. "I swear. It is a mistake." Aliyah stuffed a fifty-dollar bill into the waitress' pocket. "Here is a tip, dear lady. Now please to take it away."

Amina sniffed as the waitress shrugged and left. Amina leveled a sneering glance at Habiba. "Do I need to say more?"

Aliyah's eyes grew big. "What? *What?* That was just a little mistake. She got the wrong table, that is all."

"Girls, please," interrupted Habiba, "don't forget why we are here. We ladies are supposed to be watching the rise in sea level from global warming. We must continue our vigil until the sea level stops rising. It is our sacred duty."

Aliyah and Amina nodded their heads. "Yes, Sister Habiba. We are sorry that we keep forgetting."

Standing in unison the three raised clenched fists and chanted together: "*Halt Global Warming. Stop Earth Raping. Ban Water Now. Urrah!*"

Several restaurant customers paused in their consumption of pizza slices to look at them in annoyance.

The three sat again.

Habiba sipped from a glass of kale juice. "These are our sacred duties, girls. The Pollo Ranchero Casino has directed us Holy Bowlers to do our utmost to stop all activity by Earth-raping developers." She handed them a stack of flyers. "We must distribute more of these." She pinned one to the wooden railing. It read: 'Sponsored by: Holy Bowlers Coalition of Gay Non-Judgmental Nature Atheists Against Patriarchal Oppression of Feminist Resistance to Evil Patriarchy and Other Very Very Bad Things—*Muslim Cross-Dressers Union Local No. 36.*'

All three members of Local Number 36 nodded solemnly. There was no arguing with that.

"We will make more progress once more girlfriends like us convert and join the Union," Habiba said.

They nodded. Aliyah stood and threw a handful of flyers into the wind where the coastal breeze scattered them along the Santa Monica beach, provoking single-finger salutes from beach-goers who stuffed them into trash barrels along with the girlfriends' earlier 'distributions'.

Aliyah propped her pole higher. "Say, girls, look there. Isn't that a nice location for a new pizza restaurant?"

The others nodded. It was indeed ideal.

"I will call my father and ask for the money."

"Me too. Maybe he would like to build a hotel next to it."

An angry voice drifted from the beach. "Hey, you whores. Stop littering."

Amina leaned over the railing and thrust one arm vertically. "Fuck you, water-lover. Go drown in your poison."

"Eeeeh!" drifted the reply, with upthrust arm to match.

The shadow loomed again, cutting short the festivities. "Your pitcher of Margaritas, sir. . .I mean, madam."

Aliyah jerked back. "Oh no, dear lady, there must be some mistake again. Ha ha." Aliyah leveled another nervous glance at Amina.

"*One pitcher of Margaritas. Heavy on the tequila. Size: large. Extra limes. Signed—*"

"Ha-ha. That is enough, dear lady. Alcohol is against our religion. Ha-ha. It must be someone else's order."

"There's no one left, sir—I mean, ma'am. You're the last customers."

"Here is another fifty for you, dear waitress, just please to take it away."

The waitress smacked her gum and stepped back into the restaurant.

Amina snorted and looked away. Over the railing, her eyes fixed on a distant object.

Following her gaze, Habiba and Aliyah paused from their lighting of global warming vigil candles to peer through the growing dusk. A white whale had sprouted legs and was running on the strip of beach where the sand was firm, rapidly approaching the pizza restaurant. Before they could react, the white whale rushed up the three wooden steps leading from the beach and burst onto the patio.

He grabbed one end of their table. Heaved to catch his breath. Briefly the whale fumbled with buttons on his Hawaiian shirt as if to improve his appearance, then gave up and leaned to support his weight, yellow shorts covering his bulbous posterior.

He flung a desperate glance behind, ignoring the girlfriends. He turned back to them.

"*They're here!*"

Amina, Aliyah, and Habiba exchanged alarmed glances and peered over the railing. Dusk was swiftly plunging the beach into darkness, and the pizza restaurant's night lights flicked on but cast only weak rays over the outdoor patio. The patio seemed suddenly empty—the dark menacing.

"You've got to run," he wheezed to catch his breath. "Get away! You can't stop them—no one can."

Aliyah spoke. "Don't I know you? There is something about your face."

The whale grabbed Aliyah by her abayah, hesitated in confusion when Aliyah's sprouting beard was exposed—her gold medallion and chain popped loose and landed on the floorboards with a clang. The urgency returned. "You don't stand a chance. Don't you understand?—they'll *getcha!* There's nothing you can do. They're *inhuman!*"

"Yes," said Amina, wagging a finger. "I recognize you. It's on the tip of my tongue." She looked up and clicked her fingers trying to recall.

Habiba stared into the darkness. Blinked. "Girlfriends—something is coming."

The white whale jerked. He spun about. Rushed to the safer side of the table. Looking at the three cross-dressers, he panted, "You've got to help me. I've been running so long. Can't go on. . . They were right behind me the whole way."

Out of the darkness appeared a small smudge of white, soon matched by another white smudge, then rapidly a half-dozen more. The smudges grew. They took on black outlines. A smudge of yellow materialized below one of the white smudges; two green spots followed. Moving too quick for anything human, the smudges closed the distance in seconds and planted feet in the firm sand at the bottom of the pizza restaurant's wooden steps. The smudges had swelled to oval patches. In the midst of the white ovals appeared lips that stretched in a phalanx of grimaces.

The girlfriends put their hands to their faces.

"What—what the hell *are* they?" Amina blurted.

Aliyah staggered back a step. "They can't be real."

"No human ever lived looked like this," said Habiba.

Two newcomers put their feet on the first wooden step.

"Don't let em come near," the whale hissed. "That's how they *getcha!*"

Amina and Aliyah exchanged worried looks. Slowly, two of the ghostly figures mounted the steps to halt on the patio only a dozen feet away, the weak restaurant lights playing tricks in the night. The first white face split broadly in a fake smile, blackish almost purple lips accenting its ugliness as if calculated to offend, diamond tattoos framing violent glowing eyes. A pullover shirt cursed with unnatural black and white horizontal stripes covered the upper half of its slim body, solid black pants mercifully hiding the lower half which ended in white-on-black saddle shoes. A frenchified floppy black beret completed the thing's appalling attire.

The second pasty-face had the gall to wear a single universal garment of yellow spandex, its numbing monotony relieved only by one red star over its heart. More ugly black tattoos marred its brow and cheeks. On its head, the ultimate insult to good taste—a bowler hat one size too small.

A shudder went through the girls. "Don't these things care what they look like? Doesn't it matter to them what society thinks?"

"No," shivered the whale. "Other people mean nothing to them. They do as they please. Offend whom they please."

A third pasty-face climbed the short steps. Looming out of the dark like a nightmare from Christmas, green pants were surmounted by red suspenders over another black and white horizontal striped shirt, with another floppy francophone hat clinging disgustingly to what vaguely resembled a head.

More shocking, however, was the thing that clung to the Christmas nightmare's forearm—sitting like a doll, arms limp, legs dangling, its own face bulls-eyed by a sucker-punch of whiteness in the midst of a tiny blue blazer with a blue and white nautical cap perched on top. Green Pants slid a corpse-like hand up the doll's back and its mouth jerked into movement with a clacking of wood, its tiny white beard twitching on its grinning chin. Two horrid eyes snapped left and right.

The eyes focused on the girlfriends.

The girlfriends staggered back in horror. To keep from falling, their hands gripped the table as fiercely as did the great white whale. From the doll came a metallic creak sending shivers down their spines.

"*Huuuuuuge.*"

Amina and Aliyah looked again at each other. Their differences vanished in the face of this threat from the depths of Hell.

The doll clacked its wooden lips. Its eyes flicked left and right. "*Huuuuuuuuuge!*"

Grins split the three corpse-faces wider.

"Did ve not tell you, *Huuuge*, zat you cannot escape us." Green Pants moved his hand behind the doll's back and the doll again spoke. "No von who agrees to join us can ever leave. You know zat, Huuuge."

"You can't hold me to it, Captain French," the whale spluttered. "I. . .I didn't know what I was doing." Huge spun his eyes about searching for an escape route, but after running his big bulk for so long, he could barely stand and continued to cling to the table to keep from collapsing.

"Zere is no goink back, Mr. Buffet. Vonce you sign in blood, *zat* is all she wrote." Green Pants shook with hilarity, on his arm Captain French's lips clacking like castañedas.

Amina snapped her fingers. "I got it. You're *Huge Buffet*, the richest man in the world."

"That's right," Aliyah echoed. "You cornered the world market in buffet restaurants, buying companies left and right for years."

"But what are you doing here?" asked Habiba. "What could you, of all people, possibly have to do with. . .those *things*?"

"I didn't know what I was doing. I heard a simple slogan—thought it was harmless. I joined up thinking it would help me get chicks. How was I to know what they were up to. . .that their plan was to use me to flood the Earth?" Huge Buffet glanced back to the mimes. "I can't be a party to that, I tell you. You'll kill millions!"

"Millions—or only von? Vat is ze difference?" Captain French's mini-fingers grasped a mini-cigarette from underneath in European fashion. Green Pants moved his hand and the Captain French puppet continued its monologue.

"You promised—bratvurst."

The girlfriends could detect no movement in the doll's lips except the up and down mechanical jerks of its white-bearded chin. Again the girlfriends exchanged worried looks. Were they asleep? When would the nightmare end?

"Bratvurst, Mr. Huge Buffet. You promised bratvurst. As ze owner of all ze vorld's buffets, you promised to use zem to increase ze bad stuff in ze atmosphere. Ve already have all of ze giants of industry vorking for us. Except you. You promised bratvurst, unt cabbage, unt beans, unt—*cauliflower.*"

"You can't hold me to it, Captain French. All that gas will increase global warming so there's no going back—you'll drown everyone."

More ghostly mimes arrived, crowding behind the first three, all rocking with silent laughter.

Captain French's chin dropped. "Zat is ze idea, you dumkopf."

"Wait a minute," burst out Amina. "Are you ugly pale-faces trying to say that you're in *favor* of global warming?"

"You are not among ze qvik learners, are you—Ms. Wannabe?" clacked the doll.

Amina caught her breath and snapped her fingers again. "Oh no. You did not just go there, did you girlfriend?"

"Vent zere, took out last night's trash, took pictures, unt came back mit ze photos from Photomart."

Aliyah moved her neck sideways. "Say *what?*"

Without moving his lips, Captain French took a puff on the mini-cigarette. The smoke blew out, forming little swastikas in the air. "Unt mailed it back to myself mit a T-Shirt zat says. . .'I Raped ze Earth unt all I got vas zis T-Shirt."

The Holy Bowlers' jaws dropped. "That's enough out of you, Paleface Squad." Turning to the others, Amina yelled, "Let's give it to em, girls!"

As one, the Muslim Cross-Dressers Union pulled off their abayahs and pantsuits and threw them aside to reveal Sasquatch hairy bodies encumbered by flat brassieres and women's panties—cute shades of lavender and chartreuse. Snarling, they scraped their painted nails on air ready to scratch out the eyes of their enemies.

The mimes jerked backward and squinched their faces, for once getting a taste of bad taste which even they had not conceived of. They sucked their breaths. But not for nothing had they met with success in raising sea levels around the world. Their determination was matched by their efficiency and innovation.

From behind them another mime climbed out of the darkness, the others taking care to move well out of the way of the latest weapon in the mimes' repertoire of ferocious inhumanity.

Purple Lips and Green Pants stepped aside to reveal a scene of such horror that the others could not comprehend how any Maker of the Universe could permit such to live. The corpse-face of the newcomer was surrounded by a narrow perimeter of black greasepaint and punctured by purplish lips sprinkled with random diamond-shaped purple tattoos, surmounting an aged and bloated body that rolled its folds of flab beneath an over-stretched red cocktail dress clashing with overly bright eyeliner only partly overcome by red ruby earrings and red mid-high heels.

The insult to taste and culture was completed by the ragged blond wig that had become permanently affixed to its scalp, 'her' original dark hair continuing to obtrude beneath. Age was writ all over the creature, preserved beyond its natural years by some mysterious process, like a mummified drag queen still reluctant to retire from the Pyramid's Gay Marquee despite the passing of centuries.

The girlfriends staggered back, gripping the railing. Amina leaned and barfed. Huge Buffet let out a moan and covered his eyes with his hands. "Not Ya Egger Hooper. I don't want the Fuck in the Backside Institute," he muttered.

Rushing forward on her red heels, 'Ya Egger Hooper' grabbed Habiba by her genitals and growled. "Turn your head and cough." Involuntarily, Habiba did. He tested Amina and Aliyah the same way. "They're ok," Ya Egger Hooper rumbled. "They're not tibbets."

The gang of mimes rocked harder than ever with gales of silent laughter.

"Please," begged Huge. "You don't have to do this." He smiled in desperation, sweat pouring from his brow. "I'll give you fifteen minutes, or fifteen percent off my buffets."

"Haa haaa haaaaaa," creaked the nautical devil-doll, its pasty mime face stuck in a perpetual grin, its cigarette smoke spiraling into the patio lights. "Do you really zink zat ve shall let you go, Mr. Huge? Unt your little cross-dressing friends? Ve know how to resist ze lamentations of lesbians and the deceptions of cross-dressing wannabes. Unt ve cannot be bribed mit seeboots. Or hot dogs—no matter how good your buffets make zem look."

Purple Lips fixed a hypnotic stare on Amina. Suddenly she froze, unable to tear her eyes away from the mime's gaze, her body jerking stiffly. Without a word, Amina retrieved her abayah and draped it back over her body. Still transfixed by the mime's gaze, Amina sat at the table.

Taking hold of the table with one hand, with the other hand Purple Lips traced an arc in the air from one corner of the table to another corner, then snapped his fingers. The table doubled in size, wood materializing out of thin Santa Monica air.

The other mimes snickered.

Cupping his mouth with his hands, Purple Lips pretended to call, and though no sound could be heard, the waitress re-appeared. At the doorway she too stared straight ahead as in a trance. Purple Lips silently worked his mouth, and as if she heard and understood, the waitress returned inside and a minute later reappeared with platter and pitcher.

In a flat robot voice, the waitress said, "*One Canadian bacon, ham, and pepperoni. Size: large. Hold the pepperoni. Signed—*"

Amina shook herself awake.

"—Amina." The waitress set down the platter.

"No!" In horror, Amina covered her mouth with her hands.

The waitress continued, "*One pitcher of Margaritas. Heavy on the tequila. Size: large. Extra limes. Signed—*"

"You can't."

"—*Amina.*" The waitress put the pitcher next to the platter.

Purple Lips lay his stare on Amina and she instantly reverted to wooden Indian. By way of invitation, the mime drew his hand over the table, then paused, a waiter's napkin materializing over his forearm.

Mechanically, Amina sat.

One last stare from the mime, and Amina slowly picked up a slice of pizza. She hesitated. . .bacon grease dripped onto her plate.

Purple Lips' finger stabbed downward in a ferocious command: *Eat it!*

Amina chomped. Swallowed. Tears welled in her eyes as images of Paradise and seventy-two virgins of indeterminate gender dwindled into nothingness, but compelled by some invisible force, she could not resist. Amina finished the slice and reached for another.

Purple Lips picked up an invisible glass and poured invisible liquid in it. In response, Amina filled her own glass with refreshment from the pitcher of margaritas, then sat and stared with the glassy-eyed stare of the damned.

The mime pretended to drink and he rubbed his tummy. He pointed. Amina downed the tequila and rubbed her own, then burped.

The mimes broke out in more gales of doubled-over silent laughter.

Aliyah and Habiba stared with horror, wondering what evil might be in store for them.

Again the finger pointed. *Sit and eat!*

"Oh, dear me," shrugged Aliyah. "Look what these evil ones are doing. Oh, they are making me eat *ham!* Oh well, looks like I have no choice. . ." Snapping up two slices of pizza, Aliyah wolfed them down with frantic joy, followed by two deep drafts of margaritas. With extra lime.

Habiba began munching. "Who cares?" she shrugged. "I only converted last month anyway." As Habiba reached for the next slice of ham, Aliyah snatched it out of her hands and devoured it. Within seconds the two had eaten the rest, smacking away with such obvious relish that the mimes stepped back and scratched their heads in confusion.

Purple Lips, however, kept grinning. Reaching behind his back, he squirmed as if grasping something hidden—he turned to reveal two plastic bottles of water.

All three cross-dressers froze as if sun and moon had eclipsed. More worried glances passed among them. Would these creatures attempt the ultimate desecration of all that was holy—the ultimate abuse?

Reaching his hand behind his back, Yellow Spandex found another plastic bottle. Not to be outdone, a bottle appeared in one of Captain French's stiff puppet-like hands. Letting his cigarette drop, he shook the plastic and gripped its top as if preparing to open a bottle of champagne.

"Be strong, ladies," Huge Buffet urged. "Any sacrifice is worth the Sacred Cause."

But Aliyah stepped back from the table. She hastily donned her abayah again—whatever defense she could muster.

Too late—a spray of the deadly liquid struck Aliyah full in the face. Aliyah brought up her hands—shades of mascara dripped on her palms. "Heeelp mee," she cried. She sank to her knees, purple stains running down her delicate cheeks. "My make-up. . ."

"Is there a cosmetologist in the house?" Habiba shouted.

"Quick," yelled Huge. "Someone get a stylist!"

Green Pants took another step; Amina snapped out of her trance and jumped backward as another shot of the punishing substance arched over the table—it struck Habiba on her chest in the midst of zipping up her pantsuit. Gripping her heart, she collapsed, a loud sizzle erupting, sending bubbles into the eerie night-haunted air.

"My God," Huge gasped. "You fiends. You've scarred her pantsuit for life. It was dry-clean only."

Green Pants thrust Captain French forward full into the light. "Unt don't zink zat you vill get avay, either, Mr. King of Smorgasbords," the doll said.

Scrambling to their feet, the girlfriends bolted. Exiting the patio, they rushed into the restaurant and disappeared down the street, leaving the White Whale to his fate.

Huge Buffet froze under the hypnotic gaze of Captain French.

Green Pants drew near.

The other mimes crowded behind.

Purple Lips popped open a portable laptop and displayed Buffet's stock portfolio. Even as they watched, something sent his stocks into a nosedive one after another.

The devil puppet rattled again: "You are too late to reverse ze process, Herr Huge. Vatch unt you vill see—ouch!" Behind Green Pants' shoulder, the face of Ya Egger Hooper, the aged cross-dressing mime once known as J. Edgar Hoover, chief of the FBI, had quietly appeared. 'She' thrust another finger into the back of Captain French. "Dumkopf," yelled the devil-puppet, "Vhy do you keep mit ze poking of my backside? Vhy don't you go back to your Fuck in ze Backside Institute, Edie? You are *ze spleenig kopf*, you know zat? A nutty head!" 'Edie' said nothing but stared straight ahead. She sank slowly out of sight.

Captain French returned his attention to Huge Buffet. "Vatch unt you vill see ze consequence of double-crossing us. Von by von, your companies are goink. . .how do you say. . .'under vater'?" The doll turned its head to Green Pants and winked. "Every von of your companies zat is on ze coast-line is already drowning. Soon you shall be as poor as. . .vell, as zose cross-dressers' tailor." Again the sly wink.

The whale deflated. He collapsed into a chair, his gaze lost in the distance.

Purple Lips snapped his fingers. Turning, his hands went

busy and when he turned back to Huge Buffet, Purple Lips held an armful of newspapers. Spreading the front page of one, it read 'Wall Street Journal—Buffet Edition'. He nodded his eyes towards the other mimes and instantly Huge Buffet was inundated by more of the liquid poison soaking him from head to toes. With savage glee—though silent of course—the mimes circled Huge, plastering newspapers in ever-increasing layers, until before a minute was up, they had encased him in an unbreakable prison of newsprint, other mimes drying the paper in place with hair dryers. "Fifteen percent," came a whimper from beneath the paper, "Save fifteen percent."

Crickets answered.

Obeying another silent command, the restaurant waitress stiffly approached Purple Lips. She halted to stare across the Bay as had the white whale. Pulling from her pocket the two fifty-dollar bills that Aliyah had previously given her as tips, the waitress handed them to Purple Lips. He stuffed them into his pants. Evil Mime work, after all, was not the most lucrative of careers.

With final sniggers and condescending grins, the mimes descended the short wooden steps back to Santa Monica beach where one produced a stack of leaflets that read 'Cirque de Lumiére' and 'distributed' them into the wind.

A voice drifted. "Hey you clowns. Stop littering."

A mime in a conical hat with the letters *Fleur de Lis* printed on the hat mouthed an angry silent reply and a half-dozen forearms thrust up in universal salutes at the offensive suggestion that they dropped their pants and blew themselves out of cannons for a living.

Mustering their dignity, the mime hit-men of the Big

Green G melted into the night.

Episode 3

Pedro enjoyed his new job, even more so because he worked only every other weekend and could continue his day job at the Holy Rollers Derby Club, thus earning two paychecks for the first time ever. And, his new location being a military base, there was much less blood than at the derby rink in Los Angeles. 'Area Five-One', read the newspaper on the empty table before him. It might have made sense if he could count that high.

Merry whistles sounded through the cavernous basement as he slopped water over the concrete floors trying not to splash the liquid. For a moment he paused to glance at the five plexiglass containers that rumor said had once held 'aliens' from a foreign place—much like Panama he imagined, tales coming back to mind told by his cousin Miguel who had once serviced a place in Panama called Los Bolos where strange happenings were common, but according to his cousin, at least the hamburgers were free.

The containers had held creatures as strange as any. Years ago they had all escaped. When and how, Pedro had no idea. He had no time for gossip and rumors. His only concern was to clean the floors as quickly as possible and leave no soap scum. And make sure no more bodies appeared like that strange case of the former Corporal who was found dead on the floor with his eyes frozen open and his legs still twitching as if running as quick as he could from something terrifying. Who could explain?

Pedro glanced at his rusting watch. *El tiempo fuera!* Thrusting with special vigor, he retracted the mop, failing to notice that the strands had entangled a power cord.

The cord popped from the wall.

Wheeling his bucket, Pedro punched the elevator button. The elevator arrived, and without a backward glance, the janitor entered and left, rushing to catch the last secret military plane back to Las Vegas that night.

Above the containers, a temperature indicator began to move. Solidly in the green zone at first, it rose steadily and swiftly until an hour later it crossed into the red zone.

A light silently flashed.

Was anyone watching? Why would they? The chambers were empty and had been for years, even the scandal accompanying the disappearance of the aliens having long since died, and even the 1947 Roswell incident itself, the source of the aliens' bodies, had been long forgotten.

Something twitched.

At the bottom of one container, a hand stirred.

In the adjacent container—another movement.

Two forms slowly resumed breathing and stretched as from a long sleep, wakefulness returning along with life and breath.

A body rose on one elbow. A head followed and turned to peer through the container. It blinked. In the next container a second body did likewise. Quietly they exchanged glances. The first slid fingers into a white shirt pocket and extracted a toothpick. Sliding it into his mouth, he sucked, relishing the taste of cinnamon as if renewing an old acquaintance after an absence of decades.

"Lemon. Where the hell are we?"

"I couldn't guess, Orange. But we're breathing."

Orange Jello smiled and stood up straight inside the plexiglass tube and smoothed some of the wrinkles from his long black pants and short-sleeved white shirt.

"Glad to finally have those clowns off our backs," Lemon Jello said. "I wonder how long they stood on top of us?"

Orange Jello frowned as he thought, his eyes settling on the newspaper which Pedro had left on the table, where the date was plainly visible. The date on the Area 51 Tribune read: July 14, 2021.

"Too long, Lemon. Way too long."

Stepping out of the container, Orange Jello plugged the power cord back into the wall socket. He smiled and winked at Lemon Jello. He straightened his back. "We don't want anyone tripping over it in the dark." He inspected his pocket protector and instinctively reached for his Latter-Day Bible. The Bible was gone.

"Lemon? You got your Mormon Bible?"

Scrambling to find his, Lemon soon gave up. His too was gone.

A hard look came over Orange. "We accomplished our mission but everyone we used to know has long since died, and we've lost our Bibles. But it seems we haven't aged a day since we entered those plexiglass containers. What do we do next?"

Lemon shrugged. "Go into business for ourselves? There's always a demand for Bible-quoting hit-men. Especially the famous Jello Brothers."

***

The bright chariot of Helios had long returned to a well-deserved slumber beyond the bower of the horizon, exchanging its gilded wheels for silver wings on the feet of Mercury as the god of swiftness and the transience of life upended his divine thumb on the highway of the heavens and hitched a ride with the fair maid Luna, the sister of Jupiter, who turned her smiling face upon the affairs of mortal men ready to grant her divine favor to whomever she pleased.

In other words, day became night.

In the shadow of the Holy Rollers Derby Club, not far from the Pollo Ranchero Casino & Bowlarama in Venice, California, and closer still to the hasty construction of a brand new pizzeria overlooking the steady sweep of waves from Catalina Bay, two men in jeans and red and green flannel shirts, skulked past a façade of aging storefronts and across a pot-holed parking lot and halted in front of a five-foot bare naked picture of a young woman, the headline proclaiming 'Girls! Girls! Girls!'

They slipped inside the XXX-rated theater.

A candidate for retirement with frizzed hair, full bra, and fresh lipstick stopped them at a counter just inside.

"Take off your cap, Elmer," the old man blared. "We run a class operation here."

"Okey-dokey," said Ray. He slapped down two twenties.

The man slipped the twenties into his bra. "If you bother the girls, you're outta here."

Ray rippled his lips. He tapped his companion on the shoulder. "Come on, Bobby. We don't want to harm the reputation of this *high-class* establishment."

The man behind the counter thrust a half-smoked cigar into his painted lips and stared back without emotion.

Ray and Bobby entered the theater, parting the thick curtains, their duck-hunting caps under their arms. On the stage the actresses were performing a Shakespearean adaptation of *Joan of Narc* in the nude, alongside policemen sporting billy clubs and handcuffs.

"O dear soul of my heart, methinks thou mayhast run afoul of yon gendarmes of this fair city," one nude actress swooned.

A second actress answered. "Hark. Alas, my dire fate lies in gentle hand of appearance fair like a Grendel of the forest, fain wishing to ravish this faithful nun of God," said another, back of hand to despairing forehead. "I beg of you, O fair Grendel, keep yon billy club at your gentle side and cease in your evil molestations of those who have pawned their unstained souls to eternal purity."

Finding their seats, Ray burped. "Get her in the ass!" he bellowed. Several patrons turned and frowned at him for giving away the plot.

High heels approached with cans of beer. "Ten each," the burly old man in high heels growled.

The Fudd twins reluctantly bought one each.

"Are you sure this is the right place?" Bobby whispered.

Ray passed his narrow glance over the interior taking in the half-dozen other patrons, each sitting carefully alone in the theater. "Yep, Bobby. No doubt about it."

A minute passed.

Ray froze. Someone had sat behind them.

"Don't turn," whispered a hoarse voice. The Fudd twins immediately realized it was hoarse by disguise. "I just think it's not important for you to know who I am."

Ray and Bobby kept looking at the antics of the 'performers'. "What the hell do we care? On the phone you mentioned money, so here we are, bright and early." Ray smirked.

"I understand you never got your prize money for delivering the Squatch from Washington State to Professor Pierson." A hand covered with cloth slipped between them. "Maybe this will help."

The two exchanged surprised glances. Quickly they snatched the envelope and counted out the bills. Ray quietly whistled, till a couple of patrons frowned in his direction.

"Hot damn. Lookit this, Bobby. We finally got paid!"

"Yeah, Ray. It's easy street for us."

Ray looked suddenly serious. "Okay. It can't be this simple. What else do you want?"

The figure seated behind them turned its glance to either side, checking for eavesdroppers. "I have *another* envelope here—with more money. *Lots* more. All I need from you is to do a simple little job."

Their glances took on a sly look. "What is it? Or rather: *who*?"

"A stone in my shoe. That's all. Just a stone in my shoe."

"And this 'stone' would be. . .?"

"The sasquatch. I want the sasquatch 'fixed' so nobody sees her again. That's all."

Pocketing the money, Ray looked at Bobby. "You came to the right place. When we fix em, they stay fixed." Ray and Bobby smiled. "I think you just hired you a coupla fine handymen."

Without another word, the cloaked figure slid into the darkness and withdrew while Joan's gentle audience absorbed the rest of the evening's classical presentation with sudz and pretzels.

* * *

Locking the door on his office on the UCLA campus and with a last glance at the new departmental overhead sign that read ‘Department of Non-Patriarchal Fair Trade Astronomy’, Professor Richard Pierson avoided the disapproving stares of the all-female (for ‘balance’) teaching staff that occupied the other departmental offices. Slowly he exited the building.

Once again he inspected the printout of electromagnetic radiation distributions that detected the presence of water on a distant planet. Much water. How quick the progress in science had been in the past few years! Clicking a request into his Uber app, a car appeared before he could pocket his phone. Slowly the aged professor climbed in.

As dusk fell, the professor stood outside a simple unadorned building somewhere between Culver City and Venice, thankful for the shadows that rapidly covered him. For this job it would not do to be seen.

He watched the front entrance as dark cars with darker windows pulled up to the building, and white-jacketed attendants rushed to assist the passengers under a *porte cochére.* For the most part the passengers were heavily clothed, Pierson unable to distinguish features or glimpse faces. Finally his patience was rewarded. At the single glimpse he recoiled, questioned the wisdom of his venture.

No, he steeled himself. He must go on. He had discovered too much—learned too much. To turn back now would leave not only himself in danger—but others.

In a mirror he inspected the white greasepaint he had smeared on his face. It was far from expertly applied but given the situation he believed it would do. All he needed was to blend in with the establishment's usual habitants long enough to watch—and learn.

Steadying his nerves, he walked with his usual slow gait toward the front door. Immediately the white-shirted attendants stood alert. To his relief, instead of challenging him, they rushed to help.

"Git da do', Rodney. One of dem white-faced Massas is limpin dis way."

Rodney rolled his eyes in exaggerated concern. "Sho nuff. Now just what do yo think yo is doin, Massa, wandrin away from Home like dat? Yo need to watch yo feet. No tellin' what might happen if yo wanders away and gets lost. Not in dis heah town—nooo suh!"

"Nooo suh. Not in dis heah town. Dey don like white-faced Massas round heah."

Pierson smiled and mouthed a silent 'thank you' through his white greasepaint and slipped a coin to each.

Rodney whipped up a wheelchair.

Pierson sat.

"Git da do', Clarence. I don wanna mash Massa into da do' nohow."

Clarence let the door close—Rodney promptly mashed Massa into da do'. Pierson stifled a yell of pain that might have given him away, with unpredictable consequences, managing to stifle it with a grimace.

"Now look at what yo done gone and did, Rodney. Ain't no good bein' a Massa if low-down types like yo gone mash him into da do'."

Rodney rolled his eyes. "No point at-ol, Clarence. No point at-ol."

Clarence finally got the door open and Rodney pushed him roughly through and left him in the lobby.

Pierson shuddered. Inside were a dozen men in their dotage, doddering in wheelchairs, drool pooling on their laps, saliva trickling over white-grease-painted chins. Two exchanged weak hand signals between adjusting floppy French berets and suspenders. Two more wore decrepit chest medals that read 'Mime Veterans of WW2'. Still others—the ones with ponytails—'Mime Liberation Front' next to a picture of Che Guevara in white-face.

I made it, thought Pierson. *I'm inside the Evil Mime Retirement Home.*

One of the mimes leveled his gaze at Pierson. Without shifting his gaze, the mime slowly wheeled his chair closer. As Pierson watched, the aged mime launched into obscure hand movements that appeared to be a mix of sign language for the deaf, Indian pow-wow, and Mediterranean insults, the result a pidgin English for those who gloried in the silence of the dumb.

Pointing to a medal on his chest denoting former participation in the Mime Olympics, the now decrepit fossil arched up his pasty-painted face lined with black to receive silent shouts of acclaim which he had enjoyed in his prime. A hand traced a large box, the other hand the outline of a phone. It became clear that the mime intended to call Pierson on the non-existent phone.

Ring-ring. The mime's hand shook with the shakiness of a ringing phone, his thumb in his ear and little finger at his mouth.

Ring-ring. The pasty-face frowned.

I had better answer, thought Pierson. *But what do I say since I dare not speak a word?* Finally Pierson put his thumb to his ear and touched his little finger to his mouth. He opened his mouth to silently reply—something clicked in his brain and he realized that he comprehended the mime's hand signals.

The mime moved his feet and Pierson saw an image in his mind of the mime in his prime dressed in horizontal black and white stripes striding down a street. The mime stretched one arm and an image popped into Pierson's mind of the mime in his youth tracing boxes for innocent pedestrians, the strangers offended but the mime pressing on in contemptuous defiance of their feelings.

The mime twisted his ugly mouth and grinned as Pierson was forced in his mind to view the mime imitating his selected victim by copying his walk, grinning at his victim's embarrassment. *No*, thought Pierson, *no one could be so cruel. This aged relic could not still be reliving his glory days as a sidewalk bully, still gloating over how he made people's lives miserable so many years before. But he was*.

Without saying a word, Pierson gritted his teeth and took it. He resolved to go through with his plan, to find out the secrets of this savage cult, to find some way to beat them, and to discover their connection with the Cross-Dressers from Pluto. And when he was done, Pierson would confront those colleagues who had laughed at his insistence that Pluto remain a planet and not a planetoid. *Those fools*, he thought. *If only they had seen on Pluto what I have seen, they would not be so quick to dismiss it. How easily* they fool our flyby spacecraft.

The mime finished with a devastating barrage of single-finger salutes and upthrust arms at the innocent teary pedestrian who he had forced on Pierson's mind through the pretend phone call, and the mime lapsed into a drool-encrusted sleep. Mercifully, the connection broke and Pierson ceased sweating. A guarded glance showed no other retired mimes approaching him, and he casually but quickly wheeled his own wheelchair across the lobby and into a back hall.

He saw a sign above a doorway: 'G's World-Class Buffet – free water and hot dogs'. Pretending to follow the sign, Pierson waited till all wheelchairs and the many attendants pushing the retirees non-stop into doors had absented themselves from the hall. Then he casually rolled his wheelchair into a side room under another sign which read 'Mime Much' beside a cartoon of a grinning white face.

Shuddering, Pierson overcame his instinctive revulsion and entered. Before anyone could discover him, he stood and hid his wheelchair behind curtains. The room was large enough for conferences, folding chairs stacked behind the curtains alongside folded tables. The long walls boasted a series of pictures.

For a minute he contemplated the pictures and found himself struggling to overcome a growing sense of alarm. This was more than he had bargained for. From pictures of ancient American Presidents, the pictures branched out to include heads of foreign states, under each posted a label: 'Past Master'.

Pierson was increasingly mystified. Some of the pictures he recognized; others were strange. All had 'Past Master' posted beneath: first was an old painting of a man with a large beard, labeled 'Joseph Smith'; then a series of more men with beards, all of whom were obscure. These were followed by every American President and titan of industry of the 19th century, from President Grant to Rockefeller to P.T. Barnum, with a special commendation and grin on the latter's face.

Next came Presidents from the 20th century and other wielders of power: the Roosevelts—both of them; Woodrow Wilson; Emperor Hirohito; Fascist dictator Benito Mussolini; a Pope; Al Capone; Charles Lindbergh; some kid named Gary; a blank spot that read 'Adolf' but the picture had been removed; Joe Kennedy and all his sons including JFK; Harry S. Truman; Eisenhower; Richard Nixon; Gerald Ford (stumbling off an airplane as the picture was taken); Fidel Castro; every other modern American President up to Donald Trump, who was pictured arm in arm with Vladimir Putin, another former Worshipful Master, next to one of a smiling Joseph Stalin arm-in-arm with a frowning Adolf; Mitt Romney (arm in arm with Al Gore, yet another Past Master); and finally Gary again, no longer a kid.

Hovering over all was a plastic Big Green G hung on the wall like a frozen Art Deco clock. Beneath it a modest sign read 'Courtesy of the Joseph Smith Chartreuse Lodge of the Latter-Day Masons of Upper Middle Utah and Fish Fry'.

Still attempting to puzzle this out, Pierson alerted to a hand on the outer doorknob. He stepped quickly behind the curtain next to his wheelchair. The conference room was large but not large enough to escape notice without some form of cover.

Two figures entered. They clicked the door shut behind them. One of the figures was an ancient man wheeling himself in a wheelchair, his face painted like the other mimes in the Evil Mime Retirement Home. The other was similarly painted, but the pasty offensiveness was accentuated by a stringy blond wig, red silk nightgown, and ruby earrings, the dress bulging from a middle-aged paunch, heavy jowls contradicting mascara and artificial eyelashes. Plainly the Mime Conspiracy had extended its tentacles into unguessed territories.

Pierson shook his head to regain his sanity. To his surprise, the old man in the wheelchair stood. Standing with little effort, he addressed the mime in the blond wig. "As the new Worshipful Master, Edie, you must learn how to contact the office of the Big Green G. Walk this way."

"Thank you, Past Master Gary," growled Edie. "You have provided fine service to the Lodge and I'm sorry to see you go. But we gotta report this—pronto." Ignoring Gary's advice, Edie sashayed as 'she' followed him.

The two mimes approached the plastic back-lit sign of the Big Green G and raised their right arms in stiff Roman salutes. Gary pressed a button then stepped back as a wide black screen slowly descended from the ceiling. It leaped to life. Millions of colors reacted to a laser pointer that Gary manipulated.

On the screen, a backdrop of old musty books in an ancient library shimmered into view. An aged face took form—an enormous bushy white beard with high old-fashioned collar and tweed jacket with bow tie flanked by grey bushy sideburns under a large white forelock.

"Welcome, Brethren," creaked an ancient voice. The face moved weirdly, shouting uncanny valley.

"Hail, Elder Joseph Smith of the 333rd Degree," recited Gary, his arm thrusting stiffly again like at a Nuremberg rally. Edie did likewise.

A bottle sailed across the screen. Narrowly missing Joseph Smith's head, the bottle crashed onto the library of shelved books behind him, the splash of liquid revealing the books to be a façade with book spines painted on. A face intruded—a pretty but thin freckled woman with curly brunette hair. Her swaying red-rimmed eyes tried to focus on Elder Joseph of the 333rd Degree.

"Ya know what?" the woman slurred.

"Excuse me, O Brethren."

"*Fuck you*, Josheph. Thash what."

"Melia, this is not the time."

"Time shmime. *Hic*. . . Look at me when—*hic*—when I'm—*hic*—talkin' to you." Her eyes sought to focus on Joseph and failed.

Joseph Smith stood. The bearded face lowered and the face and its tweed jacket and high collar were revealed to be a large mask held by a big green frog in one large webbed hand. The frog stood facing the woman, his green face painted white and outlined with darker greasepaint.

"I am busy, Melia," the frog croaked.

"*Hic*—" She thrust a wobbly finger in the frog's face. "—I wantchu tell the truth. . .you. . .big-ass toad. *Hic*— You. . .you been slippin' your twin pokes to—*hic*—someone else. Haven't cha?" She swayed in and out of the screen.

"Melia must know that we are not bond-ribbets. So we had some fun, but the Great Gork has not performed any ceremony for us. I am entitled to see others." A hand slapped 'Joseph' across his huge chinless jaw—his twin chameleon eyes bugged out at the end of short stalks. "Ooooh. You are not right in the head, Melia."

She swayed full onto the screen. "Well. . .well. . .ya know what? *Fuck you, Josheph!* Thash what." Her finger swayed and pointed at the wall behind him. "I'm not. . .where'd you go? . . .where are ya? . . .there ya are. . .donshu run away like that. . .I'm not a. . .a piesh of meat you can—*hic*—you can. . .just shcrew whenever you want—*hic*—throw away when you decide to chase some green ass in another pond." Her eyes grew heavy. "Thash what."

"Melia, why do we always have to argue in front of strangers?" Joseph turned back to the screen, still clutching his human mask with the grey beard and collar in one floppy webbed hand.

"Give me tenshun. . .I want tenshun. . .nobody loves me."

"Don't say that, Melia. Joseph loves you."

She put a finger to her lips and staggered. "Shhh. . .no you don't," she sniffed back a tear, "You're jush shayin that—you gotta prove it—you gotta shlip it to me, Josheph."

"Five times a day is hard even for a frog on Bogland with two pokes, Melia. I must rest and tend to business some time."

"Thash what I've been sayin. . .five timesh a day jush ain't enough! I'm only *shuman* you know."

"Is Melia not happy with Joseph's new painted face? You like white painted faces, you said."

"I know," the tears flowed, "I know Josheph—*hic*—you're good to me, Josheph." She bawled into one arm. She blew her nose.

"And Johnnie Walker. You have the daily supply that you said you require."

"I'm only *shuman*, Joseph. *All* shumans need big supply of Johnnie Walker."

"What if we got you another plane like your former Lockheed Electra?"

She paused, sniffed. "Oooo-hoooo." The tears streamed down. "I love you Josheph. You the besht Josheph I ever had. . ." Swaying again, she lost balance and leaned against the frog who caught her before she could fall. Her hands ran down his green body. "Lesh splash," She grinned.

"No Melia. Joseph is working, not good to arouse pokes while Joseph is doing inter-galactic diplomacy with alien races on big screen." He pointed to the screen with his free webbed hand. He gently pushed her away.

She pushed forward again, her hands rummaging between his legs. "Don' care. Wanna splash," she grinned.

"Not now, Melia. Joseph is busy. Joseph has work to do."

"Fuck work. Lesh do it." From somewhere she produced a second bottle of Johnnie Walker and downed a swig direct. "Gimme kish, Joey." She presented rounded lips with smeared lipstick, only the bottle keeping her in balance. "Pucker up your cute little greash-painted face."

"No, Melia. I said I cannot splash with you now. Joseph must return to work." He pushed her back harder.

Her jaw dropped. She swayed and stared at the wall. She

pointed at a picture. "Don' turn your back on me while I'm talkin' to you, you toad. . ."

"I am over here, Melia. I did not turn my back."

Her eyes found him. "Well, ya know what?"

Joseph's chameleon eyes rolled towards the ceiling. He sighed. "What, Melia?"

"*Fuck you! Thash what.*" Joseph mouthed the words silently as she spoke them. Without warning, her arm swung. The bottle bounced off Joseph's warty green head.

"Oooowww!" He grabbed his head with two large floppy webbed hands, dropping the mask. "You have problem, Melia. I see why other josephs moved on and refused to bond with you."

"Thash what you think." She swayed and almost fell, Joseph reaching to break her fall. "Thash what you think. . .Well, ya know what? *Hic. . .ya—ya know what?*"

He sighed again.

She swayed closer and thrust another finger, pushing her face full into his. "I said: *YA KNOW WHAT?!*"

"What, Melia?" He would have put his chin in his hand if not for the fact that frogs have no chins.

"You got warts. That's what."

"Yes, Melia. I have warts. Thank you for letting me know. This Joseph became a frog and now has warts."

"See?" Melia pointed at something on Joseph's chest. He looked down to where her finger pointed and her arm swung up and landed another slap. "Gotcha, ya big ass toad!" His jaw dropped again.

"Oh," bleated Melia, "I don' feel so good. . .gotta shleep now. . .no more splash for a while." Staggering to one corner of the 'library', she did a slow dive onto the floor. With a belch she lost her lunch.

Snores echoed.

A side door opened and another green frog stuck its bullet head in.

"Xplak. Please to see that Melia is comfortable."

The other frog nodded. "Sic. Sperare moras."

Massaging the growing bump on his green warty head, Joseph Smith of the 333rd Degree returned to his audience, retrieved the bearded mask with the tweed jacket and high collar attached, and placed it in front of his green face where he held it at an angle, trying unsuccessfully to hold the mask steady while his other hand held his throbbing head. The mask resumed moving weirdly with toad science.

He cleared his aged throat. "Welcome, all. Are you following the path that our Lord has set for you, my Brothers? Are you resisting the lamentations of lesbians and the deceptions of cross-dressing wannabes? Remember to test them with water if you have doubt."

"Yes, O Elder Smith of the 333rd Degree. Thank you for your guidance," responded Gary, exchanging confused glances with Edie, erstwhile head of the Fuck in the Backside Institute, who perhaps had something to explain by 'her' membership in the male-only Sacred Chartreuse Lodge of the Latter-Day Masons.

The ancient face smiled, the dry skin on the mask crinkling. "Our sacred lodge succeeded in destroying the evil *tibbet* base in Nevada many years ago, but it has come to our attention that more evil tibbets have established bases in Las Vegas and Los Angeles. You must neutralize them."

"Yes, O Elder Smith."

"We are happy that our emissaries who were frozen at Area 51 are now free. Free to laugh at pedestrians and use their twin pokes and dance the polka and eat hot dogs with ketchup if they please and sit in nicer seats in high-class theaters without being forced to buy ten dollar beers or listen to catcalls from disrespectful patrons. And free to promote bad stuff in the atmosphere and flood planet Dryland to make it better for our race of right-minded water-loving *ribbets* instead of those evil water-hating *tibbets*."

"Yes, O Smith of the Eternal Plasma Screen. We hear and we shall throw every resource of the Lodge into fulfilling your requests." Gary and Edie exchanged worried glances. "But—we must inform you of a new situation. . ."

Smith's mask-eyes blinked. "What situation?"

"A Sasquatch, sir. One has appeared in Los Angeles and has interfered with our plans to flood the Earth via Global Warming."

The eyes blinked slowly as if consulting old memory banks. Smith nodded. "Yes. I kept a few Sasquatches happy in my time when my people first arrived in Utah, lo these many years. I had to wear an ape-suit to do that, just as I am doing now with white greasepaint. . ." He displayed a look of sadness and paused, unwilling to go there. "Darn Squatches left for Washington and sued me for child support after I took my 103rd wife. Go figure."

The mask remained held at an odd angle, destroying the illusion, warty greenness visible around one edge. Joseph continued. "I don't know. Nothing I do seems to make Melia happy. I have taught her to dance the polka and given her buffets of hot dogs with both ketchup and mustard and pools of water to splash in with many green balloons, but still she is not happy." He sighed. "Despite the Great Green Gork's instructions, I cannot keep climbing Mount Fuji forever. Two centuries is no longer young even for a Mormon *shuman* transformed into a *ribbet* on the planet Bogland."

Joseph Smith put one green webbed hand to his head to think, ignoring the mask which now sagged at a 45 degree angle, looking again like the frog alien he had become after founding the Mormon Church those many years ago.

"How about this? Since she broke into the Big Green Gork's supply of Green Goo, Melia's lifespan has extended like all ribbets—which probably means an eventual death sentence from mountain climbing for Yours Truly. The Great Gork is tired of dodging bottles of Johnnie Walker and has washed his hands of Melia Earhart, so it is up to me. I will give her a cosmodrone that looks like the Lockheed Electra she used to have, and a case of Johnnie Walker, and send her to photograph the evil *tibbet* base on Pluto. I understand that she has experience with aerial photography. Maybe we will get lucky and she will again go down behind enemy lines."

The floppy webbed fingers rubbed the lump on his head. "Meanwhile, I have a special plan to get rid of your Squatch. We can't have our plans for global warming interrupted. Come closer, my Brethren, and listen to my plan." Joseph glanced at the other frog, who had finished tending to the unconscious Melia. "Xplak, this will require your help as well."

Joseph leaned closer to the screen, and with Xplak listening, whispered to Gary and Edie so that Pierson, still hidden behind the curtain, was unable to hear.

Finally they finished their discussion and the screen went black and rose into the ceiling and the two Latter-Day Masons exited—including Edie, the aged cross-dresser and former head of the FBI turned mime. Gary reentered his wheelchair and quietly wheeled it out. Once outside, Rodney took over and mashed him into a do'.

Wheeling himself out of the Evil Mime Retirement Home, and certain no one was watching—Rodney and Clarence having gone on break the moment they saw him coming—Richard Pierson paused to stare up at the heavens while he wiped away his white greasepaint.

Everything was falling into place. Staring at Sirius, the star sacred to the Pyramid builders, he nodded. He had one more phone call to make. Then he could finally put his Master Plan into operation.

Episode 4

Eight wheels glided over a worn carpet and halted at the counter in another outlet of Maggie's favorite coffee chain.

"A regular coffee. Quick."

A barista remarkably similar to those Maggie had previously seen gave her a similar puzzled look.

Maggie repeated. "You know—normal size. Can you make it quick, I'm in a hurry."

The puzzled look deepened to confusion and the barista glanced behind her at the menu board overhead. "What size do you want?"

Searching vacant memory banks, Maggie half-closed her eyes. "Tall. Make that tall."

"Oh," said the barista. The barista accepted a slip of paper from Maggie. Staring at it, she looked up. "That's only a dollar. I need more."

Maggie reached into her pocket and pulled out another slip. Handed it over.

"Why, that's *fifty* dollars. I don't have that kind of change. Don't you have anything smaller?"

Maggie dug deeper and dragged out several more folded samples of paper with mysterious symbols stamped on them, which the non-Squatches and infidels called 'cash'. "Which one do you want?"

Her brows lifting, the barista selected one, returned the rest, and rang up the sale. Before fixing the drink, she turned back to Maggie.

"Room for cream?"

Maggie looked puzzled. "Uh, where's my coffee?"

"Room for cream?" the barista repeated deadpan.

"I don't want cream. It's too white. I'm allergic."

"Room? Cream? Will you want cream?"

"No. I don't want room, or cream." Maggie frowned.

The barista stared intently. "Room for cream? Cream for room?" She raised her voice, attracting the stares of half the customers.

"No, I don't want a room, I don't want cream, I just want my coffee, *please*."

"Tssk, maybe you've had enough, ma'am," dripped the barista, flipping her ponytailed hair in Maggie's face as she turned to prepare it. At last, she was ready to hand it over. . .

In mid-air, the barista paused.

Maggie stood frozen, hand extended but still empty of

boiled roast.

The barista stared blankly at the cup in her hand which was filled almost to the brim. A line of customers queued behind Maggie, but the barista still made no move to hand over the dark roast, despite several people shaking keys or tapping their feet impatiently.

The barista leaned closer. She fixed Maggie with a cold stare like pinning an insect.

Maggie's skates slid back an inch.

"You sure you don't want *room for cream*? I can easily pour some out. . ."

"No thank you! Just the coffee! I'll take it *as-is!*"

The barista stared at the cup. For a long moment she seemed about to hand it over, but just as Maggie's hand extended again, the barista pulled it back to leave Maggie's hand again open and ready to grasp, still ungraced by the black liquid. Slowly the barista maneuvered the coffee over the sink, her eyes shifting slowly from Maggie—to the elusive cup—back to Maggie. The barista poised there, leaning the cup ever so slightly as if about to pour the coffee out.

Again she looked at Maggie, her eyes questioning. She lifted one eyebrow. "It's no trouble at all. . ."

Maggie caught her breath.

The barista's hypnotic eyes looked deep into Maggie's. A few drops of freshly brewed coffee escaped into the sink. "Are you absolutely *sure*. . ."

"Yes!"

More drops spilled.

Maggie covered her mouth with a hand.

The barista lowered her head, gazing at Maggie, both

brows lifted. Her voice grew quiet. "You won't change your mind? After all, there's still time for. . ."

"No—"

"*Room—*"

"Don't say it—"

"*For—*"

"Please don't say it!"

The barista's hand held the prized brew just out of reach, suspended above the sink as if awaiting a deus ex machina to descend from the heavens and snatch it away. She fixed Maggie's eyes with a malicious dagger glare.

"ROOM FOR CREAM," the barista evilly whispered.

Maggie leaped the counter. Grabbing the barista by her throat, Maggie shook her. "What's the matter with you? Why can't you understand? I don't want room. I don't want cream. I don't want rooms of cream, or creamy rooms, or room for cream, or cream for room, I just want my goddam fucking coffee you stupid bean-sucking moron *if you don't mind!*" Slowly regaining control, Maggie finally released the barista and clambered back over the counter, her skates pummeling the formica surface.

The barista coughed to recover her breath. Filling the cup to the brim, she calmly put the cup on the counter and popped on a plastic top. "All you had to do was ask," she snarked.

The eight wheels rolled. . .from nowhere. . .to nowhere. . .crying for the Planet. . .not letting the bad ones interfere. By the end of the block, the coffee was gone and was chased by more Thunderbird wine.

Sepulveda came into view. Outside an upscale loft with

trendy exercise rooms on the floor below, a slab of white on wheels caught Maggie's eye. Skating to the parked car, she took in the new paper license plates, the dark sunglasses hanging from the rear view mirror, the new map of Los Angeles outspread on the front seat, the boxes of hats and new clothes strewn about the interior. Maggie's intense gaze fixed on the car's logo: Tesla Model X.

Across the street was a Sports-R-Us. Skating deftly through traffic, Maggie rolled inside the sports store and soon exited with a new purchase. She approached the Tesla, its owner still absent.

Spitting once into each hand, Maggie lifted the baseball bat. With aim worthy of DiMaggio, she sent the side mirror arcing across the street. The other side mirror followed. With a series of quick slugs she burst every side window. The back window came next. Pausing to straighten her grip, she stood by the front of the car and, taking careful aim, caved in the driver's side of the front windshield. Then the passenger side of the front windshield.

Two people stood in the entrance to the exercise floor below the lofts—they pointed and soon a small crowd poured out, matched by others rushing up from various directions. From their midst jumped a diminutive woman. Hurrying to the demolished car, she halted, hands covering mouth. A man joined her.

The woman jabbered to the man in Chinese. Gently the man approached Maggie as she pounded dents in the hood and doors without pause.

"Prease. My wife she-a want to know: Vhy you kirr her car? Ve new to your country. Her car do something bad?"

Maggie shrugged.

Letting the bat clatter to the ground, she skated away. Down the street, she pulled out the bottle of Thunderbird and drained it. Taking a pit stop at Madam G-Spot's Pollo Ranchero Casino & Bowlarama, she skated to her special room where she paused to admire her No-Bull Peace Prize despite its inedible nature. She dusted it off.

Again she hit the streets.

At the Holy Roller Derby Club, Vexinator rolled to greet her.

"What's the big news, Mag?"

"Call the crew, Vex. There's something brewing." Maggie burped, tasting coffee under the wine.

At a signal from Vexinator, the Club resounded with the scrape of wheels. Nite Shade, Suki Vicious, and Crybaby Baiter rolled up from rink practice, while Maiden Hell, Bloody Mary, Hatecrime Hattie, and Queen Cobra tied on pads and helmets.

"What's up?" Nite Shade propped hands on hips, elbows akimbo for balance.

"Where's Thrill Killa and Pussy Kicker?" Maggie answered.

Nite Shade and Maiden Hell looked at each other. "Thrill sprang a leak and soaked Pussy. It may be the flu."

Maggie tensed her forehead. "This is for *all* the Warriors. I need everyone."

Crybaby Baiter flipped her phone closed. "Pussy Kicker's on the way. And Thrill Killa's all right—they just had too much Dos Equis."

Maggie stopped shifting her wheels back and forth. For once, her movement entirely stopped. She passed her steady oriental gaze over each of her fighters in turn, who, like the nuns at the Bowlarama, could not resist her charms, despite her painted eyebrows, false eyelashes, and dyed hair.

Maggie spoke. "The Ballbusters have called a convention for all the roller derby teams in the Los Angeles area. At Griffith Park. Their Jammer—Sirius—says she has something she wants to say to everyone. Word is all over town. Every derby girl who is any derby girl will be there. We've never seen anything like this in SoCal."

Maiden Hell pushed out her lips. "Griffith Park, Mag—that's an awful long way from Venice Beach."

"Yeah. That's not our skating grounds," added Bloody Mary. "Here we rule—there, who knows what could happen?"

"Don't sweat it. I know Sirius. I trust her. She don't take room for cream from nobody."

Queen Cobra glanced at the rink's entrance. "Do we wait for Pussy and Thrill?"

Maggie shook her head. "Sirius takes the stage at 9:00 p.m. Her words were: if you want to stake your 'hood, show up—or *lose* it. Pussy and Thrill will have to catch up when they can."

Tying the last laces on their shoes and pink corsets and strapping the last velcros on their knee and elbow pads, they packed their fanny packs and rolled north on Nielson Way to the light rail terminus in Santa Monica.

Staring out of rocking rail cars, layers of derby gang graffiti reminded them of the city's underclass and the riskiness of the venture: 'Talk derby to me' sullied one graffito; 'I'm not mean, you're just a sissy,' warned another. The crew grew restive at reading 'Don't Start None, Won't Be

None'. They became alarmed at 'Keep moving and stay bloody'.

Taking courage from their leader's placid confidence, however, the Warriors pressed on while the dark L.A. gloom settled over them like a smoggy blanket.

They at last exited the Red Line subway elbow at Vermont and Sunset and rolled north, again plunging into darkness. A half-hour later they paused at the edge of Griffith Park.

Around them the deep night was filling with ghost-like figures, packs of grungy derby leaguers from all over the L.A. basin rolling towards the Greek Theater, denizens of L.A.'s derby gangs looming from the surrounding blackness only to squeak immediately back into its shaded depths with fierce guarded expressions.

From somewhere ahead came echoes amplified by a stage. Penetrating deeper into the gloom, the little band of Warriors rolled past eerie expanses of unoccupied closely-trimmed grass on the right, still strewn with small white globules as the only tragic testament of that day's shattered dreams by desperate men swinging steel rods below par. The Warriors ignored the carnage. They set their jaws and rolled on.

The crowd grew thick. From all directions the derby gangs arrived at Griffith Park, their wheels grinding dirt and dust beneath, their bodies boasting dirt and dust on top.

Maggie's eyes narrowed. Rival gangs, who otherwise would never have tolerated the Warriors on their turf, skated alongside, the dark gulfs as it were vomiting them from its depths to throw them cheek-by-jowl in with Maggie's soldiers.

The Theater took shape.

Rolling towards the front, but on the left so as to be close to the road—a habit long acquired by the olive-skinned veteran of L.A.'s gritty back alleys and mean sculpted boulevards—Maggie led her crew mid-way towards the stage. Hundreds of other derby girls accumulated before, to the right, and behind, breaking the backs of the Theater's folding seats to toss them contemptuously aside. Even Maggie, the imperturbable master of thighs, found herself unconsciously counting her followers to compare them to the more numerous derby gangs that arrived out of the growing darkness.

Static erupted from the stage. Maggie recognized the red-gold flowing shirts of the Ballbusters. Their leader must be near.

At the back—a tall figure in red-gold knee-length robe on eight-wheeled skates emerged.

The static erupted again as someone tapped a microphone.

The crowd quieted.

Rolling backward onto the stage, the figure rotated, slowed, deliberately approached the microphone. Sirius flung long locks of curly black hair back behind her dark Malibu tan, a serious look on her smooth hairless face, her eyes passing over the vast assemblage of L.A.'s roller derby underground.

A hush fell over the crowd as they viewed the most famous roller derby girl in all Southern California, leader of the Ballbusters and head of the Instant Death League, where every play was for keeps, her own Ballbusters team the largest and most vicious in the League, the Warriors' application to join the Death League still sitting in the League's Inbox waiting to be processed.

This was for real.

Sirius shook her big finger like the born leader she was.

"Sisters," she bellowed. All eyes fixed on her. She pawed the stage with the brake pad of one skate like a bull impatient to roll and raised her arms high, flashing her rink-chipped teeth. "SISTERS!" The serious look deepened and she lowered her arms. "Look around." Eyes shifted. "You come from every 'hood in L.A. Here tonight is every rink—from Long Beach to Sun Valley. From El Segundo—to Cucamonga!"

The crowd passed its gaze over the crowded seats, the number of derby rollers spilling beyond the theater seating to sprawl over the barriers and slopes surrounding the stage.

"Look at our numbers, Sisters. If we decide to move, who can stand against us? If we unite, who can resist us?" Her arms rose again. "We are *legion!*"

The crowd stirred. Cries of "Yes! We are legion!" resounded.

Again the big finger. "Yes, we are legion. Yes, we have the numbers. But still *They* oppress us. Still *They* deny us our rights. Long have we lived in the corners, accepting what *They* choose to give us, forced to turn the other cheek when *They* catch us bending over—and *slap our ass!*"

Maggie stared, a smile transforming her face. This was good. She could not have done better herself; she would have to remember Sirius' technique.

The arms rose again. "Just look around you, Sisters. We

don't have to take it anymore. If we unite, we will have this city *by its busted balls*."

Roller ranks stood. Clapping accompanied by shouts of "Yes! We have the numbers. We must unite!"

"I am here to tell you that We Don't Have to Take It Anymore. Sisters, I am telling you: Unite now—take the streets. Take the streets of L.A." She grinned. "We are the 99 percent!"

The crowd erupted. Everyone leaped to their skates. "We are the 99 percent! We are united! It's time to take the streets!" Maggie and her crew stared around with amazement. It was all good. Sirius had spoken The Truth. The Warriors stood and whistled, clapping and shouting with the rest. It was about time. After so long, after so much pain and rejection by the bad ones, the time had come for The Derby Nation to assert its power.

Sirius shouted into the mike, her arms out thrust. "Can you dig it? *Can you dig it?!*"

The crowd went wild. A chant began:

Derby to the streets!

United we roll!

Derby to the streets!

United we roll!

Pop.

The upraised arms froze—slowly dropped. The grin on Sirius' face faded. With a wooden thud she fell backwards onto the stage, crashing through to the floor beneath.

Every breath froze. Every skate ceased rolling.

From the backmost row, a short grungy roller girl with stiff hair and wide jacket collar pulled over her face stood and shouted, her voice reverberating the length and breadth of Griffith Park. “The Warriors did it! *THE WARRIORS KILLED SIRIUS!*”

Episode 5

“Try it once more. Stretch those cheeks.”

“It hurts. No matter how many times I try, it still hurts,” said the man’s voice.

“Don’t worry. You’ll get used to it. You just have to keep at it.”

Amina turned ‘her’ wig-shrouded head to look at her instructor, five o’clock stubble darkening her chin though it was only Noon. She attempted a fake smile.

Beneath a sign that read ‘Academy of Involuntary Transmittals’, Orange Jello smoothed his short white-sleeved shirt and adjusted his pocket protector. His pale face was freshly scrubbed with soap and a hint of alcohol, his hair carefully brushed and anointed, and he could see his customer in the shine of his loafers.

“Watch me. It’s easy.” As Amina stared at Orange Jello’s face, he stood straight and exhibited a wide friendly smile, showing all his teeth. “See? You just have to keep practicing. The more you smile, the easier it gets.” He held up a finger. “But the trick is to make it convincing. Anyone can stretch their cheeks. But it takes training and practice to make your smile seem natural. And it must be natural if you want to gain your victim’s confidence.”

Standing next to Orange, Lemon Jello nodded his head in agreement, the two passing their gaze over the first classroom of customers in their new business.

The Jello Brothers felt good. True, they could only afford this basement in Culver City under a sleepy mattress store. And yes, they had laid down their Mormon Bibles since Scripture dueling had gone out of style. But they were still young, thanks to their immuring in Area 51's alien containment tubes for over half a century after they had succeeded in destroying the secret Nevada base of the Cross-Dressers from Pluto in 1951. Their training as Mormon missionaries had prepared them well for a career of gaining people's confidence, then stealing their valuables. Confidence was their name; enrichment was their game.

Orange Jello breathed deeply. He was born to this.

"Okay, let's see now. . . Amina, you said your goal is to overcome people's resistance to your inner self and persuade them to listen to your deeper philosophical ideas."

"Me too, Mr. Orange Jello," said Aliyah.

Seated next to her, Habiba nodded her head.

Orange stepped closer to where Amina sat at her school desk. "Here is the technique. I assure you that your failure to recruit more 'girlfriends' into your Muslim Cross-Dressers Union is not due to your life-style, but to—"

A frown seized Amina's face. " *'Life-style'?*" She leaped up and waved one hand, wildly snapping her fingers. "This is not a 'life-style'. Who told you that? Whoever told you this is a 'life-style' understands *nothing* about Amina. Who has told you such a lie?" She ran a finger across her throat. "I shall cut their fucking throat."

Aliyah and Habiba jumped up and ran their fingers across their throats. "Like prostitutes. We shall cut their fucking throats."

"Now, now, ladies. Please calm down. Let's take our seats please." Orange Jello smiled broadly again and all three members of the Muslim Cross-Dressers Union Local Number 36 gradually calmed and sat.

"Can we say this is an expression of your 'inner self', then?"

The three nodded, still frowning, though less deeply.

"Good. Now as I was saying," Orange exchanged cautious glances with Lemon Jello, "your lack of success is not due to your 'inner self', and also has little to do with your dress, but rather—"

" *'Dress?'* " Aliyah jumped up. "This is not a *'dress'!* It is an *abayah*, a sacred expression of our love for Allah. Who said this is a 'dress'? Who told you that?" She ran a finger across her throat. "Point him out and I will cut the fucking water-lover's throat."

Amina and Habiba also jumped up. "Yes. We will cut the fucking throat of the water-loving prostitute."

Taking a deep breath, Orange Jello smiled again. "Please ladies, you are here to get my help, and I would like to help you—"

The three glared. "We are sorry, Mr. Jello. But we do not tolerate insults from water-lovers." They returned to their seats.

Orange Jello glanced at the other students in the class. Several quietly scooted their desks away from the three cross-dressers, except for a man seated adjacent who wore green pants, a polka-dot shirt, a red bulb on his nose, and an orange-red fright wig on his head.

"Why don't you faggots sit down?" he grunted. He shifted giant clown shoes, the unlit half of a narrow cigar drooping from his unshaven mouth. "I'd like to get somethin' outta this god damn class and all you faggots have done all day is jump up and down and yell."

Three jaws dropped. Almost seated, Amina, Aliyah, and Habiba leaped up again. "*Faggots?* Did you call us faggots?"

"Yeah, ya buncha homos. Why dontcha put on a thong bikini and go to a gay bar like any sane homo? Ya ain't doin' yourselves any favors wearin' those goddam bedsheets."

"'Bedsheets?' Did you call these *'bedsheets'*?" They stood stunned, their jaws still open.

The clown sucked the dead cigar, leaned back, his hands buried in his pockets. He snickered. "Somewhere there's three naked beds shiverin' from cold."

"*Infidel!*" Amina stepped closer and waved one hand sideways in the air with finger pointed up, the other hand on her hip. "Do you know what I will do to you for saying that, Blinky?"

"Lemme guess—"

She ran her finger across her throat. "I will cut your fucking throat, you water-lover, that's what I will do!"

"Freakin' surprise. Lemme know when you wanna begin," Blinky muttered. "I got an appointment with an acupuncturist at three. You can get in line."

"We will cut your throat, water-lover. We will cut your fucking throat," yelled Aliyah and Habiba.

"Gentlemen! Ladies!" Orange interjected. "Please. We all have important things to do and we want to make some progress here today." He gently waved the cross-dressers back to their seats. "Now, as I was saying," he laid a cautious glance on Lemon who returned his glance with subdued concern, "How you present yourselves to the public is very important on how you will be received. It's not your. . .*current situation*," he eyed Amina, "that is the real problem. It's confidence and control."

The cross-dressers looked at each other. This was something new.

Blinky slipped a small flask from his green pants and morosely took a sip.

"When you present yourself to a stranger," continued Orange, "something I have many years' experience doing as a door-to-door Mormon missionary—it is crucial that you be able to display a smile that is absolutely natural."

A quiet sigh escaped Blinky's lips as he gazed at his giant red clown feet. "Natural," he muttered.

The cross-dressers glared at him.

"You must practice your smile. Ten times—a hundred times a day. Watch yourself in the mirror, make sure your teeth are clean, wash your face with *water*—"

"Water?! Gonna have a bit of a problem there, aren'tcha, ya faggots," snorted Blinky.

"Faggots," yelled Aliyah. "You said it again. Look. He called us faggots." The three jumped up. "I'll cut your fucking throat, infidel!"

"Not if I'm armed with *H2O*," Blinky smirked.

"Enemy of Allah!" Amina yanked out her nail scissors and aimed them over Blinky's head ready for a downward thrust. "Allahu akbar!"

Aliyah raised both arms and one leg, ready to deliver a karate kick to the clown. "Allahu akbar!"

Habiba yelled "God is great!" Amina and Aliyah looked

at her in surprise. Habiba shrugged. "I'm not really that big on Allah. My mother was Christian, you know."

"Ladies. Ladies. Please, we have a lot to cover today," shushed Orange, passing his hand over his eyes.

Reluctantly, and with more nasty glares at Blinky, who frowned at his feet and took another tired swig from his flask, they finally took their seats.

"*Aaas* I was saying. . .after, uh, *anointing* your face so that you make the best appearance possible, you want to be able to inspire absolute confidence in the victim by giving him," the sullen glares from the cross-dressing section turned suddenly on him, "or *her*, the ability to suspend her natural distrust of strangers." Orange smiled at the class again, to make certain that his perfect set of teeth could be seen on the back row. "Don't be a stranger. That's the important thing. Your image, your face, your tone of voice, your clothing—you must not present yourself as someone who is *different*." He dropped another hesitant glance at the three cross-dressers. Orange quickly redirected his gaze to the second row where several men in suits glowered.

"You see, Mr. Bailey, this is the reason why you lawyers are experiencing social failure. It is because you wear a suit and carry a briefcase and this makes you *different* in everyone's eyes."

Bailey spoke up. "But lawyers are supposed to wear suits and tote briefcases."

"Yes, Mr. Bailey. But you can leave your suit and briefcase behind when you are not at the office. Like when you go to parties, or go shopping—or to attend a class like this. It is *off-putting*. Outside the office, a suit and briefcase make people want to run for the door."

Bailey and a companion, both dressed to the nines in suit and tie, and with not one but two briefcases each, thought deeply. It would take time to locate and purchase some dignified non-suit clothing. And more time to locate the keys to undo the chains that kept the briefcases permanently attached to their wrists.

"Believe me. If you want to gain people's confidence and set them up to be swindled, the last thing you lawyers want to do is to arrive in suit and tie and pop open a briefcase."

They slowly nodded.

"However well your swindles may have worked for you so far," the lawyers smiled at each other, "I guarantee that bigger opportunities will come from gaining people's confidence at the very first meeting. When we finish training you, you will walk away not only with all their money, but with the words 'Thank you, brother' in your ears." Orange grinned. "That's right. The best measure of your success as criminals and swindlers is when they actually thank you for taking their money."

The cross-dressers and lawyers grinned. Even Blinky seemed to emerge from his depression.

"You breaking-and-entering specialists," Orange glanced at a pair of homies from the hood on the third row sporting pullover skicaps and crowbars, "and you bank robbers expert at terrorizing a roomful of mothers and children," his glance settled on several characters sitting behind them wearing the rubber masks of past Presidents, "I think you'll find that our Academy's method is superior and almost fool-proof."

They nodded. All ears.

"Let's try a demonstration." Orange looked around the room. Everyone pretended not to notice and turned their glance away. "Come now. No need to be embarrassed. We all know what's it's like to try and fail at crime—we've *all* been there. That's why we're here today, to learn how to improve our performance and rob and steal with success."

Lemon rubber-necked toward the back row. "How about you bankers and stockbrokers back there? I know you are already expert at swindling people with derivatives every day, but that's lots of work. Wouldn't you like to learn how to swindle people more easily?"

They nodded, though none volunteered.

"I see some empty oil well promoters and played out gold mine hawkers in our group today," added Orange. "How about you?"

More smiles, but still no volunteers.

"New Jersey trash haulers, on the third row? Don't you want to help demonstrate how to gain the confidence of victims?"

One of them nudged his partner. "We perform a giblectomy. That seems to get their confidence well enough."

The class chuckled.

Orange smiled. "Yes, but we're all here for one reason—we're not doing as well as we would like. Or we want a complete change of career and we're thinking about going into a new and lucrative profession with minimal time and effort. And Trust and Confidence, my friends, is that Profession."

He looked at the back of the class. "What about you, Doctors? I know you‘ve been successful swindling your patients by staring out the window and saying 'You look fine to me—take this Oxycontin and Fentanyl and call me in the morning,' while your patients bleed out, but sooner or later you will want to go for the Big Bucks."

Throwing sheepish glances around them, the two doctors retreated behind their white upended collars.

"And you Televangelists on the next to back row? You especially should be alert to the concepts of confidence and control of your victims."

A clean-cut man with red tie and blue jacket jumped up and lifted his hands overhead. "Hallelujah Jello! We'll pray for you on tonight's show. But no photos, please." He gave an embarrassed look and sat.

"Well, how about you mimes?" Orange looked at several mimes dressed in horizontal black and white stripes, their faces painted white, seated at the back row beside the doctors. "Your French-Canadian circus, *Cirque de Lumiére*, has brought something new and evil to town, but you are right to think that evil alone won't take care of your retirement. You of all people should want to learn how to take your victims' money after you perform your evil work."

They smiled and nodded but made no move to come to the front.

"Bobby and Ray?" Orange looked at the third row. "I know you have projects in the works, but poaching Sasquatches from federal forests can't be very lucrative. And I'm sure it has few benefits."

Ray adjusted his Elmer Fudd hat. "We done well enough." Ray leveled a Don't-Say-a-Word look on Bobby. "But we'd like to grab some tips on how to game our next project."

"You've come to the right place." Orange nodded. "Blinky—how about you? You say you've had enough of taking advantage of small suckers at your traditional circus and want to graduate to the Big Top. Let's show them how a little enthusiasm can change everything."

Blinky sighed. "Why the hell not," he muttered. Thrusting the half-empty flask inside a pocket, he slowly flapped his giant red shoes until he stood in front of Orange Jello. He reluctantly took the dead stick of a cigar out of his mouth.

"Now Blinky, let's say you've lined up a chance to meet an older woman who is a wealthy investor. She's upper-class. She's discerning. She's single. And, best of all—she's loaded. Let's see, we need someone else. . .someone to play the Wealthy Widow." Orange passed his glance over the class once. . .twice. . . "Let's see. . .*whoo* should be the Wealthy Widow?"

His gaze settled. "How about you, Amina? Do you think you can play a Wealthy Widow?"

Frowning, Amina thought for a moment, then stood and stepped to where Orange pointed. She scratched her stubbly chin and glared at Blinky from under her stiff lavender wig.

A hand rose from the back row.

"Oh, excellent. Our mimes have changed their minds." Orange waved them forward and the three mimes halted just behind Amina. Recalling the 'incident' on the Santa Monica beach a few days earlier, the three Muslim cross-dressers stared at the mimes in alarm, but finally calmed when the mimes thrust their hands into their pockets and whistled *Swanee* while looking out the window, ignoring them.

Orange returned his attention to Blinky.

"First thing, Blinky, is to stand up straight."

The clown slowly put his heels together and rose to full height, clearing Amina by half a foot. He wiped some drool off his unshaven chin.

"That's good. Now: you've just met Ms. Wealthy Widow. She's loaded with dough. Like all widows, you know she is looking for companionship. So step close, look in her eyes, and give her the biggest smile you've ever given anyone. Stretch those cheeks."

Fixing his unfocused red-rimmed eyes surrounded by clown paint on Amina's sprouting beard, Blinky took a step closer. He took possession of his usual enormous frown, and slowly lifted the ends of his grease-painted mouth into a grimace to reveal a set of nicotine and coffee-stained teeth, only one of which was missing. His boozy breath filled the space between them.

Amina glared up at him with the receptiveness of a junkyard dog.

"Excellent, Blinky. Smiling is the first step in demonstrating confidence. Can you smile broader? Show more teeth?"

Blinky stretched his cheeks all the way to his upper lip, exposing his canines.

"Now to complete your demonstration of confidence, you must say something positive. Start with something easy—like the weather. Then move to something a little more risky, like giving your victim a pleasant compliment." Orange flashed his easy smile. "Let's try it. After all, what could possibly go wrong?"

Flicking his eyes briefly at Orange Jello, Blinky returned his alcohol-blurred gaze at the abayah-encased cross-dresser Amina, taking in the five o-clock shadow, the burning eyes, the petulant mouth, the hair-trigger temper, the unfamiliarity with basic hygiene.

"Do you like rain?" Blinky grunted. "It might make you smell better."

Amina shouted and stamped a foot, hand on hip. "There he goes! I knew he would say something like that. That's sexist and racist and very very bad." She turned to face Orange and Lemon. "You must tell him to have respect for my delicate womanhood—or I swear I will cut his ever-fucking water-loving throat!" Amina's eyes bulged.

Blinky looked up innocently. "Whad I say? *Whad I say?*"

"Blinky, that was a good effort to give a nice compliment, but keep in mind that you're talking to a widow, a wealthy widow. She is lonely. She wants to hear something nice from a man. You must gain her confidence. Now let's give her a compliment. Say something nice about her appearance."

Swaying as if from a breeze, though there was none, Blinky cleared his throat. He fixed his blood-shot eyes on Amina. "I like your mustache. Is your sister's just as nice?"

Amina caught her breath. "He did it again! He did it again, Mr. Jello! I will not take such insults from anyone. I swear I will cut his fucking throat in the parking lot when this class is over."

"Yes," echoed the other cross-dressers. "In the parking lot. Before six."

"Now, now, now, Ms. Amina. No need to get excited. It's

just an exercise. We are all learning here. Please calm down."

Orange Jello turned back to Blinky. "Now, let's see how you may gain control over your victim. We do that principally by always saying *No* to anything she says, but then repeating the exact same thing the victim said, but in different terms showing that you actually agree with her, thus establishing your dominance."

He looked at Amina. "Let's try that now. Amina, say something factual but unimportant."

She calmed. Breathing deeply, she passed her fierce gaze over Blinky's white-painted eyes, blurry from Old Overcoat, the reddish-orange fright wig with leaves entwined from sleeping on a park bench, the unwashed polka-dot shirt with dull faded plastic flower, green pants, huge red shoes, and his stained-tooth grimace staring back at her with narrow cigar stuffed back in. She noticed a small balloon on a bent stick thrust absent-mindedly in a back pocket.

"Last week," Amina said, "I went to a Circus of Infidels. The clowns there were happy. And funny." She aimed a harsh reproachful glare at Blinky.

"That's good, Amina. Blinky?"

He took the half-cigar out of his mouth, produced a small lighter and lit it. The acrid smoke momentarily overcame the alcohol haze that perpetually accompanied him, miraculously failing to burst into flame, and he drew himself up to full height. He stretched his cheeks, his canines fully displayed.

"No. You did not go to a Circus of Infidels. You went to a concentration camp of lunatics. Everyone there is happy and funny—especially the clowns. Boy, are they funny. They're funny when they tell someone to go to Clown School instead of college. They're funny when they make him juggle balls for hours and beat him when he drops one. They're funny when they lock him in animal cages and give him only bread and water. They're funny when they prostitute him to rich Asians looking for a good time. They're funny when they make two clowns fight and bet on who will be the winner. And they're sooo funny when they throw greasepaint and stupid clothes on him and push him in front of laughing crowds. Yeah, they're funny. We're so so happy and funny." He gulped another drink. Swaying again, he drained the flask.

"Oookay," said Orange. "Thank you, Blinky." He turned to Amina. "Do you feel like you have lost control, that some of your personal power has flowed to Blinky?"

"Yes." Amina glared daggers at Blinky. "The water-loving infidel has stolen my personal dignity by drinking alcohol in my presence. My religion prohibits drinking alcohol."

A cloud of smoke burst over Amina and she coughed. Unable to breathe, she turned blue. Aliyah and Habiba leaped up and pounded on her back until she breathed again, directing lethal looks at the depressed clown.

Blinky sniffed. "Do you like smoke? I'll bet it works as well as water."

Her jaw dropped. "Did you hear him? He did it again! Wait till I get you in the parking lot, you water-loving infidel!" She raised her nail-scissors again. "Your throat! I will cut your ever-fucking throat!"

One of the mimes stepped forward and fixed his gaze on

Lemon Jello. The mime moved his lips. As if in a trance, Lemon stared suddenly at the ceiling and spoke. In a monotone robot voice, he said, "Our-mime-guests-want-to-give-it-a-try."

The mime was clad in white and black horizontal stripes with black suspenders overlaid, holding up black pants, a floppy frenchy hat on top, his white greasepaint face accented by diamonds above and under his eyes. Purplish-black lipstick outlined an evil grin. Purple Lips turned and exchanged a wink with Yellow Spandex, his companion who was dressed in a single yellow spandex outfit with red star over the heart, black tattoos outlining his eyes, and a too-small bowler on his head.

As Amina and her girlfriends retreated cautiously behind Orange and Lemon Jello, Purple Lips pointed at Amina. The mime pretended to sashay down Champs-Elysee, one hand on his hip, the other drooping at the wrist. His pasty face took on a coy expression as his head bobbed. Pausing in front of Yellow Spandex, Purple Lips halted and femininely feigned surprise, then moved his lips.

"Why-how-do-you-do-my-good-man?" buzzed Lemon Jello again in a robot tone, his wide eyes testifying to his loss of control over his own voice.

Yellow Spandex silently laughed.

Purple Lips fixed his stare on Amina. Standing behind Orange, Amina suddenly stood at attention and began to walk mechanically. One hand on hip, the other hand uplifted and drooping at the wrist, Amina sashayed exactly like Purple Lips had done, exaggerating her hips as she walked across the room, the junk-yard dog expression replaced suddenly by a feminine coyness. In front of Blinky,

Amina shook her head as in a daze.

Again silent laughter from Yellow Spandex. He bowed at the waist. Straightening, he caught Blinky's gaze. To everyone's surprise, Blinky bowed politely to Amina, his clown eyes wide as if his body, like Amina's, were no longer under his control.

Yellow Spandex mouthed silent words. In response, Lemmon buzzed "Good-day-to-you-too-Madam." Staring at Lemon Jello, Yellow Spandex silently twisted his lips, and Lemon spoke again. "May-I-say-your-ugliness-exceeds-all-bounds-today?"

Purple Lips silently laughed with coy feminine embarrassment. "How-nice-of-you-to-notice," buzzed Lemon.

Glancing at Yellow Spandex's shoes, Purple Lips mouthed again. "Your-red-shoes-are-so-pretty. Like-you, they-need-washing," buzzed Lemon.

"Just-for-you, I-will-clean-them," came the rejoinder, Lemon still doing all the talking while Amina and Blinky faced each other, silent.

Yellow Spandex reached into a pocket and leaning over pretended to anoint the other mime's shoes with the liquid contents of an invisible flask.

As he did so, Blinky, staring into space, mechanically extracted his flask of Old Overcoat that he kept in his pocket and dumped the contents on his red clown shoes.

Standing straight, Yellow Spandex puffed an invisible cigar and dropped it. As if he were a doppelganger condemned to duplicate the mime's every move by spooky action at a distance, Blinky puffed his cigar red hot—then dropped it on his own alcohol-soaked shoes.

Flames burst.

"Oh no—oh, no, no, no." Blinky said. He twitched his feet but seemed unable to move from the spot.

Purple Lips waved his feminine hand again. "What-a-nice-flower," Lemon buzzed. "May-I-smell-your-flower?"

Yellow Spandex grinned. "Why-yes-indeed-good-Madam," continued Lemon. "My-flower-has-a-very-nice-smell."

Purple Lips bent over to view the red star on Yellow Spandex's chest. As he did so, Amina did the same, bringing her face close to Blinky's faded plastic flower.

A fire hydrant of water erupted.

"Eeeyaah," Amina shrieked. Rubbing her face clean of the 'poison', she violently shook before springing into motion. Swinging this way and that, Amina ran circles around Lemon and Orange, her hands flinging the poisonous liquid away as fast as she could manage.

"He sprayed me with poison! Blinky sprayed me with poison!"

"My dear Amina!" yelled Orange in shock. "My dear lady!"

Blinky finally broke free. Flapping his giant shoes—now roaring with flames—he flopped around the room close behind Amina. "Oh no. Oh, no, no, no."

The mimes leaned on each other, holding their stomachs while they heaved with silent laughter.

Amina and Blinky reversed course, the cross-dresser now chasing Blinky with upraised nail-scissors while he flopped back the way he had come, leaving traces of flame and ash behind.

"I'll kill you, infidel! Wait till I catch you, I'll cut your fucking throat!"

"Oh no. Oh no, no, no." Blinky flopped. "Need some help. Need some help here!"

Amina narrowly missed him with a swipe, popping the balloon in his back pocket. "Stop running, you water-lover! Slow down so I can cut your ever-fucking throat!"

While they ran, Purple Lips pretended to pull a Bible from a pocket. Opening the invisible book, he looked at Yellow Spandex and silently recited quotes while crossing himself. Reaching into his own pocket, Yellow produced his own invisible Bible, and with exaggerated outrage, recited passages back at Purple Lips in a duel of silent quotes.

From the back of the class the two televangelists jumped up and rushed to the front. "Blasphemy," they yelled. Producing a real Bible, they loudly recited to the mimes: "And the Lord healed those who were sick from many diseases and cast out many devils; and suffered not the devils to speak because they knew him."

The rest of the room's inhabitants stood, their credulity badly sprained.

Yellow Spandex produced a Mormon Bible and handed it to Lemon.

Surprised—but pleased to see his beloved Mormon Bible back in his hands after an absence of seventy years, even if it was not his personal copy 'Old Brigham'—Lemon snapped it open and fired one of its most lethal passages at the televangelists: "The scales of darkness shall begin to fall from their eyes; and many generations shall not pass away among them, save they shall be a white and delightsome people."

The televangelists staggered and fell to one knee. It was

a fierce, almost mortal blow.

Struggling to their feet, the televangelists let loose with one of their own: "And the whole city assembled at the door, and he cured many sick of various disorders, and expelled many demons, and permitted not the demons to speak."

Now Lemon fell back as if struck in the chest. Orange tried to avoid the barrage, but he could not cover his ears in time, and he too gasped—collateral damage.

Aliyah shouted: "You infidels dare to recite your infidel books in our presence? This steals our personal dignity as much as drinking alcohol." She whipped out a Koran from beneath her abayah and flipped several pages: "And Solomon said: 'We have been taught the language of birds', so an army was created for Solomon of jinns, men, and birds, and all were kept under strict discipline."

The Jello Brothers and the televangelists reeled, stunned by the passage.

Blinky skipped past, flames traveling from his shoes to the curtains on the walls. "Need some help. Need some help here."

"I'll kill you, you water-loving infidel!" Amina ran in pursuit, swinging her nail-scissors. As she ran past, Lemon snatched her abayah and it ripped off in his hands—with their usual coordination, Orange did the same with Aliyah's abayah.

"Sorry, ma'ams. We gotta put the fire out." The Jello brothers used the two snatched abayahs to stifle the burning curtains and Blinky's burning shoes, pausing only a moment to comment. "Say, ma'ams, those are nice thong bikinis you're wearing."

Amina—*sans* her sacred abayah—turned her bikini-clad Sasquatch body towards Lemon. “I will cut your fucking throat too, Mr. Jello. I will cut all your infidel fucking throats. And scratch your eyes out also.”

“Not today.” Lemon bolted up the stairs to the mattress shop.

Amina followed. “When I catch you, I will cut your fucking throat,” she yelled in pursuit, pausing only to snatch up bedsheets in the mattress shop for herself and Aliyah to replace their scorched abayahs.

“Get her, Bobby!” yelled Ray upon sighting Aliyah's Sasquatch-hairy body. Bobby threw his arms around Aliyah in between Koran quotes: “We got ya now, ya Sasquatch. Thought you could fool us by wearin bed-sheets? You cain't hide no more. Fergit that other job, Bobby! We're gonna get us that ree-ward fer sure with this un.”

“Thanks, Doc. We'll make a fortune selling your drugs to our clients,” said the lawyers, shaking hands with a grinning doctor. They stuffed narcotics in their briefcases, then turned to face the next row. With a vicious swing, the lawyers slam-dunked the oil-well promoters and gold-mine claimers with their briefcases and stole their wallets. As the lawyers made ready to run, the bankers and stock-brokers tackled them. Grabbing their briefcases, they took a step—the New Jersey trash haulers body-slammed them. Before the latter could make good their escape with the booty, the burglars broke open the briefcases and stole most of the drugs, while the bank robbers pulled out guns and robbed the New Jersey crew and the lawyers of what remained.

The curtains burning like Atlanta, the entire student body of the Academy of Involuntary Transmittals rushed the stairs to exit.

Habiba tossed her abayah aside and joined them. "This *Allah* thing ain't workin' out," she mumbled.

Lemon snuck back down, leaving Amina roaming the streets armed with bedsheet and nail-scissors. Yanking the curtains down and stamping the flames till they smoked, and the basement now empty but for Lemon hiding behind the stairflight, and Blinky who had pulled off his shoes and lay supine on the floor softly groaning, Orange took a deep breath.

"Oookay. Let's move to our second topic: How to Win Friends & Achieve Inner Calm with Positive Visualization."

Episode 6

As from an electric shock, Maggie instantly grasped the danger. They were minor league players in the heart of Indian Country, unfriendly gangs on every side ready to roll against anyone who stepped on their turf without derby league permission, and as if that were not lethal enough, their team's name was spreading through Griffith Park like a bad meme as those responsible for the death of Sirius. And not just *her* death—but the death of their chance to unite and dominate Los Angeles.

It was a grim prospect.

The hand of every derby girl would be against them.

"Nite Shade. Suki Vicious." They responded instantly,

alarm in their eyes. "You take the right flank. Hatecrime and Cobra, the left. Remember the special formation we practiced. Maiden Hell and Bloody Mary—you're Twin Jammers. Crybaby Baiter, Vex, and myself—we're Phalanx. Once you Jammers engage, we'll break up the party."

The crew exchanged glances.

"Maggie, we've never gone this far before. Are you sure we'll make it?" Nite Shade and Suki passed worried gazes over the vast crowd of tattooed frowning roller queens who were even now changing from allies into enemies, sworn to take revenge as soon as they could identify which gang in their midst had turned their dreams to dust.

A shadow passed over the moon. In the midst of the ensuing darkness, Maggie threw aside her helmet with the pivot stripe. She was in her element.

"From nowhere—to nowhere. Let's roll."

Sliding from Griffith Theater to the feeder road, they rolled toward Vermont Street, making their escape just as the moon reappeared. Around them, the other gangs were dispersing, some casting suspicious looks at the Warriors, others collecting in small clumps, mustering their numbers to strike—but strike whom? Strike where? Who were *The Warriors*? What were their colors?

The foothills eased by as the Warriors followed North Vermont southward. At Hillhurst Avenue, a small group of skaters had staked out the intersection, unsure which direction to guard but determined to prevent any unauthorized team from crossing.

"I know this team," growled Maggie. "The Ugly Puglies. They're stupid." The Warriors picked up speed. Before the Puglies knew what hit them, fiery pigtails and a half-shaved head with tattooed coffin burst from the darkness and knocked several down. Two pirouetted, attempting to engage—the Phalanx slammed them. With Maggie in front, the main body of Warriors rolled over the rest of the Puglies, sending them howling into the gutter. They clutched elbows and knees as the Warriors merged with the night.

"Don't mess with the Squatch," taunted Crybaby Baiter.

Down Vermont, they slowed. "Los Feliz and Ambrose are up ahead. There's sure to be hostiles waiting."

"I have an idea," said Bloody Mary. "Let's cue into the derby network 'Live Lips' App. Maybe the rest of the City didn't hear the Big Lie. Maybe the rolling is clear all the way back to Venice."

"Try it and see." Pausing under the light of a dull streetlamp, the Warriors punched up the iPhone App. They crowded around to listen.

The 'Lips' came into focus. Rippling across the iPhone screen without face or eyes, the Lips did their damage—and moved on—broadcasting their lie in a sultry voice to a million eager ears:

"For all you serial rollers out there who didn't make it to the Derby Convention," the Lips seductively murmured, "there has been a bit of a problem. It seems that one gang at the Convention didn't care for the Plans of our beloved Sirius, Chief Ballbuster, to bring all the derby leagues under central management. So they retired Sirius—permanently. A thousand eyewitnesses have put a name to that gang: The Warriors. Hailing from Venice, it seems the killers made their escape a short time ago from the Park and are headed back the way they came."

Crybaby Baiter and Vex looked to Maggie with open mouths. "How can they say that? We didn't do shit at the Theater. To Sirius, or anyone." The others nodded agreement.

Maggie hushed them and motioned to keep listening.

Live Lips resumed. "The derby clubs at the Convention have suggested that if The Warriors fail to make it back to Venice, no one would be upset, and they would like to send out the word to every derby club in the L.A. basin between Griffith Park and Venice, reminding them of their duty to Derby League Dot Org, which was badly harmed tonight. Therefore we have been requested, as a public service, to read the roster of Roller Derby Clubs on the named itinerary—for the benefit of You-Know-Who. If you're out there, Warriors, you might want to listen up. . ."

Silence ensued. Then the Lips again moved. "This just out, Motor Rollers. It seems the Warriors have surfaced. They barreled their way through the first derby club in their path, the Ugly Puglies, who have fallen by the wayside. It's up to the next friendly club in their path to strut their stuff. That means you, *Cherry Bombers*. Let's see if you can block Vermont Avenue better than the Puglies.

"Also on our list of volunteers we have: the Steel Knockers, the Lipstick Pivots, the Jammer Up Your Asses, the Cannibal Rocketeers, the Toxic Leakers, the Skunk Apettes, the Zombinators, the Girls Can't What & Die'rs, the DominaTrixies, the Lezzie Hatchets, the Y B Normals, the Vicious Vixens, the Fat Enough 4 U Whores, the Pink Machines, the Girlfren Squashers, the Holey Meats, the Bitchy Bruisers, the Kitty Killers, the Bare Ass Heartbreakers, the Katzen Jammers, the Vaginal Mixers, the

Queer Girl Sluggers, the Big Girl Bitches, the Angels Without Mercy, the Sloppy Raggers, the Crotchetyettes, the Bush-Mowers, the Lick My Dusters, the OCDivas, the PsychoTeens, the Homicide Dolls, the Queens of Your Bare Butt, the Sluts By Choice, the Kiss My Wheelers, the Polly Baiters, the Damned Divas and Damned if You Don'ters, the Krazy Kleptics, the Killa Bs 4 Ever, the Ball-Crushers, the Hate You Trulies, the Bloody Jammers, the Helles Belles, the Bare Ass Brawlers, the Take No Prisnas, the 69 Beaters, the Talk Derby To Me's, the Pivot Fisters, the Tittie Yankers, the White Boys Can't Derbiers, the Comet Rippers, the Butch-aholics, the Nails In Ya Coffinettes, the Lugy Strikers, the Manglers, the Bite Me Bullies, the Jammer Brats, the Brawling Bitches, the Wash This! Rollers, the Stay Calm While I Kill U's, the Donut Suckers, the Kill Em & Feel Better Betties, the Kuntalicious Korpses, the 60 in Zero Crashers, the Live Fast Play Dirty Rollers, the Revoltin' Meemies, the Vomiteers, the Left Turn Titty Twisters, the Size Forty Crushers, the Cherry Mashers, the Willow Swatches, the Legatics, the Skateitarians, the Roll Like A Girl Killas, the Piece & Just Us Dykes, the Big Squeezers, the Nut Wrenchers, the Velcro Strappers, the Toothless Hos, the Whores for a Day, the Can't Keep a Bloody Girl Down'rs, the Manic Mommas, the Killa Kommados, the I See Dumb Skaters, the Bloodyettes, the Never Take Midol So Deal With It's, the Rambling Punishers, the Roller Vamps, the I Warned U Not to Come Backers, the U Dug Yur Own Gravettes, the Death Rattle Gaspers, the Grungematics, the Corpses On Wheels, the Back-Seat Hearses, the Bad News Brawlettes, the Zombiemanics, the Betty In Your Facers, the Bastardettes, the Wight Wing Wongs, the Mothers of Insurrection, the Coffin Aromas, the Girl Reapers, the Silicon Busters, the Rolling Thunderettes, the Krazy Kunts, the Color Me Bloodys, the Screw It Good Hackers, the The's With No A'ss's, the Why Don't We Do It In the Rink'rs. . ."

Maggie flicked off the App. "We're wasting time. We have to get through Feliz and Ambrose." With a backward glance into the gloom, the Warriors ground forward, their pink corsets and blue pleated flaps with black leather skirts underneath, their colors standing out like recruits on parade, their bare hints of tail teasing like quarter moons.

Los Feliz came into view. Maggie signaled that they slow down and approach from the deeper shadow of an unlit building. Sighting several girls on skates, they paused to take positions. Maggie nodded—the Cherry Bombers, known for their tendency to slip explosives into an opposing team's fanny packs. Traffic was heavy at Los Feliz and the Bombers had not yet sighted them, but they must know from listening to the Derby Net 'Live Lips' App that the Warriors would seek to surprise them and barrel through.

Maggie risked a radical move—she split her forces in two.

Hatecrime and Cobra crossed the median to the left, and when the light turned, they slowly skated across as if returning from an uneventful evening at the Theater, while Nite Shade and Suki Vicious did the same at the crosswalk down on the right. Only when both pairs had crossed the street and attracted the attention of the Bombers, did Maggie and the others slowly glide across Los Feliz a half-block away speeding swiftly through the traffic while the

Bombers' attention was distracted grilling the advance guard.

As Maggie approached, still careful to take advantage of what shadows were afforded from the streetlights and the lights of surrounding businesses, she could clearly see the cherry bombs clutched by two of the Bombers. With a snort, she noticed they had arrived in an Escalade, their skating skills so far below that of the Warriors that they had rolled in on rubber.

Queen Cobra exchanged greetings with a counterpart among the Bombers, the other showing mild interest in Cobra's reggae braids, while Hatecrime attracted stares by her partly shaved head. From behind, Suki and Nite Shade slipped in, careful to smile and wave so as not to alarm the Bomber sentries.

"You gutter-gals haven't seen any Warriors, have ya?" blandly asked one of the Bombers, not alarmed but still not entirely assured. She tossed her cherry bomb in the air like George Raft flipping a coin to emphasize her distrust.

"Fuckin ass," smiled Hatecrime. "Point one out and I'll put her in a pine box. Imagine wasting Sirius when we could've squeezed this city's gonads till the pips squeak."

"What league are you with?" asked the other suspiciously. "They say those Warriors are expected to show up around here any time."

"League?" snorted Hatecrime. "We don' need no stinkin' league. We score with every match we have."

This worried the Bomber. Reaching to her side, she summoned Live Lips to get more info.

"Whatcha need?" asked Hatecrime.

"Colors. Live Lips just announced the Warriors' colors."

She eyed Hatecrime's pink corset and blue flaps covering her ultra-short black leather skirt, the same uniform worn by Suki, Nite Shade, Cobra, and all the Warriors. Six Bombers gathered around the phone, three more lounging inside the Escalade. Casually, the Warriors drifted back.

Out of the gloom burst The Juggernaut.

Falling on the Bombers like an out of control dozer, the Warrior Phalanx flung Bombers left and right, smashing their phone without hope of repair. Maggie's impetus, with Crybaby Baiter, Maiden Hell, Vex, and Bloody Mary close behind carried the Jam all the way to the Escalade, where Maggie—who had snatched both cherry bombs—crunched them through the air vents. They rolled to the engine.

"Oh fuck," yelled the Bomber behind the wheel. She flew out as if sprung by an ejector seat.

The other Bombers scrambled out of the Escalade as fast as their half-laced skates could manage.

The explosion blew the hood up and crumpled it, filling the interior with acrid smoke—that car would never deliver cherry bombs again—or Cherry Bombers.

Crybaby Baiter blew an energetic kiss at the pile of bodies, moaning on the ground. "You just got a hand-delivery from the Warriors. How do ya like it, little girls? Does it smart?" She and Suki laughed out loud as they mustered behind Maggie.

They quieted. Bloody Mary was staring at her hand. The tip of a finger was missing.

A hard look took hold of the Warriors.

Mary raised her hand over her head and bathed her hair in the blood. "So much the better," she grimaced. "No one can ever say that Bloody Mary lives a lie."

The others nodded agreement. Now they were truly veterans.

Tying her finger with string, Mary skated forward.

"Let's roll," said Maggie.

Propelling down Vermont they soon came to the next intersection—Ambrose Avenue. Looming in the streetlights were over a dozen hulking brutes on mountain bikes. They were not capable of overtaking the Warriors' street skates, but they could use their bikes to run them down, and the added weight would make it more difficult to jam them into submission. Maggie eyed the size of the women and their masculine flared salmon collars and nodded in recognition: the Transvesdykes.

"What are *they* doing here?" asked Suki in thinly veiled alarm. "The Convention was only for derby girls."

Flipping open the cell phone, Maggie brought up the Live Lips App again. The lips resumed their former movement: "We've had some feedback from the Vermont Front, conventioneers. . . The Puglies may have folded like bad origami, but the Cherry Bombers stepped forward for the greater good and did battle with the Warriors. They went down in flames and lost a new Escalade in the process, but they report that they inflicted a serious injury on the Enemy. So all is not lost, friends. It's clear the Warriors are heading for the Red Line Subway to get back to their home turf as quickly as they can, but Derby Leaguers—you have friends out there. Several have pledged to stop the Warriors before they reach the Red Line. We thank the Transvesdykes for stepping up to the plate."

Maggie flipped the phone shut. The growing looks of

alarm on the faces of her soldiers made consulting Live Lips something to be done only intermittently.

"We've learned a lot. They're stupid. They think we don't know who's in front of us, and what we're dealing with. Now we know. And we know where they expect to find us."

The crew nodded, optimism returning.

Maggie looked at Crybaby Baiter and Hatecrime Hattie. "It's time for Bait & Switch. The Transvesdykes will have some people at Ambrose Avenue, but the rest will be halfway down, expecting us to try a go-around. That's just what we'll do—but with one change."

Skating right-ward, they infiltrated the residences and soon found what Maggie sought. Then, sliding across Ambrose a half block down, they were instantly sighted by the Transvesdykes and the mountain bikes leaped in pursuit. Turning back eastward, Maggie found a gap between two houses bathed in darkness. While the other Warriors rolled into the shadowed gap, Maggie and Maiden Hell stood in the light of a streetlamp.

"Hey, girlicues," called the Dykes. "Don't think you can hide from us. Wait up. We've got a little gift for your breadbaskets." On the Transvesdykes came, with packs of cigarettes and marijuanettes rolled up in their T-shirt sleeves, and tattoos of girlfriends on their shoulders, their mountain bikes picking up speed.

When they arrived, Suki and Cobra yanked the rubber hose to chest level.

Tumbling like sloths at the wheel, the Transvesdykes flipped crewcut heads over loafered heels to finally slide to a stop at Maggie's feet. Suki and Cobra lowered the hose. From the opposite direction came the rest of the Transvesdykes, hurrying to close the pincers, unaware that one pincer had fizzled.

Up went the hose again. Down went the rest of the James Dean wannabes.

They lay in the bright moonlight, legs caught in a tangle of bikes, faces upturned in the silver rays, despite their defeat unable to tear their eyes away from the gorgeous visions that presented themselves, verily unto angels sprouting from the earth.

"So you—you're the Warriors?" The dykes caught their breath as they contemplated the loveliness of the victors. "If we had only known. . . If we had had the chance to cast our eyes on you before this. . ."

Suki placed her derriere on the nearest face with a smirk; the dyke sighed and puckered up.

"Us too," lusted the rest as Maiden Hell and Hatecrime Hattie offered their rears in turn to the rest of the dykes, laughing over their victory, teasing the downed dykarellas by swinging their bra-less breasts in their faces and blowing kisses for good measure.

"Can't have it," taunted Maggie, swinging her hips. "Only in your dreams."

The team rolled, disgorging the turf, but having won the reputation.

Skirting Vermont, now too dangerous to risk, they traveled New Hampshire Avenue. In a short time, an expanse of greenery opened.

"The Vermont-Sunset Subway is cattycorner—over there," motioned Maggie. "Once we get on board, we'll have a clean ride to Santa Monica." The Warriors passed cautious glances over the grassy expanse that was poorly lit by outdated street lighting, two passersby stumbling about scrounging bottles to gather pennies and nickels for their next dime-bag.

The way was clear—*too* clear.

Maggie put an arm before Hatecrime could step out of the shadows. “Every derby gang in L.A. is tuned into Live lips. There is not a single derby girl, or friend of a derby girl, who doesn’t know that we’re headed for this Subway entrance.”

They exchanged glances again. “So what do we do?”

Crybaby Baiter whined, “How do we get outta this mess, Maggie? I didn’t sign on for this.”

The others looked at Crybaby Baiter in surprise. Her attitude was new. The tension was beginning to tell.

“We gotta just plough through, bitches,” said Queen Cobra, fingering the hidden copper strips in her elbow pads. “They may win, but they’ll damned well know they’ve been in a fight.”

Hatecrime sneered. “A *fight?* Are you fuckin kiddin’ me? I’ll kill em and eat their livers.”

“Look,” hissed Vexinator. “There’s something moving in the park!”

They focused, and sure enough, something glinted as it moved between the trees. Not quite the height of a human, it flashed and glinted like metal on metal.

“I think we should—”

It was too late. Nite Shade and Suki had already taken off, skating onto the concrete walkway that encircled the park. The rest hurried to catch up, Hatecrime and Cobra watching their flanks, the Phalanx guarding behind.

Between two copses of trees, they realized their mistake. From one copse rolled forward a herd of golf carts—from the other, another squad of the same. Behind them, the trap was sprung as more examples of the most efficient engines on the planet closed the ring around the Warriors at an inexorable two miles an hour. At the controls frowned an efficient corps of retirees ready to lay down their lives for their scarce part-time jobs, their first careers already under their belts. Having received their orders, nothing would be allowed to interfere with their part-time employment, martyrdom a small price to pay to preserve their privileged sinecures. Golf caps graced their aged heads. Steel golf clubs angled from their electric steeds, ready for use at a moment's action.

Maggie thrust out her lips in annoyance. 'Going Gocart' could be as lethal as 'going postal', and she had no desire to expose her soldiers to another confrontation that may result in further casualties if there was any way to avoid it.

But they were surrounded. There was no way out.

Two octogenarians crept from their carts, and placing hands on the small of their backs, managed to stand straight after a minute or two of stretching. They brandished their golf clubs, the mean steel glimmering with moonlight.

"Didn't plan on the *Gocart Furies*, didja?" smirked one.

The other adjusted the green baseball cap that matched his green pants with vertical white stripes. He grinned. He had a black bruise around his left eye—a scar from a lifetime of marital dueling—and with triumphant malice, as he stood he lightly tossed the golf club from his right hand to his left, then back to the right. He grinned again and took a practice swing. Hatecrime Hattie stumbled and fell backward, and for a moment her nose took the place of a divot as the angry oldtimer tried to get a nose in one.

He missed by a mile. Upended by the force of his swing, he tumbled and for a minute lay on his back groaning as he struggled to catch his breath.

"Damn the fate that makes us hurt each other like this," mumbled Crybaby Baiter. "I didn't want this. No one did."

Two more Gocart Furies closed with the Warriors, stumbling forward like zombies, still gripping their steel rods with the distant memory of a former life, though having long forgotten the purpose of the instruments.

One paused in front of Cobra. "You look like a nice young lady. Have we met?" he smiled, leaning on his club.

"Get em, Bill," the other said. "Don't you remember? We gotta stop 'The Workers'."

Bill looked at his companion. "I thought you called them 'The Carriers', Al."

"The Carriers? Is that what I said? You sure?"

"Of course, I'm sure, goddammit. Whadaya think I am—senile?"

Al turned toward Suki. Brandishing his golf club, he yelled "Where the hell is our mail? What have you Carriers done with our mail?"

Confused, Suki looked back at Maggie.

The club narrowly missed her skull.

"Oh, you did NOT just do that!" Snatching the golf club from Al's hand, Suki grabbed the old man by one arm. Yanking his pants down, she wrestled him over her knee and let him have it with his own golf club, pounding his cheeks until the club snapped in two.

"Ooooh," he moaned.

As one, the golf carts jerked to a halt. The Gocart Furies crept out and slowly made their way to Suki, their golf clubs upraised. Bill was first in line. He smiled. "Say, I hate to bother you, young lady, but I—uh, I don't suppose you could. . ."

With a frustrated but indulgent smile, Suki ordered Bill to remove his pants and lie over her knees. Soon she had broken his golf club over his rear end as well.

"Me next," groaned another octogenarian, grinning like a hackneyed coconut.

"Say, little hotties," said two others, staring imploringly at Queen Cobra and Nite Shade, "Can you. . .?"

The Warriors sighed. Sitting next to Suki Vicious, Queen Cobra and Nite Shade and Vexinator strong-armed the rest of the Gocart Furies over their knees with their pants pulled down amid squeals of pleasure and soon broke the rest of their clubs bruising their aged hineys.

When they were done, the Warriors rolled across the park, escorted by a grateful parade of happy Fury gang members in their carts, vigilant and determined to make certain no one prevented 'The Carriers' from delivering their mail to the Vermont-Sunset Subway entrance.

As the Subway rattled in their ears, launching swiftly southward, Live Lips announced, "We must hand it to the Warriors, derby lovers. Despite the best efforts of our Roller girls and their friends across the L.A. basin, they have not been stopped. They gave a ferocious fight, but the Gocart Furies have dropped the ball, made an error, and the rabbits are solidly on first base."

"It is a cloud-bank that croaks. Is it a cloud-bank that croaks, Margie?"

"It is a cloud-bank that croaks. Is it a storm that blows, Marigold?"

"It is a storm that blows. Is it a storm with no water?"

"It is a storm with no water. Is it a storm that blows for tibbets?"

"It is a storm that blows for tibbets. Is it a wind that blows no good for tibbets?"

"It is a wind that blows no good for tibbets," croaked Margie.

From the center of the cloud-bank emerged a 1936 single-wing Lockheed Electra. Spiraling swiftly down through the thin atmosphere, the plane descended onto the mile-wide stretch of bowling lanes that adjoined the communications building.

The plane braked jerkily to a stop.

A horde of hopping toads gathered, exchanging looks with jaws open and chameleon eyes swiveling on bulging eye stalks.

Inside the plane, a young woman removed headphones and adjusted a leather head-hugging cap. She paused. She surveyed the crowd of green bullet heads gathering about her plane. She half-stood. Draping one leg outside the cockpit, she momentarily stumbled and caught herself with both hands, then slowly let herself down till her Depression-era boots touched ground.

She broke into a grin.

"Made it." Descending to her knees, she kissed the concrete, there being little else natural material remaining on Pluto after more than a century of tibbet colonization:

"Mwa-mwa-mwa," she kissed it. At last, she struggled clumsily to her feet.

"Hail Mary, the Saints are with me. I'm so happy I could dance a jig." Before the gaping mouths and wide eyes of the growing crowd of toads, Amelia Earhart leaped in place, slapping hands on knees and behind on feet, executing the best little jig she'd ever done. Reaching into her back pocket, she popped open a bottle and took a swig.

"That was a long trip. A whole thirty minutes without even a sip. It was *in-shuman*."

Margie closed her chinless toad mouth. "You have recited the holy phrase," Margie croaked. Her stalk-eyes surveyed the ever-growing crowd of awe-struck toads. "What are you?"

"Just a gal from Kansas. Here to *set things right*." She burped as the swig hit bottom.

Margie exchanged eye-stalk glances with several other toads. "How do you know our holy phrase?"

"Set things right?"

No response.

"In-shuman?"

Still no response.

"Kansas?"

A flicker of response. Then nothing.

"Hail—"

The crowd caught its breath.

"—Mary?"

The toads dropped their jaws again.

"Oh, that's easy." She took a breath. "Hail Mary—"

They sucked their breaths.

"—full of geese—"

Non-webbed hands flew to cover toad mouths.

"—the Lord is with me—"

From the crowd of toads a low-level croaking answered: "Blessed are you by women, blessed is the fruit of thy loon, Jessie Christina. . ."

The visitor cautiously took over: "Holy Mary, Mother of God, pray for us—"

No one dared breathe.

"*-hic-* singers—"

The toads bubbled with happiness. "*Folk*-singers. This strange visitor knows our tibbet secret code. Blessed are the *folksingers*."

Together they finished the prayer: "—now and at the happy hour of our rest, amen."

The bulbous crowd exploded, croaks and hisses resounding across the dead face of Pluto, non-webbed hands grasping the Lockheed Electra, eager to touch the divine aircraft, more webless hands and toes touching the Visitor Herself.

"Watch it there, toad. No white-face, no entry. Ya get my meaning? Amelia Earhart ain't dropped all her standards just yet. Ya gotta show a little respect, after all."

Margie the tibbet toad hopped onto the Electra and croaked louder to grab the others' attention. "Fellow tibbets. In our sacred mission here in this lonely outpost of the vast *tibbet* galactic empire, charged as we are to stop the spread of those evil *ribbets* who refuse to limit their outrageous spread of water across the galaxy, we have been graced with the privilege of welcoming the new Saint Melia to our home away from home."

A chorus of croaks sounded approval.

Margie the toad jumped back down. Bowing her green bullet head to waist level, she looked up again. "O Holy Saint Melia. You who know all our secrets and our language—" Amelia glanced up at the translation device provided by the ribbets that was well hidden by her leather cap "—can you teach us your sacred dance? Saint Lucia the Holy Bowler revealed to us the sacred ritual of hurling balls at nine-pins in Her Third Secret of Fatima. Your appearance here today proves you are a Sister of Santa Lucia of Fatima, and you have brought us another sacred ritual."

Amelia's brows alternately contracted and expanded. "Sacred dance?" She glanced at the ground. "You mean—?"

The crowd stepped back. "Yes, Saint Melia. Please to show us." They were all eye stalks.

Slowly, after bolstering herself with yet another sip of Johnnie Walker, Amelia repeated the chief entertainment that she had learned on the planet Bogland in her rare moments of sobriety when the cases of liquor had temporarily run out. She hopped on one leg, slapping the opposite knee. The toads hopped and slapped in imitation. Then she hopped on the other leg, slapping the other knee; the toads did likewise. Then she hopped from one to the other, slapping her hands alternately to her feet behind her. As the crowd did the same, she paused.

"You know, I really need some music to do this right."

They breathed ecstatically. "The sacred dance also has *sacred music*?" Eye stalks swiveled with pleasure.

"Yes, indeedy. I have the flash drive right here."

Executing the file in the communications facility, polka music blared over loudspeakers:

John Jacob Jingleheimer Schmidt
His name is my name too
Whenever he goes out
The people always shout
John Jacob Jingleheimer Schmidt

Within moments, the entire planetoid of Pluto echoed to the sound of millions of water-hating toads hopping ecstatically while croaking in unison to a Polkafied rendition of John Jacob Jingleheimer Schmidt.

Margie paused. "Saint Melia of the Holy Polka. You have made our tibbet race very happy. What else do you have to offer us? And what can we do for you in return?"

To Margie's surprise, Saint Melia grabbed Margie between the legs. "Turn your head and cough." Happening too quickly for Margie to think of any other response, Margie coughed. "Never mind." Amelia sighed, her disappointment visible. "It was just a thought. You're not exactly like ribbets, are you?" She opted for Plan B. "I don't suppose you can synthesize a certain combination of organic molecules?"

Margie bowed and spread her toothless toad jaw in what passed for a smile among toads. "Are you suggesting, O Saint Melia, that you have something better in mind than Thunderbird wine?"

***

"You idiot. How could you lose her? Don't you know what she means to us?" Ray and Bobby stood on Sepulveda Boulevard reconnoitering. "You had her in your hands. How could she get away?"

"I don't know, Ray." Bobby stared ahead without emotion. "She just did. There was something about her—I don't know—I just couldn't turn her in to Professor Pierson. It was like—like she was almost human."

"Human?" Ray smacked his friend on his shoulder. "Are you kiddin' me? Squatches ain't human, ya jerk! No way, no how. They cain't be. Not with all that hair." He again scanned the open street, searching the darkness for any sign of Aliyah. "That Squatch means a cool fifty grand to us. Another fifty, that is."

He turned to confront Bobby. "Now what do we tell whoever the hell it was hired us during Joan of Narc? We took their money but let ourselves get distracted by this Aliyah Squatch."

Bobby shrugged. "Maybe we should forget about Aliyah and do what we were paid to do."

"Yeah. Maybe. But it's gettin' late. And from what I hear, there's a gang convention at Griffith Park in this lousy town tonight. That will make it dangerous for a couple Joes like us to walk the streets. See, the traffic is already less. Even the rich bros and bitches don't wanna get caught on the mean streets of L.A. tonight."

Glancing about, Bobby nodded. "Yeah, I see what ya mean."

His eyes froze.

"Ray."

"And I don't wanna get caught up in the same damn thing—"

"Ray. . ."

Ray followed Bobby's stare.

"You see what I see?"

He peered into the gloom. "All I see is a white car parallel parking outside that old retirement home across the street, by a ceramic mime holding a lantern."

"Look closer, Ray. What do you see inside the car?"

Edging to the street, they paused at the curb. "Is that what I think it is?"

A movement inside the car morphed into a person as it exited and stood by the car.

"No. It cain't be. Not in the middle of the Big City. And not driving a new Tesla Model X."

Ray and Bobby exchanged amazed looks. "Let's get a closer look." As the figure approached the Home and passed through a gate, they hurried to the corner, and without waiting for the light to turn green, raced through the desultory traffic where they arrived at an old-fashioned iron fence encircling the Mime Retirement Home. Finding the gate locked, they scrambled over the fence and penetrated the woody brush in time to see the Tesla owner more clearly while it briefly conversed with a pair of black attendants under a wide overhang before entering the establishment.

Ray hit Bobby in the shoulder again. "Ya moron. Cain't you do nothin right?"

The enthusiasm drained from Bobby.

"It's just another human in an ape-suit like what we saw every day in the woods of Washington."

Bobby shook his head. "You're right. We shoulda guessed from the way it parked the car. Only a human would parallel park a Tesla like that. I mean, if it was a

Squatch it would have parallel parked better! Yeah. I guess that was just another human in an ape-suit like all the others we saw in Washington. But there's still Aliyah—she was definitely a Squatch, if I ever saw one."

"Fuckin A," Ray replied. "That damn bedsheet didn't fool me for a moment. Fergit that ape-suit. But we cain't keep wastin' time lookin' for Aliyah—not when we know where the other Squatch is. Let's go do what we were paid to do: get the other Squatch—the one we brought to L.A., and then lost."

Bobby pushed out his lips. "Mought's well. I'll call Uber. You oil the duck rifle and make sure Etsy still works."

Episode 8

"Gimme a nopalito," Maggie grunted. Maiden Hell offered Maggie some Thunderbird wine and she gulped twice and handed the bottle back. Wiped the back of her hand. "That'll do." Maggie gazed at the slitted eyes glimmering two cars behind. There was something odd about them.

Maggie inspected her soldiers. Midnight was approaching, but in derby time the night was still young. And though they had seen some action the Warriors still had plenty of energy. A few pills helped. Maggie refused them—but when the chips were down, a few uppers fit the bill for the rest of her crew.

As the cars rocked, the Warriors gazed at their newest challenge. From the darkness the slit eyes grew, as if eager to close with their prey; as the eyes approached, the subway lights extinguished—the better to cover their moves? Who knew what weapons these newcomers may possess?

Maggie lay a serious look on her brood. This was indeed for keeps.

The Red Line rattled south toward the Vermont / Santa Monica access, the Warriors seizing hold of whatever they could grasp to keep from tipping over. The lights in their car were bright—uncomfortably so—especially contrasted as they were with the shadows of the car immediately behind where the lights had dimmed.

The eyes grew larger. Red could be seen in the pupils, a circle of white entirely surrounding them, like an archipelago of fires in the night sky.

Vexinator traded worried glances with Bloody Mary and Hatecrime.

The eyes were getting close. Only one more set of doors separated them, and still they could not see faces.

Maggie whispered to Queen Cobra, Maiden Hell, and Suki Vicious. They withdrew to the back of the carriage, leaving the front guarded by Nite Shade, Bloody Mary, Hatecrime Hattie, Crybaby Baiter, and Vexinator, with Maggie anchoring the center. They took up positions behind two rows of seats—creating a channel where anyone entering the car would be forced to bunch together. Behind them, a pair of Bloods halted their attempted mugging of two Cripps and all fled the car. The kind of trouble derby gangs brought, no one needed.

The Vermont / Santa Monica exit sped by, no pedestrians willing to board—and no bystanders remained on board to exit.

The rails beneath the car popped rhythmically.

Vex and Crybaby shook themselves alert. Drowsiness now could be lethal.

The back doors opened. . .

Darkness.

A labyrinth of forms appeared suddenly, twisted like willows in a storm. Rushing into the car, the forms separated into a half-dozen corpse-white ghosts with diaphanous shrouds trailing—shrieks burst on the Warriors' ear drums as all the intruders let loose at once.

"It's the PsychoTeens," shouted Bloody Mary.

The Psychos skated forward, jaws open, lungs erupting, and as they grappled with the Warriors' front line, a second wave of corpse-lights crowded into the car, while behind a half dozen larger figures barreled in on skateboards, dressed in leather jackets and beach-shell necklaces, their faces painted like pizzas—with bacon. Depositing a DJ station, the two largest figures rapped into portable mics waving their arms.

"And the Insane Clown Pasta!" yelled Nite Shade. "With their band of gigolos!"

As the lights in the car flickered, and the Warriors staggered under the weight of the shoving, screaming PsychoTeens, the Pasta Duo spread their savage hip-hop lyrics across the madly scrambling tangle of asses and elbows.

One Psycho grabbed Nite Shade and shrieked in her ear: "You can't wear that blouse! I bought the very last one at Hot Topic!" Falling back, stunned, her place was taken by Bloody Mary who sprayed the teen's face with mace: "Go to your room! Young ladies don't talk to people like that!"

Another tumbled over seats entangling Crybaby Baiter: "You promised to drive me to Stella's by 6:00 p.m. Now nobody likes me!" Suppressing a sympathetic tear, Crybaby tied the PsychoTeen to a chair: "That's enough out of you. Time Out for five minutes—and not a moment before."

The Pasta Duo bellowed into their mics at max decibels:

Killa momma boom boom
hit em with my zoom zoom
give em room for cream cream
listen to em scream scream

The mics were snatched from their bloated hands and the pizza faces upended in confusion as the mass of struggling bodies stood still, the shrieks ceasing.

Maggie, Maiden Hell, and Suki Vicious stood behind them, smirking.

"Uh-oh."

Throwing the intruders' mics out the door, the three Warriors pounded the Pasta Duo from behind with rabbit punches to the kidneys, sending them slamming into the band of pizza-face gigolos, who scrambled out the windows, the night's assignment suddenly looking too much like work. Pounded from behind and in front, but without the possibility of deriving the remotest pleasure from the experience, the PsychoTeens panicked.

Mace and elbows quickly flattened the lot, leaving the teens bruised and crying amid a tangle of reddened shrouds, while the Warriors mustered for a recount. Bloody Mary recited: "Rule One for PsychoTeens: Whack Em good. Rule Two: Repeat Rule One."

"That was brilliant, Maggie," said Cobra. "I would have

never thought of climbing on top of the car, scrambling to the back, and dropping down behind them."

"It was easy. They're stupid."

Maggie paused in her count. The Warriors were one short.

Peering behind the seats, they soon found Crybaby lying face-down. Maggie gently lifted her. She painfully opened her eyes.

Crybaby murmured. "I got soft—listened to her sob story—how her mother made her come home by 3:00 a.m. each night—I felt sorry for her." Crybaby closed her eyes and swallowed. She opened them again. "Then the little bitch kicked me in the shins!"

The Warriors traded hard looks. Sympathy helped no one.

"Leave me. I'm done for." She caught Maggie in her grip. "Just lift me one last time. . .before you skate away." Nodding, Maggie lifted Crybaby up on one elbow. Crybaby leveled a glare at the bruised Psycho-teens. "Na-na-na-naaa-na. Wee showed you-oo." Then she lapsed into coughing that shook her delicate frame and her eyes closed again. Crybaby Baiter lay and grew silent, not to move again till the St. Derby Rescue Squad could bring a Frappucino and pig in a blanket. It was a fitting end to a fallen Warrior.

Maggie stood. Still undefeated, she skated in small semicircles. "We can't wait here. They will send more."

Skating to the front of the train, Maggie pointed to the doors that separated the cars from the cabin that housed the drivers. With a gesture from Maggie, Cobra slid a copper strip into the lock and popped it. The doors opened.

Two sleepy drivers with blue caps and bulging paunches looked up in surprise, hastily hiding full-color centerfolds.

"Look straight ahead, boys. Didn't your mommas teach you that it's not safe to drive without watching the road?" Maggie and Vex smiled and flexed rippling biceps in their faces. "You have a new schedule. You don't stop till we tell you to stop." As she spoke, the subway raced through the Vermont / Beverly station and the Warriors glimpsed gangs of angry-looking derby girls lined up on either side: the elite Bloody Jammers, Helles Belles, and Take No Prisnas.

Lucky them.

Soon Wilshire / Vermont sped past, this time no gangs visible on the platform. Then Westlake-MacArthur Park, skates skulking half visible in a darkness that obscured their colors.

Vex touched Maiden. "Metro Center almost here." They looked to Maggie. "We'll have to exit this time."

She nodded. "Light rail to Pico."

The Warriors looked at each other. They knew what that meant. Aside from the certainty of trouble at the Center, the light rail tram, unlike a subway, afforded ample opportunity for agile gang members to climb on, whatever speed they might travel. And after commandeering this train, the authorities would block the Warriors from repeating that maneuver in the future.

"Listen up." Vex thrust the Live Lips App into their midst.

"Our hats off again," crooned the smooth double lips on the screen. "We have to hand it to the Warriors. They survived our very own derby team, the PsychoTeens, even with backup from your friendly neighborhood hip-hop band, the Insane Clown Pasta, and their pretty gigolos. But don't cancel your bets yet, derbycators. There were casualties on both sides, so the Warriors' numbers are dwindling. In memory of our beloved Sirius, we call for a draft of more troops to right the wrong and put these pretenders in their place. Here's to seein' you in the trenches—and the Warriors in their coffins. Live Lips off—till your next update."

The drivers finally allowed to perform their appointed task, the Red Line subway slowed. Metro Center hove into view. Exit was possible on only one platform, then they would have to climb one level to grab the Expo line to Culver City.

Maggie gathered her troops about her. Like plates of armor they formed a cohesive whole, a phalanx that she knew could ram through any combination that rival derby gangs would dare field. Maiden Hell and Vexinator took the front row. Queen Cobra and Hatecrime took the left, and Nite Shade and Suki Vicious the right. Maggie positioned herself at the center with Bloody Mary watching behind.

The carriage slowed.

A last bump and it jerked to a stop.

The Warriors gazed out the windows into the dim interior of the Metro pits, two levels remaining between them and open sky. Their mouths opened. No derby gang was visible in the flickering florescents. Maggie and Vex exchanged suspicious glances.

It had to be a trick.

Bunched like a mailed fist, the Warriors carefully exited

the carriage, noting again the sparsity of casual pedestrians, the few who appeared taking one look then bolting for the exits. Derby trouble had a way of clearing paths everywhere they went—except for those intent on suicide by skater.

The silence of the station was overwhelming, and with each step seeming to echo regardless of how quietly they crept, Maggie put a finger to her lips. If they could avoid attention, maybe they would survive the night.

They crossed the platform.

On the ground rested a package. Moving slowly towards the stairwell, Maggie noted the red and white wrapping tied neatly with red ribbon. What was this? Her brows contracted. Entering the stairs, they climbed halfway up. She raised an arm—they halted.

Behind—around a corner—something jerked back.

She narrowed her eyes. Whoever it was had no skates.

Maggie waved the Warriors on.

Further up the stairs they slowed again. Another package was on the turn in the stairwell. More happy wrapping, this time white snowflakes on a background of blue. A suspicion grew. But Maggie motioned them on again.

They kept climbing.

"There," whispered Bloody Mary. "Someone is behind us." She looked upward at Maggie, perched two steps above. "We're being followed—or surrounded."

They exchanged more wary looks. This time they heard the quiet grind of wheels.

Another platform and they would emerge on the Blue and Expo level and they could take refuge on the train to Culver City. If they were merely being followed.

They crept up and forward again, their wheels softly touching concrete.

A metal trashcan appeared and Nite Shade leaned to peer inside. It seemed bottomless and Nite finished off an Eight-Hour Energy spray and casually tossed it. To her surprise it dropped soundlessly for what seemed an eternity. Finally it hit bare steel bottom with a quiet tink.

The band resumed their climb.

They froze.

From somewhere a mournful echo sounded, emanating as from Metro Center's unplumbed depths, and the little band listened with growing alarm to drums in the deep as they thumped. Fell echoes drifted up from its putrid depths: 'Ta-rat-a-tat-tat. . .'

Turning to Nite Shade, Maggie hissed, "Fool of a roller girl. Next time roll yourself in."

Nite Shade returned a sheepish look. "I didn't know, Mag. How could I? It's been years since the Roller Derby League owned Metro Central."

Climbing faster, they became aware that the volume was increasing, like the rattling drums of little drummer boys signaling menace and rage from those whose slumber had been interrupted. It was suddenly replaced with the ominous notes of a vile tune: 'Rudolf the Red-Nosed Reindeer. . .'

From the lower levels of the Inferno, the Warriors finally rolled from the accursed stairwell and emerged onto the platform offering access to the Expo and Blue Line trams, their alert gaze scanning every crook and fanny of the few pedestrians on that level, naïve as to what was about to happen.

Quick—on either side—more packages brightly wrapped and tied, the walls festooned with the silver and green wreaths of their death and resurrection cult, the latter being impossible without committing the former. Threatening crosses were sprayed on the walls—warning signs of who now owned Metro Central.

Down below. Running feet climbing the stairs behind them, accompanied by grinding wheels. The mournful ringing of bells accompanied harsh shouts of 'Seasons Greetings!'

"Run," yelled Maggie. "It's the Santa Claws! They never take 'I gave at the office' for an answer. They will drag you down to their special Hell where the same Christmas music is played year-round over and over and you can never escape it or change the station. No matter where you go, Christmas music will always be there, just like you never left their Hell behind."

At the edge of the platform they stopped short—the Expo Line had not yet arrived. The empty tracks loomed before them like an iron and steel cemetery, no possibility of escaping the nightmare horde about to burst upon them. Behind them blew the lethal strains of 'Feliz Navidad', repeating without regard to the fact that every person living had already heard it a thousand times, which was a thousand times too many.

Erupting from the stairwell came a tangle of red fur with white lining, curly white beards split by open mouths smiling with fake sincerity, lethal bags filled with coal and bricks slung over their hefty shoulders.

"Ho-ho-ho, *you ho's!*" The smiles turned to sneers. "Merry Christmas to you and yours." Skating into the shape of a quarter moon, the fiery red Santas surrounded the little band of Warriors like snow-sprinkled demons from the north pole of Hell where midget slaves were worked to death under the threat of naughty lists to make skates and lawn weeders.

"You do know what Christmas is *really all about, don't you?*" demanded the biggest Claw, Nick the Knife, displaying a new three-pronged lawn weeder in one hand with razor-sharp edges and twirling a bag of bricks threateningly with the other. With a shock, Maggie noticed tufts of red hair hanging from the Santas' belts—the scalps of red-headed elves who had questioned the purpose of Christmas. Behind him a little drummer boy tapped Taps on his drum, which he had learned from reruns of Branded.

Nick the Knife skated forward, and braked. Swinging his heavy bag, he squinted at the Warriors. "You're on Nick's turf now. So tell me: do you think Christmas is just a pagan festival taken over by Christians? Or is it *really about the birth of Christ?*" He leaned forward in anticipation, a large Christian cross dangling from his sweaty neck, his angry face red as a beet waiting for Maggie's answer.

While waiting, several Santas thrust wrapped boxes at the Warriors with sly smiles on their faces.

"Don't accept them!" Maggie called. "Or you will be stuck with gifts you never wanted and will just have to regift them."

Hatecrime had already extended her hand—accepted the box with its pretty blue and white snowy decorations. Before she could react, the ribbon dropped and the wrapping came off in her hand. Unable to resist the pretty white box, she opened it.

A polyester tie.

And no receipt.

Throwing her free hand to her forehead, she swooned. "I can't stand it. I'll have to re-gift to someone else." Then collapsed on the platform amid triumphant sneers from the Santas.

"We can bring her, Maggie," yelled Suki. "I'm strong. I can carry her."

The Squatch shook her head. "No. She knew the risks and volunteered anyway. We all did." A fierce look took Maggie, determination on her face. "We can't take her. If I did the same, I would expect you to leave me too."

Maggie and the others continued to back across the platform toward the Expo Line.

Another box flew towards them. It missed and broke open on the ground. Cardboard belts and hospital socks spilled out.

"Ugh." Nite Shade spat. "How dare they try to give things like that to human beings." She stared at the paunchy bell-ringers with infinite contempt. "Have they no pity?"

Nickie the bulbous bell-ringer swung his heavy bag threateningly again and brandished his weeder. "Well, little girl? What's your answer? Think carefully. You don't want to go to the top of my *naughty* list, do you?"

The Squatch frowned. Opened her mouth. She paused.

From behind, the Blue Line creaked to a stop and disgorged a mass of teeny-bopper skaters in blue-grey pajamas, twin floppy ears matching puff balls on their derrieres. Rolling rings around the clumsy Santas, they snatched their red hats and rolled away with their packages, making it impossible to give their wrapped curses to the Warriors, re-gifting not being an option for tweens.

"Pagan festival, Sanka Breath. How many times we gotta tell ya? You're livin a lie!" The tweeny Easter Bunny spun a pirouette cackling in soprano, her little freckled face grinning happily.

The Santa's beet-red face turned white-hot. "Birth of Christ, you little fucker! Come here and I'll twist your goddam Easter-lovin' ears off. Ya little Jonas Brothers groupies. Show some respect for your elders, goddammit!"

With a hop and a swish, the Bunny skated beneath his outthrust arms and laughed again.

The Santa lurched, and missed. "I'll shish-kabob your Satanic bunny ass. Just wait till I catch you." The Santas lumbered forward, clawing air with their lawn weeders and swinging their brick and coal-laden bags. "Some roller derby club you are! Just a bunch of goddamn candy-ass tweens in Bunny costumes. You're an embarrassment to roller derbies everywhere."

"Maybe so. But we caught the Warriors—not you."

Both halted in surprise.

The Warriors had gone.

Above ground, the Warriors were rolling along South Flower Street under the starlit sky of 2:00 a.m. Los Angeles, propelling southwest. The Pico Station lay a half-dozen blocks away.

At the bottom of the Metro stairs, two figures emerged, and in their hurry to catch their quarry, collided with two others. The first pair had pizzas painted on their faces, their humiliation and anger showing through the sausage and cheese face paint, and they limped from pains in their kidneys. The second pair wore Elmer Fudd green plaid jackets with hunting caps and brandished an ancient rusted rifle.

"Goomba wearin Fudd duds," rapped one of the Insane Clown Pastas, waving his hands in the air.

Ray and Bobby stepped back. Suddenly Bobby waved his arms gangsta style. "Huntin' fer a Sas-quatch."

The Pizza Clowns looked at each other, eyebrows raised. "Lookin' for a girlfren."

"To put her in a bath-tub." Ray grinned back.

A huge green frog suddenly appeared at their side, also swinging his webbed hands in the air gangsta-style. He continued the rap, croaking:

Joseph volunteer now
fly with me to Bogland
get a shot of mojo
grow another poker

The toad stopped rapping and looked at Ray and Bobby with his chameleon eyes. "Are you Josephs? Xplak is recruiting all the Josephs that Xplak can find for quick conversion to mimes. Emergency mobilization."

"Heyll no. Ain't neither of us named Joseph Whoop-de-do, you big uglified lump of fungus." He cocked the rifle for emphasis.

The toad looked the Fudd twins up and down. "Maybe yes, maybe no, but even with current emergency Xplak must consider quality control. You two are 4F."

Xplak turned to the Insane Clown duo. "Xplak is recruiting Josephs. The Great Gork's Plan has immediate need for more mimes. Benefits include happy Retirement Home where loyal servants take great care in how they push your wheelchair. Risk of job is—overrated. Are you Josephs?"

A guilty look came over the pair. "Actually. . ."

Xplak aimed a silver device. A flash, and the Duo froze in place.

"Thank you for volunteering, Joe B. and Joe U. You have made my quota for tonight. The Great Green Gork will be pleased. You will be happy as evil street mimes who molest innocent people—you are already mostly there." Lifting the two effortlessly, Xplak carried them up the stairs past several discarded Christmas packages whose ugly thoughtless contents were strewn on the concrete, to a blue and green trash dumpster at street level, the loud grinding of wheels from Santa and Easter Bunny posses skating after their prey, which dwindled in the distance.

Maneuvering the frozen Josephs over the side and into his cosmodrone disguised as a dumpster, Xplak hopped inside. With a grunt indicating annoyance that the Great Gork had demoted him to using this primitive version instead of assigning him the new business-class version that enjoyed walk-on access, Xplak twisted some dials and flipped some levers.

Another moment and they were plunging into the nearest available worm-hole.

Episode 9

"How does she do it?" Margie looked at Marigold then back to Saint Melia, instructor in the new sacred dance called the Polka. "No matter how many organic molecules our beloved Saint Melia consumes, she is still able to touch hands to knees and toes without mistake."

The two tibbet toads looked at the room full of acolytes striving to emulate their new eponymous leader, ranked equal with their beloved Saint Lucia the Holy Bowler, but constantly failing after consuming liberal quantities of the new concoction that Saint Melia called 'Johnnie Walker'.

Margie hopped on 'Jingleheimer' and tried to touch her back toes on 'Smith' but staggered to one side, even her giant floppy feet failing to restore her balance. She turned her wide inverted bow-like jaw to her friend, who was no more successful than she in mastering the complex dance.

"Our race performed well until Saint Melia commanded we consume quantities of 'JW'. What are we doing wrong?"

Marigold hopped higher in another attempt to touch her back toes. Again she failed and stumbled as she alighted. "My stalks are not moving where I tell them. My eyes cannot focus. I am not sure if I am standing or sliding. Could this be the state of ecstasy that Saint Melia has described?"

"Perhaps this state is not to be found on our little planetoid Pluto. Perhaps it is only to be found elsewhere."

Margie tried to focus her chameleon eye-stalks on Marigold in an expression of surprise. They both stopped hopping.

"Is Marigold saying what I think Marigold is saying?"

While the rest of the toads on the bowling lanes continued trying to perfect their polkas while in a state of sacred inebriation, Saint Melia, dressed in leotards, emptied yet another bottle of 'JW' and tossed it at a toad in the front row. "Thash what you get," drifted across the lanes. "Do what I tell ya, ya goddam toad!"

Sliding quietly out of the bowling palace, the two toads rested and exchanged looks. They peered about to be certain they were not overheard.

"Melia is our Saint. Is her dance not sacred?"

"Her dance is sacred. Is she to be obeyed like Saint Lucia of the bowling lanes?"

"She is to be obeyed like Saint Lucia of the bowling lanes. Are we happy with current situation of Saint Lucia?"

"We are happy with current situation of Saint Lucia—whom we sent to Wetland. Did Wetlanders accept Saint Lucia?"

"Wetlanders accepted Saint Lucia at the little town of Fatima a century ago. Did Wetlanders like Third Secret of Fatima where Saint Lucia revealed the sacred activity of bowling, with purple mannequins as their reward?"

"Wetlanders liked Third Secret of Fatima and sacred activity of bowling, with purple mannequins as their reward, and especially liked Saint Lucia's tendency to remove her clothes and accept payment for sex, which we tibbets on Pluto found. . .unhelpful. Will Wetlanders also like this new Saint Melia and her tendency to smile at whiteness and dance the Polka while drinking Johnnie Walker?"

"This tibbet is certain that Wetlanders will like Saint Melia of the Holy Polka. Will Wetlanders like Saint Melia who appears in Lockheed Electra?"

"Wetlanders will like Saint Melia who appears in Lockheed Electra. Can Wetlanders dance the polka and bowl nine-pins after consuming quantities of 'JW' organic molecules?"

Margie stared into the vast expanse of space, which was

dotted with innumerable stars that never dimmed in their outpost on Pluto far from the Sun. "That's *their* problem."

***

Striding purposefully on her long mountain legs into the Evil Mime Retirement Home, Gilda adjusted the stylish wide-brim white hat perched fashionably on her head, and bypassing the white-faced dotards with evil grins staring at her with ancient knowing glares, she advanced to meet two figures.

The first was an anciently aged—yet still preserved by some mysterious mime process—plump figure in a red nightgown, red pumps on her feet and ruby rings on her ears. A raggedy blond wig refused to detach itself from her scalp despite the dire need for a replacement; white and black greasepaint refused to be cleaned from its face despite the fading and smearing of decades of wear.

"Hurry the fuck up," Edie growled.

For a moment Gilda paused, a frown crossing her recently shaved face.

The second stared up from a wheelchair, aged even more drastically than Edie, but ever eager to play the good cop in tune with his primordial training as a door-to-door Mormon missionary.

"Good of you to come, Gilda." The aged and wrinkled Gary, at one time the youngest Worshipful Master the Latter-Day Masons had ever had, but now the oldest, leveled a quietly reproving glance on Edie. "Please forgive us for the late hour. But as you will soon see, we could not wait until tomorrow to meet with you. Thank you. We profusely thank you."

Before Gary could speak again or Gilda interfere, Edie stepped forward and grabbed Gilda between the legs. "Turn your head and cough." Gary caught his breath.

Haack. Gilda complied before she could think.

"She's okay. She's not a tibbet. She's *all* female."

Gary sighed in relief—more for the fact that Gilda had not bolted for the door than to hear what he was already certain of.

"This way to a private room."

Gilda cocked her white hat and adjusted her tailored white silk dress making sure that sufficient hairy cleavage was showing in front, and most of her werewolf-hairy back framed by a plunging V. "I'm not sure that's such a good idea, *gentlemen*," she stressed the last word sarcastically.

"Pologies," blurted Edie. "But we had to make sure. In this business we can't take any chances."

With a feminine turn of her hairy head, Gilda acquiesced, and the three—with Clarence pushing Gary's wheelchair and not colliding with doors for a change—entered a sparsely furnished room. Clarence shut the door as he left.

"Now, Ms. Gilda," Edie grunted, "I would just like to point out that after you came here from that forest in Washington, it was we who got you that flat in Malibu, and we who funded your bank account and got you that *very expensive* new Tesla car of yours, and it was *we* who bought those fancy clothes that you so proudly flaunt everywhere you go in this town."

Gilda stared out a window.

Leveling another 'Down-boy!' glance at Edie, Gary stepped from the wheelchair and stood straight, though he

remained two feet shorter than the seven-foot tall Gilda.
"*Aaand*," Gary interjected, silencing Edie, "we are very happy that you chose to help us in our quest to save this fair city from a threat such as it has never experienced before: evil tibbets and their agents—meaning first and foremost, Maggie P. Squatch, who you must know due to your—uh," he risked another side glance at Edie, "*intimate* association in Washington state, is not a true Sasquatch like yourself. Yet Maggie is garnering all the benefits of pretending to be one."

"Are you certain of that, gentlemen? How exactly would you know?"

Edie and Gary looked at each other in astonishment.

"What exactly *do* you know about Maggie?" Gilda continued. "Do you really know anything at all?"

"We know enough," growled Edie.

"Yes," agreed Gary. "We know what we know. And we know enough. Now, to put it bluntly, Ms. Gilda, you accepted our money and our favors, which have transformed your entire life from one of scavenging nuts in a forest to a privileged life such as few people enjoy."

Gilda continued to stare out the window.

Edie frowned. "What's the idea of taking our money and then ignoring us?"

Gilda glanced at her carefully manicured nails and her werewolf hairy palms.

Gary the good cop took over. "We don't want much, Gilda. It's real simple. We just want you to file a palimony suit against Maggie—something that will entangle her in the legal system, suck up her time and her money till she has nothing left. Of all the people on this planet, only you can do it. All you need to do is move into that bowling palace where Maggie currently resides and make things stick just long enough for your lawyer to file the lawsuit."

A smile crossed Gilda's freshly shaved face. "I kind of like it in Malibu. In fact, I think I'm getting used to living there."

The bad cop returned. "We remind you again, Ms. Gilda, that we are responsible for setting you up, and any time we like we can send you back to scrounging in the woods with that Sasquatch goon squad you call a family in the foothills of Mount St. Helens"

"Sorry, gentlemen. That won't wash. You see, I have landed a role in a sitcom about Sasquatch family life that's paying me lots of cash. I'm no longer interested in living in a run-down Loonitarian bowlarama in Venice City. If you want me to lower my lifestyle, you'll have to pay me more money—a *lot* more money."

It was Gary's turn to get excited. He wriggled in his wheelchair. "*More* money? But we don't have any more. Do you have any idea how expensive it is to run a French-Canadian Cirque de Loony-air circus and a chain of concierge Mime Retirement Homes?" He cast a 'no-offense-intended' glance at Edie.

"Sorry, gentlemen. Give me a call—when you can afford me." With that, Gilda stood and walked out.

As the Tesla drove away, Edie and Gary exchanged outraged looks. "Why, that ungrateful bitch! I can't believe she would do this to us. We can't afford to pay her any more money. After all, evil mime work isn't cheap."

"Well," said Gary, "we can keep going for a while with the circus receipts. But things are fragile; one more shock may bring everything to a standstill. But not to worry just yet. I was afraid something like this might happen. So I've had something else in the works."

Edie laid an inquisitive glance on Gary. "Something else?"

Gary nodded. "On the veranda. The show starts now." Struggling to his feet, Gary slowly crossed the veranda, Edie following behind. Gary halted at the edge and stared into the tree-lined verdure that stretched to an iron fence behind the flowery gardens that the retirement home's inhabitants enjoyed during daylight hours.

When it was clear that the gardens were empty and that only Gary and Edie were present and no other mimes or attendants were watching, a shadow separated from the other shadows in the back. Cautiously it approached.

Gary eyed the shadow knowingly. "Nice to see you again."

The figure was wrapped in a blanket. The eyes peered left and right as if it would not do to be discovered. "You too, Gary. And you, Ms. . .Ya Egger Hooper." Edie winced at the name. The eyes slid about again. "How's the Fuck in the Backside Institute?"

"Fucked as always. But I have my contacts."

"I'm sure you do."

Gary fixed the stranger in his glare. "Why didn't you finish off the Squatch?"

Hesitation. "Those two stooges I hired failed to do the job—they let themselves be distracted. You know, it's damned frustrating to pay someone to do a job, and then they have the gall to do nothing."

Gary and Edie looked at each other. "Tell us about it."

"So I took matters into my own hands. At the Convention in Griffith Park earlier this evening—I myself shot at the Squatch. But I missed and I hit some derby girl named Sirius. I had to think quickly, so I did the next best thing—I blamed the Warriors for killing Sirius shouting loud enough for the whole Park to hear. Now every roller derby girl in L.A. believes that Maggie and her Warriors are responsible for killing Sirius. And they're all out to get her."

Gary and Edie smiled, their brows rising across their foreheads.

The stranger continued. "No way will the Squatch survive tonight. She will never see Venice again."

Pulling out his cell phone, Gary punched radio buttons. "We gotta keep track. Cause if she breaks through to her home turf, we're gonna have Big Trouble in Little Mime-a."

The Live Lips App came up and the three pressed their ears to hear.

Edie set her jaw—akilter. "She's on South Flower Street! Headed south."

Gary looked up from his wheelchair in alarm. "That means she's headed for Pico Station." He frowned. "We're gonna have to send in the big guns. We gotta stop her—no matter what it takes." He waved his arms. "Buzz the Circus! Wake the white-faces! It's time. . .to *Release the Crackers*."

"By the way, how'd you get to Sepulveda so fast, when the Warriors are still stuck in Hollywood?"

"Uber." The mysterious stranger turned and disappeared into darkness.

Episode10

His eye focused intently on the latest Live Lips broadcast, Professor Richard Pierson hurried down Pacific Avenue until he arrived at his destination. He paused a moment to view the neon nun marquee whose exposed derriere flashed blue and red enticing the innocent to bowl and gamble—and do what else? The smiling nun winked. The neon sign read 'Madam G-Spot's Pollo Ranchero Casino & Bowlarama for Upper West Los Angeles – Precinct 9'.

It said much—and nothing at all.

Pierson had learned a lot from the Mime Retirement Home and suspected much about Madam G-Spot's place. But tonight he was on a different mission. His plan to unite every roller derby team in southern California and turn them against the evil mimes from the Cirque de Lumiére had failed. And now Maggie was in trouble.

For a moment he observed the customers. Though the time was after 2:00 a.m., every few minutes another ordinary dressed customer would enter, and almost as often someone would exit. But the latter seemed drastically changed—a man in a pretty summer dress and fulsome black wig with artificial eyelashes and off-color lipstick almost stumbled into him. "Pardon me," the man growled, and paused to look Pierson over as if suspicious of *his* looks.

The man in the summer dress departed.

Next a woman in formal men's suit complete with placid tie and hint of mustache exited. She muttered in a high voice, "Goddam global warmers—I'll pound em to a pulp," then she also paused to glare at Pierson. Finally, running a comb through her freshly trimmed hair as if having just visited a men's barber, she walked away without a word, but still eyed him as if not entirely sure he could be trusted, and Pierson began to wonder if he should perhaps apply some rouge to his own face just to avoid suspicion.

But more was in the works tonight than cross-dressers despite their vastly increasing numbers across the L.A. basin. On the façade of Pollo Ranchero, underneath the neon marquee, hung a large vinyl sign: 'Third Annual Dervish Festival' and a number of people were frequenting a pathway strung with naked light bulbs that led, with a sharp leftward turn and down a half-block, to Venice Beach. Celebratory noises rose from the direction of the beach, and a steady stream of nuns, entirely clad but for face and hands in broad habits of black or brown, hurried to and fro with happy comments.

He had no time for creature comforts, however. Pierson climbed the steps to the Holy Rollers Casino and entered.

Inside, he was struck by the large number of bowlers spinning their balls down immaculate wooden lanes to pummel white nine-pins, the dark huddled forms of more nuns visible at the far end re-setting the 'sacred' pins. Others—to his shock, barely covered by skimpy two-piece swimsuits to reveal taut youthful female bodies, their names all being some variation of 'M'—pranced back and forth bringing pizzas and beer to the bowlers, while more assisted the clients in putting money into one-armed bandits and other slot machines between bouts of bowling.

Again, he had no time for balls or slot machines. It was the rumored Madam G-Spot he wanted.

Up ahead, on the corridor leading to the VIP area, he saw a clutch of fabric-encompassing intent-looking nuns heading for a platform where several Dervishes in traditional spinning top skirts and absurdly tall chef hats twirled endlessly to a band that banged out Turkish folk music. The music filled the bowling palace, interrupted only by bowling balls striking pins and the quiet buzzers and bells of gambling machines propped at the far end.

But it was the figure whom the nuns surrounded who attracted Pierson's attention. Short-short, stubby legs, spindly arms, and a body as preternaturally round as any ball that ever graced a palace lane. It skipped to keep up with the larger and heavier nuns like a child striving to stay with her parents. But when the little sphere spoke, the others paused to listen.

"Oh my, my, my. Oh, oh, oh. Things are so tangled, Maureen. However can we manage?" the little spindly voice babbled as the small band of nuns neared Richard.

"We'll just have to manage somehow, Madam G. We can't let our Dervish guests down," replied a nun. "Just look at them, Myrtle. If only Jessie Christina would allow us the leisure time to stand and twirl, maybe we could achieve inner peace also."

"Wouldn't that be nice," Myrtle said. "Then things would be a lot more relaxed around here."

"Yes, indeed," Madam G-Spot echoed. "Less trouble and more relaxed is what I always say. Just like the good old days."

Myrtle and Maureen exchanged quiet glances at this remark but continued escorting Madam G-Spot toward the front door.

The little voice spoke again. "But all we can do is pray to Jessie Christina and Santa Lucia to give us strength in our busy tasks. And look how successful we are." Madam G-Spot passed her glance over the many customers in Pollo Ranchero, the frequent reward bells, and the steady stream of cross-dressers exiting the VIP area after collecting their rewards. "Proud I am. Sinfully proud."

"Oh, Madam G-Spot," called one of the nuns. "You said the 'p' word."

She caught her breath. "Oh my, my, my. Yes indeed. I must recite a Hail Mary now."

The half-dozen nuns halted in stride and lowered their heads while G-Spot sank to her knees, veritably disappearing amid the hulking squat bodies of the other nuns.

"Hail Mary, baked in grease, the Lord is thy recipe, blessed are you by women, blessed is the fruit of thy broom, Jessie Christina. Holy Mary, Mother of Virgins, pray for us folksingers, now and at the happy hour of our best. Amen."

She stood and the band of nuns turned toward the entrance.

A stranger blocked their way.

"Oh my, my," said Maureen. "What can we do for you, my good man?"

Richard could not help but notice the transformation of the nuns from grandmotherly servants of God discussing recipes into bar bouncers running security for the Casino, several bending their arms as if to call strong biceps into play.

"Be careful, Myrtle. This one isn't a spring chicken, but he's still a man. Watch out for his violence."

Myrtle shifted her eyes from side to side, intimidated despite the protection of greater numbers and the obvious old age of Professor Pierson.

"Excuse me, sir, but we are very busy. Oh, so very busy." The nuns began to squeeze past him.

Pierson spoke: "Please, good women of God. I have come a long way and I must have an answer to my question before the night is out. Time is of the essence."

"The two-piece nun-maidens are over there. And the beer taps are over here. And the bowling balls are in between. What more could a man want?"

Pierson again blocked their passage. "That's not why I'm here, good woman. Please. This is an emergency. My question concerns a certain person who resides among you, by name of—"

Bypassing him again, they headed for the doors.

"—*Maggie*."

As one, the group of nuns halted. More quiet looks exchanged among them. The protective cocoon parted and Madam G-Spot stepped forward. She looked up at Richard.

"Are you here to serve a summons?"

Richard laughed. "No."

"An invoice?"

"No."

"A bill?"

He shook his head, smiling. "Not at all! I'm Richard Pierson, Professor of Non-Patriarchal Fair Trade Astronomy at UCLA. I'm a friend of Maggie. I must talk with you about her—tonight. Right now, in fact."

She turned to the other nuns. "Wait outside, dears. This will only take a moment." As her escort exited, G-Spot stared up at Richard, the guarded look still about her as if he may turn out to be a bounty hunter or private eye. They stepped to a quiet corner where no one could overhear. "What do you want, then? Please make it quick. I have a Festival and customers that need my attention, and Maggie is not here tonight."

"You are Madam G-Spot?"

Slowly she nodded. A smooth triangular smile appeared on her weird neckless face.

"Then only you can help. Maggie's in trouble."

"Trouble?"

"The worst." He took a breath. "Yesterday I called a derby gang leader named Sirius and asked for her help in uniting all the derby gangs in Los Angeles to fight a new and powerful enemy that recently came to town. Sirius immediately understood—she called a Convention in Griffith Park tonight. But as Sirius spoke at the Greek Theater last night," Richard glanced up, a tear coming to his eye, "someone shot her."

Madam G-Spot looked puzzled. "And?"

"The Warriors also went. Sirius and I planned to make Maggie co-leader of all the derby clubs, along with Sirius. But before Sirius could mention this, she was killed. In front of hundreds of roller derby girls, the killer shouted a lie—that it was Maggie who had shot Sirius! Now every derby gang in SoCal is hunting her, like a dog."

G-Spot stared into the distance.

"We have to save Maggie, Madam G-Spot." He raised

his arms. “She’s tough, but no one can survive hundreds of bitchy roller derby girls once they start rolling. Not even Maggie and her Warriors.”

“What can anyone do?”

“Send out your nuns. Block the Expo Line. Stop the other derby gangs cold; give Maggie an escort to bring her back to Venice, bring her back home safely to your Pollo Ranchero.”

Again the distant look. “You are right, Professor Pierson. We owe her that much. Here is what I propose—”

A chorus of shouting erupted from the front of Pollo Ranchero. Glancing out, Pierson saw the nuns around the Casino’s entrance explode in a frenzy of jabbering. Madam G-Spot hurried outside to join them. Through the glass, Pierson watched them exchange frantic words, their arms waving, then all rushed around the corner towards Venice Beach.

Looking about the interior, he watched as more nuns, learning the news from some obscure source, hurried to the entrance, leaving customers adrift, depositing pizza and beer orders untended, even the Dervishes slowing their perpetual twirling to snatch a glimpse.

This bore investigating.

Following the growing crowd of nuns, pedestrians, cross-dressers, Dervish admirers, and a few cross-dressing Dervish-admiring pedestrians, Richard trailed the hanging light bulbs the half-block to Venice Beach where he halted.

Stunned, he could only stand and gape.

Plunged into the half-wrecked tent set up by the Dervishes and Pollo Ranchero nuns and the local Unitarian Church with its ubiquitous signs of water bottles X-d out in red, cross-dressers and bowlers and hordes of the curious lined up to watch with open mouths. . .at a 1936 Lockheed Electra, its wheels at the end of a long double-trench ripped into the white sands of Venice beach.

Even as Richard watched, a slim young woman released her protective belts and staggered out of the cockpit to alight with some difficulty at the foot of the airplane.

"Well, whatsa matter?" she laid a bleary gaze across the crowd. "Ain'tcha gonna give a welcome to Amelia Earhart? I finally made it!"

One pedestrian glanced at his watch. "*Amelia Earhart?!*" He laughed out loud. "Who are you kiddin'? This is the 21st century."

She halted as if attempting to digest this, trying to focus. "What year did I take off?"

Several pedestrians and late-night beach-goers fooey'd their hands at her. "The *real* Amelia Earhart left in 1937." They laughed again. "This is the year 2021! Welcome back, *Ms. Century-Old-Whoever-You-Are-Humbug!*" They drifted away, the cameras that several reporters had set up turning off.

Confusion settled on Amelia's face. "21st century? But all I had was a little delay with some fuckin' toads."

She hesitated as a crowd of black and brown nuns gathered round, growing smiles gracing their eager faces. A small nun, round as a bowling ball, stepped from their midst. "Forget them, Ms. Earhart. We know who you are. Welcome home, Saint Melia of the Holy Polka!" A shout of joy erupted from the nuns, with Dervishes and cross-dressers joining in.

Melia's face lit up again. This was more like it.

Taking her on their shoulders, they paraded her up the block and into Pollo Ranchero where she was put to work instructing them in the new sacred dance that was all the craze on a certain planetoid which they carefully avoided naming out loud. Within minutes the nuns had set up a second Shrine dedicated to Saint Melia of the Holy Polka beside their first Shrine to Saint Lucia the Holy Bowler, and began teaching new customers how to dance the polka while they bowled. Not to be left behind, the Dervishes switched from seeking nirvana by twirling in circles, to seeking nirvana by dancing the polka while spinning and guzzling JW.

Following the crowd back into the Casino, Richard noted that one by one, after visits to the rear, some Dervishes were also turning into cross-dressers and he wondered if their new wigs and lipstick and brassieres aided or interfered with their spinning. Under their giant chef hats and white skirts, they were quite the entertainment as they danced and spun in their new bras, mid-high heels, and lipstick. As someone passed around fifths of hard liquor and the Dervishes attempted to add knee-slapping to their spinning, Pierson thought, *this should get interesting*.

But what about Maggie?

Pulling out his cell phone, Pierson caught the end of the latest Live Lips report. The smooth voice purred, "The rabbit is sprung and running for its life. It thought it could evade the Christmas Capers and Tween Machines at Metro Center, but escaped only temporarily. Our soldiers are in pursuit and more loyal rollers are preparing to board the Expo Line—helped by several friendly neighbors. More from the front lines soon."

The danger was worse than ever.

Pierson gazed over the expansive interior of the Pollo Ranchero bowling palace which was now resounding with polkas danced to the tune of 'John Jacob Jingleheimer Smith' in between rolling balls at nine-pins. Two nuns approached and Pierson recognized Myrtle and Marigold. They looked tougher and more assured than earlier, though maybe it was just a trick of the light, or the lateness of the hour.

The nuns broke into pleasant smiles. Suddenly a pair of scantily-clad nuns joined them, their smiles even broader. Each took one of the Professor's arms.

"Madam G-Spot has asked you to be her special guest in the VIP area, Mr. Pierson." They grinned. "That's quite a privilege. You don't even have to roll any balls, or dance any polkas."

He blinked. "Uh—are you sure? I need a quick answer."

More smiles. "She will meet with you again shortly. Very shortly. In the VIP area. She will be glad to help you in there."

"Okay." Richard stood uncertainly. This was not what he expected. But where else could he turn? As he watched, other nuns ushered 'Saint Melia' to the VIP area. If it was good enough for the famous Amelia Earhart. . .

The nuns in bikinis pulled him, thrusting their smiling faces into his. Indeed, even at his advanced age, the lure was difficult to resist, his eye finding its way to bare midriffs and blossoming chests. He soon returned a smile of his own.

Up the side corridor and to the right they hurried. Before him a wide carpeted lobby-like area opened up with a string of doors. On the right, a long row of cubicles were occupied by a dozen nuns who had returned to their ceaseless activity setting up nine-pins with minimal assistance from labor-saving devices.

On the left was a door under a sign that read 'Holy Kitchen', and another door that read 'Holy Bivouac'—with indications of scorching on the door and the carpet as from repeated encounters with flames, and Pierson noted several fire extinguishers propped within easy reach, along with medical kits including especially, and mysteriously, a stack of eye-patches. Next was a large door under a 'Nun Such' sign, with strange noises emanating from behind as from a constantly-running mechanical contrivance—guarded by the biggest nun yet with muscular arms folded and a 'do not come hither' expression on her glum face. Finally they arrived at an irregularly shaped door as if forming a stylish entrance—under a large crudely constructed sign that read 'Back-To-Nature Wigwam' in big leaf-green letters.

"This is your lucky day. 'Richard', is it?"

He nodded.

"It's not often that guests are allowed in the VIP area, Richard. Our little establishment is very exclusive."

His brows rose. He recalled the constant stream of 'lucky' winners he had seen coming back here and the equal volume of cross-dressers who had exited.

They escorted him to the Wigwam's entrance.

He frowned. "What about Maggie? Madam G-Spot said—"

"In here, Richard," the nun smiled, interrupting. "Madam G will soon meet you in our Wigwam. Just as soon as she can break away from her many duties." Opening the door, one of the bikini-clad nuns stepped through, taking care to pause with her bare behind fixed for a moment in front of Richard's face, and she began lighting candles.

Richard climbed through the symbolic entrance and sat cross-legged on a recyclable fiber rug in the center of the tall teepee. On the walls in the semi-gloom he saw ersatz deer hide on the walls, pictures of Western nature scenes, and incense burners in the midst of hanging pictures that read 'Peace & Justice', 'Earth Day', and 'Unleash Your Fem'.

Another nun sat on the floor before him. It was not Madam G-Spot, but Marigold. While he looked, Marigold lit the incense and its smoke soon spiraled about the teepee to pause at the top before finally escaping.

Positioned about them were imitation deer hide drums, Indian peace pipes, and Fair-Trade pillows, together with—and most surprising—an old Western-style wooden rocking chair with a purple mannequin sitting within, a brunette wig propped at an angle on its bare purple head.

The squeeze-box nuns sat on either side of him, and with their sincere smiles turned coy and their fulsome, nigh, bare breasts thrust shamelessly forward, Richard found it increasingly difficult to focus on anything negative or form any objection. By force of will he recalled Maggie back to mind, only to lose focus again before the nuns' adoring stares and caressing fingers which constantly reassured him and boosted his frail over-the-hill ego, yet a third one entering to sit behind him, the swimsuit tops of all three barely-clad nun-maidens seeming to come loose and 'malfunction' as they pressed smilingly closer.

"First we must say our prayers. We are in a church, after all," exclaimed one of the nuns.

"Oh my. Would you like to lead the prayer, Marigold?"

The nuns held hands and formed a cross-legged circle around him.

Marigold recited: "Our Mother, who bakes in heaven, Jessie be thy name, thy kitchen come, thy cook be done in baking as it is unleavened. Give us this day our daily bread, and forgive us our recipes as we forgive the recipes of others; and lead us not into conception; but deliver us from the sinfulness of men."

If that don't beat all, thought Richard. *No telescope could have prepared me for this.*

Inhaling the incense through his nostrils, Richard found it more and more difficult to focus his mind on anything but the gorgeous femininity around him—excepting the dark lump that was Marigold. *I guess we should get this over with. The sooner we get this done, the sooner we can get back to helping Maggie.*

"Repeat after me," smiled Marigold.

"Yes, Sister," everyone replied.

"Momma knows best."

"Momma knows best," repeated Richard with the others.

"Don't mess with Mother Earth."

"Don't mess with Mother Earth. . ."

"Zero children is best for the planet."

Richard felt dizzy. "Zero children is best for the planet. . ."

"Smoking is a crime against Nature—except for marijuana peace pipes."

"Smoking is a crime against Nature—except for marijuana peace pipes. . ."

"Development rapes Mother Earth."

"Development rapes Mother Earth. . ."

"I must stop global warming," Marigold's smooth voice continued.

The tones were deep and rich. Before Richard knew it, his own voice had responded, "I must stop global warming." Breathing deeply with eyes closed, he failed to notice the gleam that had appeared in the eyes of the purple mannequin seated in the rocking chair before him. From somewhere a drum circle sounded, its thumps rising steadily in his ears soothing his soul and calming him as Andean flutes joined in—louder and louder the drums sounded—faster and wilder the pipes played—then an image of an olive-skinned face that reminded Richard of distant leaden seas, a mere hint of oriental in her sloe eyes, her indigo shoulder-length hair with bottom fringe upended, and tastefully mascaraed eyebrows from her exposure as a child to the first Nevada atomic bomb explosion at Frenchman's Flat in 1951, filled his mind and all else was shut out.

He must save his Maggie.

With an effort, he opened his eyes.

To his surprise, the other nuns were staring at him with sullen expressions. To his even greater surprise, the purple mannequin in the rocking chair no longer sat, *but stood*—its red animated eyes stared into his own. And for a fraction of a moment he could not be certain if he was sitting and looking up at a mannequin, or if he stood and stared down at an old man looking up at him.

Suddenly he understood the full meaning of what he had

contemplated without resolution for the past sixty years, ever since he had first showed off his telescope on Stirling Peak as a twelve-year-old boy boasting to a pretty young girl whom he had just met—his best and only friend: Maggie.

And he understood that the glowing meteors which he had glimpsed in his telescope departing Pluto and landing in the growing number of chicken-ranch bowlarama-casinos run by the nuns of Opus Dea *were* the purple mannequins, one of which even now sought to steal his soul and transform him into yet another Cross-Dresser from Pluto!

As he sat and watched, his mouth open with horror, he saw the red glow increase in power, and his polo shirt and tan jacket grow brittle and dusty while the mannequin sprouted a new polo shirt and jacket *just like his*.

Reaching into a pocket—which gave off dust and split apart when he touched it as if suddenly anciently aged—he pulled out the greasepaint that he had carried about since he had infiltrated the Mime Retirement Home and been forced to take the 'call' of the retired mime in the wheelchair. Summoning his last reserve of strength, Pierson unscrewed the top and smeared whiteness over his face.

"Eeeeew!"

As if shot, Marigold jerked backward. Her jaw dropped in disgust.

Disgust and anger seized the other three nuns and they instantly released Richard from their unholy holy grip. They too jerked back.

Smearing more paint across his jaw and cheeks and forehead as rapidly as he could, Richard held out the grease-pot like garlic before vampires, and the nuns leaped to their feet and retreated in horror to the back of the teepee.

"My god! What kind of fiend are you?" they shouted. "Don't you know it's dangerous to bring a medium out of a trance like that? She was only trying to help."

"That kind of help I don't need."

As he watched, the mannequin—no longer purple, but an exact duplicate of himself—stumbled. With a shiver and an eerie whine, the mannequin disintegrated into dust.

The nuns glared in pity at the pile of dust. "You don't understand, Richard. Cross-dressing is in your nature. You must Unleash Your Fem. Let your inner self take control. The only way to do that is to stamp out your toxic masculinity *once and for all*."

"No," yelled Richard. "You lie! I know better now. Once upon a time I might have believed you, but now I know your real plans. You Cross-Dressers from Pluto have no intention of helping the Earth. You're not here to save anyone but yourselves. You're exactly like the Evil Mimes from Bogland and their *ribbet* masters. But where the Evil Mimes want global warming to flood the Earth and drown everyone to make it safe for their water-loving *frog* masters—you and your *tibbet* leaders want to dry the Earth out and make everything die of thirst, so you can make it safe for water-hating *toads!*"

The nuns looked at each other with more sullen glances. "Mr. Pierson. . .you know too much."

He thrust out his grease-pot. "I know you'll never cross a line of white paint. I'm breaking out of this joint." Leaning over, he smeared a finger line of white paint on the floor and the nuns jammed together in rage. “That’s so you don’t try to follow me.”

Gnashing teeth and fixing lethal glares on him, the nuns could do nothing, and Richard backed out of the ironically named ‘Back-To-Nature Wigwam’. He headed for the Casino’s back door. He knew now that Madam G-Spot would not appear, would not help, and for some incomprehensible reason would not help Maggie.

On the way, he brushed past a bookshelf and his eye passed over the titles of its books: *Walden, Silent Spring, The Doll House, The Feminine Mystique, No Logo, The Authoritarian Personality, A People's History of the United States, and of course. . . Autobiography of a Yogi.* Pausing in his flight, he dumped the shelf over in outrage, and rushed toward a side door.

Then froze—

Episode 11

Fleeing, but still organized, the Warriors belted down South Flower Street heading for the terminus to the Expo Line—and the safety of Santa Monica. Maggie took the lead, glancing frequently behind to ensure the rest of her crew were still with her. Maiden Hell and Nite Shade rolled in front, with Suki Vicious, Vexinator, and Queen Cobra behind, and Bloody Mary bringing up the rear despite her injured finger. She spat on pain.

Far behind, in the direction of Metro Center on 7th Street, drifted distant sounds.

Up ahead, on 11th Street, was the platform to board the

Expo tram.

Beside loomed a logo of a coffee cup—Maggie's favorite. She slowed and entered, the rest of the Warriors followed behind.

Several customers stood in line. A young man in sandals and Mohawk with silver chains hanging from his faded jeans and jacket looked up in alarm, and before he could react, Maggie rolled over his sandals, sending him limping to the sidelines. Again. The rest of the line made way.

Behind the counter lounged an overweight teen, his unwashed hair dripping to his shoulders, dull placidity reflected on his face, his fuzzy mouth crinkling with disinterest.

"Yo," he muttered.

Maggie caught her breath, leaned forward. "Gimme a regular."

No response.

"A regular. Coffee."

Still no movement. For all Maggie could tell, the barista was a totem pole.

"You know—the black stuff. In a cup."

He finally cocked his head.

She tried again. "Tonight. Like, right now."

One brow raised. He turned and passed his placid gaze over the expansive menu dominating the lobby. Raised a finger to his cheek. But kept staring.

Nite Shade elbowed Maggie. "This place does serve coffee, doesn't it?" She arched an ear to sounds from the direction of Metro Center.

An idea dawned. She traced an image of a coffee cup in the air. "You understand 'cup', right?" She spoke loud but clearly.

He mouthed a sudden 'Oh'. "Coffee." He smiled. "In a cup."

The Warriors exhaled with relief. He got it.

Taking a cup, the barista turned and made as if about to pour coffee inside—he paused. He turned back and put the cup down.

"Gimme some money first."

Sullen looks. Scrambling in her fanny pack, Maggie extracted a piece of paper and tossed it on the counter.

He looked it over, his brows contracting. Finally he looked up. "This is a Franklin!" Both brows rose. "Wow. Never seen one of these before." Lifting it to the light, he ooh'd and ahh'd, admiring its appearance. "Howdaya like that?"

Maggie leaned closer. "Is it enough? It's all I got."

He threw it back down on the counter. "Can't make change for Franklins."

"Here, I have money," Vexinator said. Reaching into her fanny pack, she pulled out two bills and put them down as Maggie took back her hundred.

After a quick inspection, he threw her bills down too. "I can't make change for Grants, either. Gimme something smaller, or clear the way for *real* customers." He eyed the guy in the Mohawk who was still nursing his toes.

Nite Shade and Bloody Mary tried their luck—no deal. Their money was all Canadian.

"We want coffee, too," said Cobra and Suki and Maiden. Their money was instantly rejected as well—the quarter flung down by each was not enough.

The Warriors frowned.

Finally a tall gentleman with a clerical frock stepped up with a friendly smile. "May I help?" Pulling out his wallet, he handed a stack of ten-dollar bills to Maggie and deftly took the hundred from her. "I'm sure one of these will be quite acceptable to this young man, Madam."

The barista nodded.

Accepting a ten-spot from confused Maggie, the barista motioned her to pocket the other bills, while the pastor stood rocking happily on his heels in satisfaction of his good deed, and the other Warriors, equally confused, watched in silent wonder.

The barista paused. He glanced at the empty cup in his hand.

"Tall!" yelled Maggie, Suki, and Maiden all together, the sounds from Metro Center coming nearer through the open door.

He smiled and proceeded to fill the first cup. It computed.

Behind the Warriors several more customers entered to join the others who had made way for the derby rollers and the lot now queued grumpily behind them.

The hour was past late and was now early. The Warriors were beginning to tire, and even Maggie, although she nibbled on her stash of dried nopalitos in her fanny pack and took quiet swigs from her flask of red Thunderbird, was starting to feel the strain.

The distant sounds from up the street were becoming noise; shouts and bangs became discernible as the Santa Claws and Easter Bunnies went at it. Time was as short as the pleated blue flaps and black leather under-minis that graced the appled rumps of the Holy Roller team, which attracted more than their share of casual stares from many in the coffee queue.

The barista again halted.

Slowly he turned.

Step by step he neared.

Inch by inch.

With the insane focus of a certified instructor of OCD, he stared into Maggie's eyes, and said: "Room for cream?"

Every Warrior caught her breath. Exchanged stares. "No, Maggie. . . He did not just 'room for cream' you, did he?" The entire queue took a shocked step backward, several stifling gasps. One whispered to his companion, "That barista. He room-for-cream'ed that lady. Can you believe it?" The other gave a look of pity. Wondered if a 911 call would be answered at this hour. Even the pastor gripped his fists in anger at witnessing the disgraceful event.

A tear came to Maggie's eye as the words echoed in her mind. True, she had been room-for-cream'd before, but she had gotten over it. Thought—hoped—it would never happen again. For a moment she stumbled, confused, embarrassment coming over her that some puerile teenage boy would dare to shame her by making such a comment. In her confusion, she blurted, "No—I mean, 'space for cream'—no, make that 'no space, no cream, but yes some room." Finally Maggie fell silent, too shocked to continue.

Pitilessly, the brute drove home his insult. Angling his head, he leaned forward, locked his eyes on hers once again. "I said: *room for cream?*" Followed by a triumphant ugly smile.

"Dude," said the guy in the Mohawk, "did you just *room-for-cream* her?" He looked disgusted. "That just isn't done."

Finally Maggie recovered. "I don't drink cream. Don't like it. Don't touch it. I'm allergic—I'm whatever. So don't keep asking me if I want to put the stuff in my coffee."

Puzzlement. Did not compute. Again the barista blared the offensive words, even more loudly: "*Cream? Room? Cream in your room? Rooms of cream?*" Not satisfied with insulting Maggie, he turned his dull expression on her companions. "How about you three: *room for cream? Cream for room? Creamy rooms?*"

The pastor gasped and put his hands over his ears, then put them over the ears of an old lady in the queue. The guy in the Mohawk doubled over to retch. Suki, Maiden, and Cobra, along with the rest of the Warriors rolled backwards stunned, their mouths open.

At the entrance a fat guy in a red suit and red cap on eight-wheels halted in shock. Turning to a pair of Easter bunny ears next to him, he gasped, "That guy. He *room-for-cream'd* them!" The bunny ears shook her head in sorrow.

Maggie frowned.

The pastor took out a bottle of water and took a swig. Stepping to the counter, he pointed to the barista. "You should be ashamed of yourself. Don't you know it's not polite to say Room for Cream to anyone?"

Cowed, the barista finally filled their Tall coffee cups and shamefully handed them over.

The pastor looked down his nose. "I think you owe this young lady an apology." Gesturing to the barista, he accidentally spilled water on Maggie's arm.

Maggie aimed a shocked and angry gaze at the pastor. "Sinful evil water man!" Snatching the bottle of water from his hand, she poured the contents over the pastor's head. "Drown in your sinful poison!" She threw it aside.

Enough was enough.

With a single smooth motion, Maggie whipped her telescope bat from her fanny pack, snapped it to full length, and let loose on the coffee shop's counter: screen registers, glass partitions, flavor pumps, cookie packages and paper cups flew in a tornado whirlwind, leaving the barista stunned on the floor staring at the ceiling.

"NOT FAIR!"

Taking up her Tall cup filled to the brim, she yelled, "You're stupid! You Failed!" and burst through the surprised Santa and tween, leaving twisted bunny ears in her wake.

Maggie barreled back onto South Flower Street, and rolled toward the Expo Line, her Warriors cheering as they rushed to catch up, 'Not fair!' and 'You're stupid!' echoing behind.

The Santas and Easter rollers re-grouped and gave chase.

At the next intersection a long string of cars appeared, crossing the Warriors' path like a train, forcing the derbyers to pause. Their amazed gaze fell upon a self-driving car, no one behind the 'wheel' except a house cat staring intently out the car's back window. Another self-driving car followed, the only occupant a large dog, barking incessantly, its eyes fixed on the cat in front. As they drove past, two more self-driving cars appeared, hooked together. Inside were several ragged forlorn-looking children little more than skin and bones, clinging to bars set in the windows. One had posted a sign in crayon: "Save me from Daycare Macht Frei." Last in line was a self-driving car covered with seaweed, no one at all inside, and only a little Dutch flag torn and flapping in the wind next to a tiny sail like a Flying Dutchman on wheels—who knew for how long? Or how far?

The little convoy passed into the night. The Warriors pressed on.

Just in time.

"Ya think that's gonna save ya, ya pagan dream-killers? Think again. We'll get ya for Sirius," the Santas shouted. The grinding sets of eight wheels resounded off the surrounding buildings as the Easter bunnies joined in. "If those elf-slaving Sanka-drinkers don't getcha, we will," they added.

At last 11th Street arrived and the Warriors roared past. On their left, the Expo Line emerged from the depths and a block later they found the platform, a double-car tram rolling to a stop before them.

From the wrong direction.

As the Warriors stared, with threats of "You're on our naughty list!" growing louder, the tram screeched to a halt and the doors slid open to reveal a phalanx of flesh in black leotards in each carriage.

"Oh, no," muttered Nite Shade.

The first hideously painted face smiled and answered. "It just ain't your lucky day, is it, Warriors?"

"It can't be," added Vex. "Not the 'Fat Whores'—"

With a grin the Whore yelled, "Fat Enough 4 U!"

With that, the Whores spilled out onto the platform, their skates groaning under their great bulks, their black leotards holding in their masses of flesh just enough to keep their arcs and turns from tumbling the Whores onto the ground, flab over flab. Before Maggie could hatch a plan, the two gangs merged into a confused mass, flesh absorbing elbows, half-drunk coffee flung onto the Whores' greasy hair without effect, sprays of mace evoking only cackling laughter from the triple-chinned faces, protected as they were by massive layers of skin base and cheap lipstick with fake eyelashes long as Nixon's nose.

"We'll be done with you little bitches quicker'n a twenty dollar local," called their leader, sliding her fists rudely over cylinders of air directly in Cobra's face.

"Like anyone would touch you for less than that," yelled Nite Shade in reply.

The chief Whore narrowed her eyes. "Wait till I slam-dunk you," she shouted. "You ain't been jammed, till you been jammed by a Fat Whore!"

The two teams rolled parallel back the way the Warriors had come, ramming each other. The Santas were almost upon them.

"Pivot," yelled Maiden Hell as the Chief Whore rolled toward her.

Maggie zipped from behind. The Juggernaut slammed into the Whore. Though Maggie was stopped in her tracks as by an eighteen-wheeled donut truck, the Whore sailed off the platform, the impetus of her roll unbreakable.

The Santa gang leader looked up—saw the approach of grey doom. With the blast of a cannon, the great amoeba flattened him like a piston crushing a car, elf scalps and red shreds of unwashed fur exploding.

The Warriors succeeded in guiding the rest of the Fat

Enough 4 U Whores onto a collision course with the other Santas, triggering a new series of explosions as the globes of flesh, studiously accumulated over a lifetime of supine transactions, found their antimatter in the form of bloated subway-dwellers in red suits swinging bags of bricks—where matter failed to meet antimatter, Santas and Whores rolling side over side in unholy pairs.

"You touch it, you own it," shouted the Santas, attempting to pawn their brightly wrapped curses on the Fat Whores. "You touch us, you rent us," they shouted back, attempting with equal fervor to force various unidentifiable appendages into the Santas' reluctant callused hands, evoking equal expressions of revulsion. Several Easter Bunnies went down as well, being un-masked as tweeny boys opting to sample the vague wares of those Whores who were too dizzy to demand their customary payment.

Two Whores remained on the platform, and as the last remaining Santas and Bunnies followed the Warriors back up, it looked like the end may have finally arrived—Cobra caught her reggae locks in the deep crevasse of the nearest Whore, who despite her own attempts to break free, was unable to loosen her folds of flab sufficiently to do so.

In desperation, Cobra thrust an arm inside to free her braids. The Whore ceased trying to break free. With an evil grin, she began to shake, the ripples drifting across her leotard-prisoned flesh sucking Cobra more deeply into the fleshy crevasse till her entire arm disappeared.

In tears, Cobra glanced at the rest of the Warriors. "Leave me," she cried. "You can't save me. No one can. I'm caught like a fly in a Venus trap. I'm doomed to digestion."

The others peered at her with pity and despair. As more

Santas appeared, forcing them to dodge swinging bags and more pretty packages tossed at them with sly grins, they looked to Maggie—what could they do?

A west-bound tram slid to a halt. From its doors sprang a bald woman with tattoos on her face, alongside a brightly smiling slim and elegant skater. The first wore the pink corsets, black leather shorts, and pleated blue flaps of the Warriors—Thrill Killa had finally arrived. The latter was dressed in clean white shirt, high school tan skirt, white headband, pearl necklace, and pink sweater—Pussy Kicker, the veritable image of Donna Reed or June Cleaver.

One look and they instantly took in the situation. Pussy Kicker skated to the Whore who had caught Cobra. A swift kick between the legs, and the Whore gasped, expelling Cobra like a cork from champagne. Thrill Killa grabbed the Whore's hands between her legs, and dragging her backwards from behind, propelled her off the platform where she landed on the feeder lane with a bounce. That Whore, at least, would not disappoint any more clients.

Pussy Kicker yelled in triumph.

Skating circles around the remaining Santas, while the Bunnies were preoccupied with their male comrade tweenies attempting to ride the groaning islands of flesh lying in the street making little distinction between black Whores and red Santas, the Warriors succeeded in boarding the next train to Santa Monica.

With a last few skated feet thrust into angry protesting red Santa and black Whore bellies to block them from boarding, the doors closed, clipping several bunny ears in the process—with all the Warriors on board, the tram rocketed from the station.

Maggie finally breathed. "Let us pray." They formed a line. Together they knelt, their hands together: "Hail Mary, baked with steaks, the Lord is thy recipe, blessed are you by women, and blessed is the fruit of thy moon, Jessie Christina. Holy Mary, Mother of Virgins, pray for us folksingers, now and at the happy altar hour of nopalitos and wine, the flesh and blood of Santa Lucia the Holy Bowler of the Third Secret of Fatima amen."

Episode 12

In front of the open door leading to escape from the Holy Rollers' Pollo Ranchero Bowlarama & Casino there appeared before Professor Richard Pierson a slim young woman whose gaze transfixed his own. As Richard angled to squeeze past her to freedom, he saw her mouth open and her eyes widen with wonder. She broke into a bright smile.

"Excuse me." He paused, politely returning the smile. "Say. You really do look like those old pictures of Amelia Earhart in those black and white flicks from way back. Welcome home. Gotta go now." He broke away and hurried toward Venice Beach, hoping the Dervish Festival was still in operation so he could lose himself in the crowd.

It was.

As he settled to rest and down a drink—somehow only Thunderbird wine being available, due, he supposed, to the nuns' and Dervishes' odd sensitivity to H2O—it occurred to him in the back of his mind that just maybe he might find a Pollo Ranchero nun not entirely opposed to rescuing Maggie, someone—anyone—who might listen to his call for alarm.

A footstep.

He turned.

Amelia had followed.

In surprise he stepped back. Famous Amelia Earhart was one thing. Amelia Earhart stalking him in the night was another. The lights strung about on wires were still lit, despite the mid-morning pre-dawn hour—3:00 a.m. to be precise—and a few curious and sundry still roamed about staring at her Lockheed Electra and the remains of the damaged tent which had been taken down, and in a clearing surrounded by Bermuda grass and white sand a number of spectators had gathered around a squad of Dervishes who still spun in place on a stage in their eternal effort to achieve nothing-at-all.

Amelia stepped towards him, eyes rimmed with red, hands clenching and unclenching at her sides.

"What—what do you want?" Pierson asked.

She broke a smile. "You—something about you—draws me on."

Richard threw glances to left and right. Though the Festival still carried on and other people still walked about, the darkened corners were growing as they drifted away one by one. He felt uncomfortable under her penetrating glare.

His jaw slid open. "Me?"

Her smile broadened. "I want you."

"Are you sure you mean me?"

"Like a butterfly to a flower." She stepped closer.

"I'm just an ordinary guy. Why would you want me?

You're famous—a big shot. The famous Amelia Earhart. You can have anyone you want."

A downcast look came over her. She looked down. "I've lost my fans. Nobody believes I'm me." She sniffed back a tear. "They all think I'm a fake."

His face tried to express ambivalence. "Well, after all, you don't exactly look 120 years old."

"I was kidnapped. Forced to develop photos. Make tiny cameras. Made to eat nothing but rice and sake—"

"Oh?"

She put a hand to her forehead, eyes closed. "Wait. That was something else. . . After that, I was kidnapped again. Force-fed Johnnie Walker. Raped all day by fiends in striped shirts."

His brows rose higher. He continued to eye the exits. "Do tell. . ."

Again she lay her dull clouded gaze upon him. "I got away. They tried to make me stay, but I escaped their Hell. Came back. To help my country. To warn about Hitler's secret base in Panama and stop that devil Hirohito and the Mormons."

"Do do tell. . ." He still eyed the exits.

"The fiends wore *greasepaint*."

Suddenly Richard remembered. The white paint from the Back-to-Nature-Wigwam was still plastered on his face. He was whiter than white.

As they spoke, Richard had backed away from the better lit areas of the Festival and he found himself next to bleachers hastily set up by the nuns for the crowd. The crowd which Amelia's errant Electra had chased away.

Step by step she came closer, driving the aged Pierson

behind the bleachers.

"But why do you want to stalk me? I'm a nobody."

"You're a fan. You know me, you like me. The truth is—I'm nobody without my fans."

"This isn't right. Amelia, I think that if you don't leave me alone, I'll have to hire a bodyguard to keep you away."

"I'll get through to you anyway. I'll phone you at odd hours, leave breathless 'I love you' messages at your home. Email all your ghost email addresses. Lie in wait at your favorite coffee shop. You're a fan—you know it comes with the territory."

"Amelia, this can never be. You're just another famous person to me, like thousands of other famous persons."

"No! You must love me! I have no one else in my life. I've worshiped you from afar for. . .almost half an hour."

"No, Amelia. There is nothing between us. There can never be anything between us. For me, being a fan is just business."

Pawing the grass, she rushed upon him. Pushed him down on his back. With a maniacal grin, she tore off his shirt and tossed it aside.

"No! Oh, no!" he cried. She was too strong to resist. He swallowed and closed his eyes, afraid to fight her off, what she might do to him, or to those he loved. He choked back tears as Amelia's vulgar hands touched his body. His belt came off, then she unbuttoned his jeans and with brutal strength dragged them entirely off, exposing his underwear. He bit his knuckle, his eyes closed, his face averted. The dishonor!

Off they came.

With a glint of triumph in her wild eyes, she glared viciously into his, and inspected the object of her irresistible passion.

The fire died.

Her glare by degrees turned surprised, savage, disappointed, depressed. "Go ahead and cough," she muttered, rising to her feet.

As Richard rolled over and cried into his discarded shirt, Amelia let loose a single swift kick at his jeans, sending them flying. "I should sue you for false advertising." With that, she staggered away.

Richard slowly dragged his clothes back on, and with a feeling of utter degradation and humiliation, slunk away in the darkness, unable to show his white face in public. At the first water fountain, he hastily scrubbed the white away, rubbing and scraping till his skin was raw, concerned passersby pausing to stare. Never again could he wear whiteness with pride and dignity. Never again put on the greasepaint. "That's not me," he cried quietly to himself. "It's not me, I tell you. I'm not one of them. *I'm not white!*"

Back at the Festival, Amelia trod the grass in a glum mood. "God damn *white-tease*," she mumbled over and over. "How dare he lead me on like that—I'm only *shuman* you know. Even inviting me behind the bleachers!" She pushed out her lips in defiance. "And he better not go telling people this was anything but consensual. He asked for it." She stopped. Taking out her flask, she took two big gulps. "Imagine that—only one poke!"

Suddenly her gaze fixed on another figure, even more unexpected than a slutty teasing Professor. Back in the Casino, among whirling Dervishes who had emerged from

Madam G-Spot's Pollo Ranchero as cross-dressers and were now twirling about dressed in wigs and lipstick, was another figure who aroused her deepest feelings.

Attempting to spin with the best, but reeling with the worst, was an unshaven figure in green pants, polka-dot shirt, red bulb on his nose, and a reddish-orange fright wig on his head. From his lips dangled an unlit thin cigar. His giant red clown shoes bore scorch marks cross-printed with stains as if they had recently burst into flames and been hosed out. What attracted Amelia's eye the most, however, besides being intrigued by the man's innovative attire, was the white paint forming semi-circles around his eyes.

Pay-dirt.

Stumbling, Blinky thrust out a giant red shoe. He paused. Standing straight, he regained his balance. He grunted and frowned. This nirvana thing wasn't as easy as it looked. Not even the heavy white skirt that the stone-faced Dervishes had reluctantly attached to his red plastic belt had been enough to counter-balance his baggy pants and huge shoes. What else could he do? Their giant chef hat would not fit over his bright orange hair and his chubby arms got tired too easily to hold them out while he spun. He lay his cynical gaze over the other participants and watched them twirl effortlessly. *They must drink their booze in the morning*, he thought.

Struggling to strike a match, he finally lit it and transferred the flame to his dead-stick cigar stub, puffing it back to life, acrid smoke tearing his eyes. Larger cigar stubs were hard to find in the park. As were decent cast-off lighters. Casting suspicious glances about—to make sure those goddam Mimes were nowhere in the vicinity—he downed another swig of Everclear. Purity, the Dervishes had said. That's what's important. Like family.

His eye stuck on something.

Off the stage, half enclosed by the darkness beyond the open front doors, stood a slim figure—a woman—a young woman. With freckled clean face and eyes that were focused on him. She smiled and let loose an exaggerated wink.

At him? He glanced around again—it must be a mistake. But no one else on the stage was standing still as he was. The mystery deepened till she passed her slim hands over her head in the shape of a fright wig and pointed and smiled again.

Him indeed.

For a moment he reviewed the day's events for misdemeanors and felonies, then the past month's. No—his transgressions were either too light or too old or too concealed to attract the attention of law enforcement, though a nasty memory of his youth re-surfaced when he had worked the clown circuit at children's parties and once mistakenly packed a children's piñata with condoms instead of balloons. 'Get outa town and join the Circus', the cops had viciously told him—'or we'll prosecute'. He stifled his misery again with a drink and blinked through the haze.

She was still there.

Emerging from the shadows, she stood in plain light, smiling and waving, both her eyes and her arms giving 'Come hither' messages. With a last confused glance, he removed his Dervish skirt, took the cigar from his mouth, gulped, and stepped off the platform.

Motioning him to follow, she backed away like a gossamer enchantress.

Blinky followed. True he still had no idea who she was, or why she summoned him, but another search of his alcohol-drenched brain produced no living memory of encounters with the opposite sex either. Except for that blind Eskimo in Anchorage, but that was a different story. . .

He was overdue.

He followed her the half-block to the tent on the beach, where, lit by the light of a harvest moon, she paused in her flight and allowed Blinky to approach. Seductively, she leaned back against a post, her lips averted. As he came close, she suddenly turned to face him directly. Her red-rimmed eyes stared deep into his own blood-shot orbs. Attempting to turn too quickly, she stumbled—Blinky caught her in his arms.

"This—this can't be," she blurted. "You. . .were just standing there, silhouetted in a field of spinning tops like a Monet surrounded by a living exhibit of Art Deco." Unable to endure his gaze, she put her hand to her forehead and closed her eyes. Then opened them again. "I could not look away. The beauty of your form has seized me like a fever."

Blinky dropped his gaze and took in his polka-dot shirt, green pants, and red stained shoes ten sizes too big. He scratched his jaw with its week's worth of growth. A boozy burp surfaced. "I juggle a lot," he said.

One feminine hand stretched out and caressed his yellow suspenders. "I'll bet you have to know a lot for your profession. I mean, you must spend an awful lot of time preparing for performances." She smiled demurely.

He smiled—his first in a long while. Swallowed again, glowing cigar in hand. Leaned against the pole nonchalantly. "You know," he swayed briefly then caught his balance with the other hand, "bein' a clown ain't what most people think it is. There's the tossing balls around without lettin' em fall. There's droppin' your pants over and over till you get it just right—it's not as easy as it looks. If you get blown out of a cannon before you drop your pants, that's okay. But what if you drop your pants first, and then get blown out? Now that's a problem!"

She nodded in pretended surprise.

He took a drag on the cigar, feeling like Bogart. "It's tough under the Big Top."

Nestling closer, she fondled the plastic flower on his shirt till he hastily covered it up—after all, she might be allergic to water like those prissy cross-dressers he had recently encountered.

"What do they call you, Pale and Handsome?"

He coughed, stifling bile. "Blinky." His dull stare lay on her like pesticide on non-organic grapes.

"Oh, that's such a nice name. How ever did you come up with that?" she smiled.

Downing another swig from his flask, he sucked the cigar and blinked profusely as the smoke spiraled into his eyes. "It's just a nickname. The other fellas at the Circus gave it to me."

"Did they?"

"Yeah. They laughed." He grew serious. "They *always* laugh when I'm around." He sighed as if to cover up something deeper.

"You know what they call *me*?" she asked, all innocence.

Blinky shook his head.

"You don't know? From looking at my face?"

Again the vacant look.

A frown appeared on her face. "Amelia."

Still nothing.

"As in 'Earhart'?"

He shrugged.

More forcefully: "As in *Amelia* Earhart, the world-famous flyer who crossed the Atlantic and flew around the world? I was a bit late getting back."

"News to me, lady. But I'll drink to that." He knocked back and drank another gulp of his Everclear.

She stared at the ground sadly while Blinky puffed up a storm. Finally she looked up again, her eyes tracing the outline of white grease-paint around Blinky's hypnotic eyes. She forced a smile. "You know what?"

He shook his head. "What?"

"I need a drink. That's what."

Smiling, he offered his bottle and before he could stop her she drained half of it. His mouth dropped open and his eyes narrowed in anger. "What the—?" His fist briefly raised, causing Blinky to lose his balance and stagger. He clutched the post to stabilize himself. "Now why'd you go and do that? It ain't easy to find half-empty bottles on the street, ya know."

A bleary but bright smile coursed over Amelia's face as the alcohol re-entered her body. Three hours was just too long.

"Lesh kiss."

He leaned back, his turn to be surprised. "Huh?" Once

more he glanced around. Did she actually mean him?

"Thash right! Your little pale-face turns me on. I wanna fly to the moon tonight."

Another glance to left and right—this time for comfort. "Are you sure? I mean: you—and me? We just met."

"Don care. I wanna ride your twin pokes."

Confusion.

Blinky shook his head. "Whatever. Your place. . .or your place?" he said, preferring not to mention the cardboard box that he called Home.

"Don' care 'bout that, you little Josheph you. There's some real nice bleachers right over there. Thash good enough for me." She grabbed Blinky by his red bulbed nose and led him straight-away toward the bleachers without regard for who might be watching.

"Ow ow ow! Careful with the nose, Amelia baby. I had it sewed on in a former life and it don't come off no more."

"No problemo, Blinky. You jesh bring your little Joseph-face over here and pump up the works, caush Melia's gonna fly her plane tonight. And she don' care who knows it."

A last painful groan, and after carefully depositing his Everclear behind a trash can, Blinky found himself tossed on the ground behind the bleachers—the ground unaccountably rounded as if already prepared—and Amelia leaped right into the matter. The polka-dot shirt flew. Then, as Blinky leaned back on his elbows in stunned amazement, his suspenders and shoes followed. *Could this be real*? he reflected. He pinched himself and jerked. Then he pinched Amelia and she squealed in delight.

Real.

With a gasp of pleasure, he pulled off Amelia's blouse and yanked it free. His eyes focusing on the *objet d'arts* that lurked in his dreams, he savored his first contact with female mammalian glands since that time in Imperial Valley when he gave pro bono performances for blind farmers' kids. But that was a different story. . .

He rubbed his gritty face on her breasts while her hands worked frantically to undo his belt. Again he leaned back and watched while Amelia tore off her own pants and proceeded to strip him of his.

Off they came.

Exquisite pleasure settled on her face as she sat on his legs—both she and he covered by nothing more than underwear. With a last sigh, she pulled off his boxers.

"Come on, baby!" Blinky shouted. "Go for it! It's all for you!"

Ice.

Cold as the North Pole. Or South Pole for that matter, zero being zero wherever it may be.

The smile died. Her mouth closed. Her eyes teared. Yanking her eyes away, she burst into tears and covered her face with her hands. "Why me? What have I done to deserve this?"

"Uh. . .whassa matter?" Blinky looked between his legs where his member had come back to life after a hiatus longer than he cared to admit. Nothing wrong there.

She glared hatred. "What happened to your *second poke*?"

"The hell you say." He looked again. "I can give you a second, third, and fourth. But ya gotta have patience."

She leaped to her feet. Dragged her pants back on.

"Wait, baby. You ain't seen nothin yet," he said.

"How dare *–hic–* you trick me like thish," she staggered again, reaching for her shirt and bra. Replacing them with some difficulty, she stepped back. "Draggin' me back here—back behind these bleachers *–hic–* and tryin' to force me to have sex with you."

"What?!"

"Even pulling my clothes off me. You know what?" She pointed an accusing finger at Blinky.

Quickly dragging his own clothes back on, he stared back in confusion. "Uh—"

"*Fuck you!* Thash what!"

"I thought that was the idea, dear Amelia."

"Thash what you think," she staggered back several paces, "thash what you think. . . Well, ya know what?" A hand disappeared behind the trash can.

"Baby, whatever it is, I can fix it." He finished putting his shirt, pants, and giant red shoes back on, and took a step toward her.

"You got warts. Thash what."

Another puzzled look at his own body. "Amelia Dearhart—or whatever your name is—give me a chance. Don't you understand? I love you, baby. You're for me!"

"Well, ya know what?"

He stopped in his tracks, starting to get the message.

"*Fuck you!* Thash what!"

"But what about my Monet clothes? What about my pale-face? You love me, don't you, Dearhart?"

She swayed in the lack of wind while Blinky puffed frantically on his cigar. "No, you god damn 'Binky', or whatever your fuckin' name ish, here'sh one from me!" Her arm swung. Before Blinky could dodge, the bottle of Everclear exploded on his head, drenching his fright wig.

He grabbed his wig with his hands—then remembered, his eyes locking on the cigar.

"Uh-oh."

Like the Hindenburg, flames exploded, the orange-red dye instantly transformed into an orange-red inferno.

"Oh no. Oh, no no no." Flapping his giant red shoes like a scarlet version of the blue-footed booby, Blinky flopped into the night, his wig a pillar of fire sufficient to guide any number of lost desert tribes. "Need some help. Need some help here," faded into the distance on Venice Beach.

Sniffing back a tear, Amelia turned. She shuffled away. Leaving the Festival of Dervishes, she walked aimlessly up the beach, the comfort of crowds and lights dwindling together, leaving it all behind—for all time, as far as she cared. Another trash can came into view and she sighted another half-drunk bottle of something-or-other and she snapped it up and drained it down. Sighting yet another, she clutched it and staggered on.

What kind of hell have I landed on? I remember Earth being a lot more fun than this. Sniff. . . Nobody knows me. . . Nobody loves me. . .

She stumbled on.

At last she paused. On the beach before her loomed a tangle of huge tents next to the Santa Monica Pier. A subdued sign suspended on the side of one tent read: 'Cirque de Lumiére'. With a lonely sigh, she pulled a flap aside and entered an untended back entrance.

Not far behind, a pair of eyes, narrowed and quiet, followed.

Episode 13

The Expo Line sped west at a steady clip, the early hours of a routine Los Angeles pre-dawn passing swiftly. Maggie P. Squatch, Professor Emeritus of Sasquatch Gay Feminist Studies at the U. of C. at L.A., recipient of a No-Bull Peace Prize—her name recently submitted for a Pulitzer for superior social commentary in the form of a short four-line poem about piggy toes written daringly on a coffeehouse bathroom wall—passed her steady gaze over her crew.

Their buns were tight but tired under their pleated blue flaps and their black leather short-shorts left little honed hiney to the imagination. Bloody Mary's red pigtails were trashed and she continued to ooze blood from her missing fingertip. Suki Vicious had lost two cords on her pink corset, leaving one side flapping with every breeze, exposing too much breast—or not enough, depending on one's point of view.

Maiden Hell inspected scrapes on her tattooed coffin in her reflection. Nite Shade re-tied her skates after examining a swollen toe stomped by an Easter Bunny taking martial arts. Vexinator sat and took the moment to close her eyes, not even a second Energy drink keeping her going. Queen Cobra tried to re-braid her hair where an irate Santa had hung caltrop ornaments. Only Pussy Kicker and Thrill Killa were still up to speed, Pussy touching up her lipstick and adjusting her June Cleaver headband, and Thrill running a Headblade over her tattooed skull.

23rd Station passed.

Jefferson / USC.

Expo Park.

Vermont.

They began to breathe easier and no longer felt badly—while marveling at the grammatical paradoxes of popular speech. Maybe—just maybe—the night would finish without further combat.

The double carriages slowed. . .

Western Station hove into view, and the Warriors knew that such was not to be.

On the platform, arranged in order on either side, were a roller derby gang which the Warriors had heard rumors about, but had never previously encountered. As the tram ground to a halt, they viewed their latest opponents from their position in the first carriage and soon understood why they bore their name.

The doors slid open.

"Step back, Warriors," said Maggie's steel voice, as the new gang skated on board the second carriage. Muscle shirts and Moe-haircuts combined with stern looks and tattooed arms to throw a pall over the former good times. Each newcomer flexed massive forearms and biceps, carefully developed through long hours at the gym to live up to their *nom de guerre*.

"Left Turn Titty Twisters," Maggie recited hollowly. Not even she looked forward to encountering these specialists in mammary mutilation.

The Warriors cast worried looks on each other. None were prepared. Brassieres were not part of the Warriors' usual uniform.

The tram resumed its motion, headed towards Crenshaw.

With a malicious grin, the two foremost Titty Twisters skated up the carriage aisle, their muscular fingers snapping like metal vises, rushing to twist unsuspecting nipples like undocumented maids twist wet towels for hotel managers named Patel, ready to squeeze them equally dry.

Blocking the passage from the second carriage to the first, the Warriors herded them into the narrow corridor like the Spartans herded undocumented Persians at Thermopylae. Undeterred, the Twisters crammed through, sweating confidence.

Vexinator and Cobra met them head-on. In a flurry of fisticuffs, they managed to deflect the hammer-like blows of the Twisters' extreme musculature, protecting their vulnerable nuggets. Vex darted a squeeze at the lead Twister's own breast and contacted; with a vicious turn, she attempted to disable the Twister with a dose of her own medicine—and met metal.

The Twisters' own breasts were protected by metal bras!

Rattled, Vex fell back. Nite Shade and Suki Vicious took her place, both striking at the lead Twister simultaneously, aiming their snake-like nips at her exposed flanks and belly. Squeals of pain did not deter the Twister, however. On she came, a dozen vises made of flesh and bone reaching from behind her to grab the Warriors' titties like tentacles of a giant squid.

A tentacle contacted Nite Shade and twisted left. Nite gasped in pain. Unable to continue, she retreated. Bloody Mary leapt into the gap. Slapping the Twister with a deadly series of open-hand slaps, she sent her sliding to the sidelines, her bloody finger leaving red tattoos on her face like a Maori.

Two more Twisters took her place.

Suki looked back, her face grimacing. A Twister had Suki's breast full in its grip. Again the savage turn. Tearing free, Suki fell backwards over a tram seat and huddled in a corner, holding her breast and crying.

Mary tried slapping the Twister harder—but her injured finger spouted more blood and she was out of action.

It was Maiden Hell's and Queen Cobra's turn. Rushing into the center of the Squid-like gang, they landed cobra fists on their metal-sheathed mammaries like hammer blows, sending several staggering back into the passage, where their skates slipped on their own sweat, sprawling clumsily, and tripping up more Twisters.

No use—more vises closed on their nipples and twisted left, forcing them to yank free with howls of pain.

Outside, Farmdale Station came into view and the tram slowed.

No longer could the Warriors keep the Titty Twisters crammed into the passage between the two carriages; they were being forced steadily back, each covering an injured breast with one hand, while slapping the Twisters' faces with their free hand.

Maggie had held Pussy Kicker and Thrill Killa in reserve until she could discern an opening. Watching the Twisters, her eyes glinted.

With a quiet jerk, the tram came to a halt—the doors to the first carriage slid open to reveal a new phalanx of stern faces. Onto the first carriage behind the Warriors poured yet another roller derby gang—the Big Squeezers.

Before the Warriors could turn to face them, the Big Squeezers pulled metal tubes from fanny packs and extended them to their full length of three feet. At the end of each tube a piston-powered grip snapped and unsnapped. Instantly, the grips clamped home on several exposed Warrior buns.

Jumping as if stung, Thrill Killa and Pussy Kicker alighted on top of two seats and swiveled to face their new challengers. The Big Squeezers laughed savagely and snapped their metal grips like piranha jaws.

Their smiles faded.

Maggie had leaped entirely over them and now stood behind the Big Squeezers. Reaching the carriage doors, she pried them open with a strength that no one suspected rested in her coiled biceps. Pulling her metal telescoped club from her fanny pack, she snapped it to full length, and skating straight into the midst of the Big Squeezers, deflected each metal rod to close with the nearest Squeezer. Lifting her bodily, Maggie slid back to the open doors and tossed the Squeezer out.

The rest of the Squeezers paused. This was more than they had signed on for.

With a flash, Maggie returned, flipping tubes out of the Squeezers' hands like D'Artagnan wielding his rapier. Maggie grabbed the second in her own vise-like grip and tossed her overboard.

Next, brightly smiling Pussy landed a series of slam-bumps between the legs of the rest of the Squeezers while Thrill ripped their metal rods from their hands, and Maggie booted them out the door.

Now was the turn of the Left Turn Titty Twisters.

Barreling down the center of the aisle, Maggie dodged their frantic attempts to twist her own titties and responded with fingers aimed at face level.

"Owww!" The first staggered back, clutching an eye.

"Ooooh!" A second yelled.

A third followed.

Behind Maggie, brandishing metal rods taken from the ejected Big Squeezers, came Thrill Killa and Pussy. While the Twisters hung back nursing poked eyes, the clamps closed on their metal-bracketed opera-style brassieres—and pistoned them into a crumple. Howls of pain rose. The rest scrambled back into the second car as fast as they could backwards skate.

Another rush from the Warriors, with Maggie's fingers aimed at their eyes, and a dozen snapping turtles going for their breasts, the Twisters pried open the doors to the second carriage themselves and jumped of their own accord into darkness en masse.

The Warriors paused to count their losses.

Again they had survived, but Bloody Mary was permanently out of action with a twisted titty and again-bleeding finger. Vexinator was also done for—kicked in the shins, both nipples wrenched to hell, and two dutch rubs on her frizzled head. Maiden Hell also could not go on, with two twisted titties, a dutch rub, and an Indian burn that had crippled one forearm.

Maggie inspected them and harshly pronounced: "It's Uber for you. Next station."

Jefferson Station came into view, the tram swiftly decelerating.

The carriages stopped. For a moment the tram waited, the doors open to accommodate the next band of Tombstone skate-slingers willing to roll the dice in another attempt to halt the Warriors.

There—at the far end, a host of skaters were coming, the first having just reached the edge of the platform.

The doors began to close.

Outside, the darkness spewed a mass of skaters, faces screwed with hate, fists raised in anger, the platform growing black with their numbers.

"Nobody exits here," said Maggie. "They'll tear you to pieces."

The doors shut.

As the nearest roller derby gang banged on the doors and pressed their noses against the plexiglass—Maggie recognized them as Stay Calm While I Kill U's and Cherry Mashers—the tram bolted down the tracks, leaving them behind.

In relief, the Warriors slid back into graffiti-covered seats—the Warriors always had time to mark their turf—and grabbed a few minutes of shut-eye.

In moments, the clicks of the track lulled them into rem-sleep, enabling their youthful batteries to quickly recharge, and in half an hour, as pre-dawn finally began to make itself known, they arrived at Culver City Station.

Unexpectedly, no gang of roller derby girls awaited them here. Instead they witnessed a motley collection of protesters who marched to and fro over the platform brandishing signs. Barreling closer, they could read various slogans scrawled on their white placards: 'Diversity Unite', 'Ban White from Rainbows', and 'Mass Transit Unfair to Horses'.

As the tram came to a stop, Maggie pursed her lips distrustfully. Something about the slogans didn't make sense.

Her eyes lit on a sign in the back that read ‘Unitarians Against (insert here)’.

With a swish, the doors opened.

“Look out,” yelled Maggie. “It’s the Mothers of Insurrection!”

“Ah-ha,” yelled the protesters. Rolling on board, they immediately tangled with the Warriors, swinging their signs at them as if the Warriors were College Administrators who had unwisely invested in non-union coconut production.

“Don’t listen to them,” Maggie yelled. “They’re against everyone and everything. They’ll never be satisfied till all roller derby girls are wearing grass skirts and skating around mud huts.”

“Divest everything,” screamed one protester, thrusting her wooden two-by-four sign at Suki. “Switch pipelines to manure and ethanol,” yelled another, while a third clubbed Thrill in the ankle, crying “Frack this!” Thrill toppled over, taking the protester with her, but more Mothers jumped into the void, screaming and shaking their signs in Pussy’s face. “Non-gender bathrooms now!” “End patriarchal zombie deforestation!” “Un-mask the Diet-Koch Conspiracy!” “Mosquito Lives Matter!” “Drop Mr. and Ms. for Mx-y-zir!”

Suki yanked a sign and threw it to the far side of the cabin.

“Bomb patriarchy! Peace now! Arm the Amish! End military intervention!” The protester shouted in Suki's face.

More swung their signs at them. “Peace and Non-violence! Zero tolerance for deadbeat transgender dads! Death to albinos! Eat organic children!”

With her free hand, Mary grabbed and threw another.

The outraged protester screamed at her: "Ban science! Nature forever! Hands off our artificial reproduction!"

Nite Shade turned a confused look on Maggie. "Do these people ever make sense? Don't they ever stop contradicting themselves?"

She shook her head. "All you can do is ignore them and hope they'll return to meditating by empty ponds."

In short order, the Warriors managed to strip the remaining signs from the Mothers—none of whom, as it turned out had any children of their own, though a few had adopted infants from Tierra del Fuego, carefully passing over the many disabled Fuegian infants to settle only on those whom the latest scientific testing had confirmed were top-most in health and intelligence—naturally.

The remaining Mothers were blockaded in the second carriage where they stood with their hands in the air, chanting in unison: "Hands Up Don't Shoot! We're the .99 Percent!"

Having passed the Palms Station, the tram arrived at Rancho Park. The platform being empty due to partial construction, the Warriors easily tricked the Mothers by pretending to exit, and after the Mothers leaped out to further harass them, the Warriors leaped back in and blocked the doors to both cars.

As the tram jerked back into motion, the Warriors tossed the Greek salad signs out the windows, while the Mothers of Insurrection turned their attention to an 'Equal Rights for Fathers' office and promptly swarmed the sidewalk in front, shouting their opposition to this blatant outrage to fairness and equality.

Maggie passed her glance over their growing ranks of injured. Huddled together were Vexinator, Maiden Hell, and Bloody Mary. All Maggie had left now were: Herself; Thrill Killa, suffering from a bruised buttock; Pussy Kicker, who had suffered a squeezed buttock and an Indian burn; Queen Cobra, one twisted titty, but able to go on; Nite Shade, with one kicked shin; and Suki Vicious, also one titty twisted. It was a brutal accounting. But Maggie rejected any notion of giving in.

The Live Lips App sprang to life, casting its depressing pronouncement over the group: "Back with ya, rockin rollers. The data is pouring in and the meta is pouring out. The rabbit bounced off the Ladies of the Night—better known as the Large Enough 4 U Horrors—and also escaped the clutches of the Big Squeezers and the Mammary Maulers. We have to tip our hat to the intrepid Warriors, but when the morning comes the smart money is betting that our rabbits will have to pass the hat for cents and sympathy. For more roller derby girls are waiting and there likely ain't no gold at the end of the Warriors' rainbow—if the latest rumors are true. Their soldiers are falling like nine-pins, and ain't nobody gonna set em up again—if you get my meaning. We renew our call to skaters everywhere: all who cherish the memory of our dead leader Sirius and the Dream that was killed in Griffith Park last night, should bring these offenders to justice. The sooner, the better."

From nowhere. . .to nowhere. . . Maggie set her jaw. *I'll never be room-for-cream'd again.*

True enough—yet another squad of silken skaters hove into view at the next Station, Sepulveda. The Warriors retreated into a compact body behind the tram drivers. Maggie was taking no chance that these skaters might ambush them from behind like the last ones—or seize control of the train, as the Warriors themselves had done earlier in the evening, and anchor them in one place to be overwhelmed with sheer numbers.

The tram slowed. Jerked to a halt.

Sliding to either side, the doors opened onto—nothing.

The Warriors stared outside, the first rays of dawn stabbing their eyes, warping their sight.

As the doors returned shut and the tram resumed its ramshackle grind westwards, they looked at each other and exhaled in relief. The latest gang must have bolted in fear after one glimpse.

Then they froze.

In the second carriage a score of thin wiry girls with sneaky smiles and smooth silky clothing wended their way forward until they surrounded the Warriors on three sides, moving so swiftly and climbing the seats so deftly that they hardly heard them till too late.

"Big Sis," said one, a tragic expression on her face, "I know you have your share of problems, and I hate to bother you at a time like this, but," she sniffed back a tear, "do you think you can spot me a ten?" She tried to smile, but the cloud of sorrow soon returned. "My boyfriend wrecked my car and got me fired from my job."

Suki and Cobra exchanged surprised looks.

Beside her, a second skater wheeled forward. Reaching into a pocket, she poured a bag of sand on the floor and humbly groveled. "Please, please. My husband deserted me. He used my credit cards to buy land in Nevada and left me with six babies and two poodles. We don't have enough to eat. I had to leave my kids at the dog kennel."

Nite Shade felt a tear coming on.

More crowded in, their pale hands extended. "My Starbacks card is empty." "The neighbor stole my e-cigs and pet litter." "I can't pay my parking tickets, so they took away my driver's license." "I got sick but the emergency room turned me away—all I need is a lousy grand. Can you spare it till Tuesday?"

Mary felt herself inwardly crying.

"All I need is a quick hundred to buy a tire to visit my sick aunt—you know I'm good for it!" "They say my cancer is in remission, but if I don't get more chemo I'll die. My kids will go to an orphanage." "Grandma got hit by a truck and Momma burned my house down and wandered off with amnesia. Now I got no place to live."

Even Maggie felt tugs on her heart-strings. Mary began to cry out loud, while Vex blubbered into her hands.

"I'm low on milk." "I had to switch to store-brand beer." "My mother will lose her Medicare housekeeper if I don't slip her an extra hundred." "I need a fast five thousand to bail my brother-in-law out of jail, or my sister will commit suicide and it will be *all your fault!*" A line of distraught whining faces bawled before them. "Our skates are too worn—we can't qualify for the La Cienega League."

"I can't stand it," moaned Vex. "Here. Here, I'll give you my skates. Just stop crying. Please." Untying her skates, Vex handed them to the closest skater, tears streaming down both their faces. With a grateful mouthed 'thank you', the skater humbly accepted them and silently slid to the back.

"Stop. Stop," interjected Thrill Killa, sniffing back a tear.

"I can't take any more." Reaching into her pocket, she exposed the top part of her wallet.

"Wait a minute, crew," said Maggie. "Before you—"

Blindingly fast, the closest skater snatched Thrill Killa's wallet. Popping it open, the cash burst into the air like confetti—the skater grabbed it faster than a pimp deposits pesos.

"Ah-ha!" the skater yelled. Snapping out her own wallet, she thrust Thrill's money into her own over-stuffed billfold.

"What the—?" gasped Thrill.

"Sucker," boasted the skater. "Never knew what hitcha!" She laughed out loud. "What an easy touch."

Before the others could recover, the skaters snatched every fanny pack that the Warriors wore, including Maggie's, and bolted for the back carriage.

"You just got hit by Silky Sue's Krazy Kleptics," yelled their leader.

Maggie and Suki skated in pursuit, but the skating Kleptics managed to hold shut the door to the passage between the two cars until the tram screeched to a halt at Bundy Station. As the doors opened, the Kleptics rolled into the growing dawn, the Warriors not daring to pursue them into more Indian territory, smoke from hidden fires and wardrums sounding throughout the vicinity, summoning more bands of Sues to the war-path to resist the invaders.

The cars jerked into motion once more.

Maggie surveyed the damage: without skates, Vex was done. She could never keep up. And the Warriors had lost all their fanny packs, including their money, even if no Warrior could read the denominations—and Nite Shade's stun gun that she was holding in reserve, and Maggie's police baton. They were indeed as naked as their bra-less breasts and exposed hineys suggested.

Other than that, Bundy was empty, and as the cars accelerated towards the Bergamot and 17th Street stations, Maggie for a moment felt a slight lump of hope that perhaps the worst was behind them, that they might survive the evening after all.

The light of dawn spread its warming rays over the vast agglomeration of sticks and cement erected by the latest incarnation of Homo Erectus in her perpetual struggle to banish Nature from her life, patiently rebuilding them whenever the males of the species failed and resorted to smacking little white knick-knacks on freshly mowed greens to express their frustrations, all being forgiven by the females in exchange for regular ignitions of monster trucks.

And thus the world turns.

Maggie took stock once more. Bloody Mary and Vex lay flat on the vibrating floor, unable to contribute any more. That left: Maggie, Cobra, Pussy, Maiden, Nite Shade, Suki, and Thrill—the bald and tattooed Killa emotionally devastated by the equally bald deception of the young woman whom she had briefly seen as under her wing.

Bergamot Station loomed before them, the suns' growing light reflecting off the new shiny roof of the most expensive public works project since Tsar Nicholas massacred every tribe in the Caucasus, inducing sympathetic but misguided academics the world over to label every pale refugee as 'Caucasian', failing to note that every last 'Caucasian' was actually a Muslim, thus triggering an existential conflict with pale Druids two thousand miles distant who resented the implication of kinship with the *prostitutki*-condemning dwellers of that distant range of mountains.

Not that the Radiated Lesbian Nun gave a dam—or damn—one way or the other. As the tram slowed for the Bergamot Station, the latest roller derby club seeking fame through vengeance rolled to the platform, ready to give it their all to squash the assassins of their idol—while from the back of the speeding tram an infrared bullseye meandered across the cabin in search of a certain Squatch.

Episode 14

On the planet Bogland, meanwhile, things were jumping.

"Maybe we should double up and queue around the building," suggested Joseph Smith as he waddled his green froggy bulk forward. With suppressed alarm, he observed the influx of new josephs, which had overwhelmed the ribbet staff assigned to process them. "Should we double up and queue outside?"

"We should double up and queue outside. Should we recruit more ribbets to inject them?" replied Xplak, flopping forward on his own giant frog feet.

"We should recruit more ribbets to inject them. Is Great Gork in agreement with recruiting more ribbets to inject the new influx of josephs?"

A third toad, larger than the other two, turned his placid froggy face upon the chaotic scene, more josephs arriving by galactic transport by the minute while the earlier josephs pushed and jostled. Several josephs produced Mormon bibles and whacked obtruding elbows.

"Gork is in agreement with recruiting more ribbets to escort josephs to Dryland. Do Xplak and Joseph Smith think that recruiting all descendants of Joseph Smith also named Joseph will be sufficient to halt the Squatch from returning to what the Drylanders call Venice Beach?"

Joseph Smith and Xplak exchanged looks, their chameleon eyes swiveling deftly. "Yes."

Gork overlooked the rude lack of protocol indicated by their omitting to end a statement with a question. "Recruit away, then," he replied in kind.

The loudspeaker erupted again. "Attention all josephs! Josephs form two lines to the left. All josephs who are descendants of Joseph Smith proceed to line A. All josephs who are baseball players or belong to dioceses or Sicilian gangs proceed to line B. Planet Bogland and the Great Green Gork thank you for volunteering!"

More green frogs waddled into the reception warehouse and set up stretch barricades to guide the newcomers, while others appeared with syringes and distracted the newcomers' attention by rubbing their heads while injecting them, followed by a happy "Good boy."

The lines of Earthlings named Joseph entered a darkened aperture at one end while out of the other end a line of Evil Mimes stepped lightly out, arrogant grins on their white-plastered faces, floppy French berets perched snootily on their heads, horizontal black and white stripes on their pullover shirts like hosts of Apache dancers looking for lost nightclubs, double bulges in their crotches reflecting their newly minted twin pokes, all of which were the result of the Great Gork's experimental injections.

As fast as they exited, Xplak and his ribbet assistants crammed the mimes into the latest upgraded 'Cosmodrones' and launched them on autopilot to the closest wormhole, bound for distant Dryland, otherwise known as Earth, where the mimes arrived within only minutes of launch due to the ribbets' unmatched kung fu in physical science.

The Great Gork turned to Joseph Smith—the original Joseph Smith of Nauvoo, Illinois, who had once stared a second too long at a picture of Whistler's Mother in 1844, was injected, and thus became the first 'volunteer' to help Gork.

"I want total mobilization," Gork said. "Bogland has been thrown into chaos, but we cannot allow this simple Squatch to upset our plans for Planet Dryland."

"Yes, Great Gork. Let us hope we are not too late. Every roller derby league in Los Angeles is attempting to halt Maggie's progress, but so far none have succeeded. She must not break through."

"Bad results for all if she does. My plans for global warming on Planet Dryland must not be interfered with."

"Brrt. Tipsie dixit."

The ribbet Joseph Smith frog-waddled back to the communications room with the fake book spines—now happily free of airborne bottles of Johnnie Walker—and clicked back into conversation with the ribbets' chief representatives on Dryland: the Current and Interning Worshipful Masters of the Chartreuse Lodge of Latter-Day Masons of Upper Middle Utah and Fish Fry – Branch 63, Santa Monica. Joseph Smith picked up the mask with the white beard and hair and resumed the long-punctured illusion that he was still a *shuman*.

Edie and Gary turned toward the screen to receive the dispensation. “O Elder Smith of the 333rd Degree.”

“Welcome, my devotees, slaves of the Big Green G. Are you resisting the lamentations of lesbians and rejecting the claims of cross-dressing wannabes?”

“Yes, O Smith. But we remain concerned about the Squatch and her minions. Maggie has invigorated the evil tibbet cause in the City which the Drylanders call Los Angeles. Her name has spread over the entire Southwest. The Live Lips App, which we believed would finish her, has only made her more famous. Her fame is growing among roller derbies nation-wide, making nopalitos and red Thunderbird wine popular, boosting evil tibbet bases in L.A. and Las Vegas and elsewhere, and also making Back-To-Nature water-hating more popular—even making Unitarians look sane and rational.”

“Be calm, followers of the Great Green G. Keep faith. Reinforcements are on the way. Many more mimes are about to arrive to help you. Xplak is bringing them to the Cirque de Lumiére tents by the Santa Monica Pier. You are to prepare them for unleashing on all of Los Angeles this very day. Unfortunately, sending Melia in her Lockheed Electra to the tibbet base on Pluto did not work to stop those evil tibbets. They just foisted her off on Planet Dryland—making things even worse for us because the Drylanders made her a Saint, which enabled her to harass our agents even more.”

Edie and Gary exchanged cautious looks.

Joseph Smith continued. “You are to expel all retired mimes from the Mime Retirement Homes—recruit them at once to go stop Maggie and her Warriors. We are mobilizing all mimes into the largest silent army that Earth has ever seen."

With that, the plasma TV flicked off. Edie and Gary departed to implement the Big Green G's instructions—with many a worried thought. Whipping out his cell phone, Gary made a quick call, then hung up.

Exiting the back hall, Gary at first wheeled his wheelchair himself, but once in the lobby, despite his age, he exited the chair and proceeded to walk. At the lectern by the door he rang the alarm bell to attract the attention of the crowd of mimes in their dotage still smirking in wheelchairs in the lobby.

"*Attencion! Attencion!*" he yelled in the microphone with a thick French accent, acquired from the Latter-Day Masonic Lodge's long association with the *Cirque de Soliel* that had appeared years earlier in the frenchified city of Quebec. "Ze Big Green G has decreed Total Mobilizacion. All mimes currently resident in zis Retirement Home are to proceed to ze Front to combat ze Enemy. We must stop *Les Boche*. Pour l'Emperor! Pour la gloire! Pour les pantomimes glorieuse!" He flapped a green flag with a big G embroidered and saluted it while the mimes in wheelchairs stared open-mouthed.

The front doors popped open and Clarence and Rodney rushed inside, pushing a herd of three-wheeled scooters. They immediately began dumping mimes from their wheelchairs and assisting them up on canes and onto the scooters amid a veritable storm of angry silent protests and clenched fists. "Now don' you fagit to git da do', Rodney. Don' yo be mashin' da massas into dat do' like yestidy."

"Yowza," answered Rodney, promptly slamming one mime after another into doors and walls, even sliding one mime under the waiting city wheelchair bus before extracting and placing his semi-conscious body onto a new scooter.

After an interminable hour of chaos and confusion, the first batch of retired mimes had been packed into the huge van along with their new scooters, and the City Special Van for Wheelchairs and the Disabled creaked off to head for Ocean Avenue, though many were disappointed when they discovered that the avenue's appealing name suggestive of water had been changed to Nielson Way, which suggested only an over-the-hill actor. A last minute turn, however, brought them back to a street named Ocean Way—only to be disappointed yet again by being deposited onto the even less interestingly named Appian Way. Here squads of mimes marched out of the Cirque de Lumiére tents dressed as police and thrust fizzy sodas into the retired mimes' hands and left them clogging the street with canes and scooters.

Unable to resist any opportunity to harass the innocent, the fake mime police, meanwhile, made ugly faces with their fingers, scaring children in back seats of passing cars, while using their batons to direct angry drivers deliberately into traffic jams, then laughing in uproarious silence, mimicking the drivers' frustration behind the wheel.

Behind them, on Colorado and Ocean, chains of self-driving Uber cars and Cosmodrones from Bogland arrived, dumping their newly knighted galactic Evil Mime cargos into the chaos, where gangs of them chased and mocked pedestrians with growing viciousness, while Gary and

Edie tried with increasing futility to establish control.

Episode 15

Rapidly the tram decelerated, jerking to a halt before a platform with a large lit sign that read 'Bergamot Station'. Even before it ceased rolling, Maggie knew the Warriors faced an entirely new kind of trouble, something that even she had no stratagem to defeat.

The back-carriage doors slid open and the newcomers rolled in, the Warriors having sufficient numbers remaining to block only the one door to the front carriage. As the tram resumed its nightmare ride toward an ever-more brightly lit horizon, the latest freaks spawned by the night's freak-storm burst onto the scene.

Maggie and Cobra confronted them in the narrow space between the two cabins. An expressionless face hummed up at them, plastic lips and fake eyes moving in programmed sequences, metallic limbs flexing in ways that distant authors of nameless algorithms calculated would attract paying customers. "Please do not be concerned," said a flat mechanical voice. "I am your personal ISeeMoHo pleasure companion. Please deposit coins or bills to experience immediate gratification."

"I don't think so-ho," said Maggie.

The ISeeMoHos rolled forward on roller skates and briefly halted as they tightened into a single mass, their programming not sophisticated enough to enable them to penetrate the corridor that joined the two carriages together.

"We didn't send for an ISeeMoHo," said Cobra.

"Not to worry," hummed the robot, "We ISeeMoHos have been programmed by our friendly global corporation to actively solicit pleasure partners. We now respond without invitation. This is—as you would say—a courtesy call."

The tracks clicked beneath them and Maggie glanced back at her Warriors, and especially at Vex who had lost her skates, and at Bloody Mary, who had more than lived up to her name. Only Pussy and Thrill were in any shape to give battle; Maiden, Nite Shade, and Suki still nursed their twisted titties, dutch rubs, Indian burns, and pinched buttocks. None were capable of resisting lithium-powered streetwalkers.

"There is no need for an ISeeMoHo here. We cannot pay you."

"Not to worry, customer-san," came the happy reply. "ISeeMoHo accepts credit."

"We have no credit cards. That is, none that belong to us."

"Not to worry. ISeeMoHo will happily check your credit for free and proceed to provide instant gratification in style Americans prefer."

"We have no credit score either."

"Not to worry. ISeeMoHo will happily extend new credit to you as additional service from our global pleasure-providing corporation. All ISeeMoHo needs is a sample of your DNA to verify ID, and ISeeMoHo will instantly extend credit and begin providing immediate relaxation."

The robots managed to untangle themselves.

"No! We don't want robo-sex. We refuse to pay."

The ISeeMoHos continued to approach, skating like slinky if clumsy women, pausing every few moments to assume exaggeratedly feminine poses. "Do not be alarmed. ISeeMoHo is here to fulfill your every desire. We have been built to stimulate and satisfy all human needs. If you do not care for me as your personal pleasure companion, maybe you will like a different model."

The first robot, which was feminine but nondescript, skated slowly backward while another ISeeMoHo skated in front, allowing Maggie and Cobra to briefly reclaim the aisle between the two carriages.

The next robot had the hips of a Baltic peasant woman and wore a scarf over its head and a red plaid lumberjack shirt. "How's it hangin' honey?" it barked. "Hand me a beer and turn on the game. After I chop and stack the wood, I'll be ready for ya—If ya get my meanin'." The robot winked one artificial eye, shouting uncanny valley.

"No!"

It skated backward and was replaced by a doppelganger for Pussy's Donna Reed image: "Maybe it's the college girl look you prefer?" hummed the robot, sporting a clutch of books and papers and a short skirt that repeatedly lifted to reveal humanoid anatomy.

"Not today."

"Sleazy half-drunk blonde?" A robot with fake blond hair and a perpetual pout skated forward, wearing only a bikini over rock-like breasts.

"No!"

"Japanese schoolgirl?"

"No way!"

"Nappy-headed ho'?"

The Warriors briefly scanned the cars for an announcer in a cowboy hat. "No!"

The first ISeeMoHo spoke louder, pointing to other robots. "We have male model ISeeMoHos as well as female, and everything in between. We are guaranteed to satisfy."

"Don't care! Get lost!"

The robots changed their tone. "You are instructed to cooperate. We have received information that a third party has extended credit for you. Please to submit to energetic rub downs. Do not leave. Do not seek to depart. We are fully licensed and trained." They skated slowly forward, their uncanny eyes flicking and swiveling. "We are here to help. Please to deposit coins or click your App for instant payment."

The ISeeMoHos paused in unison as if simultaneously listening to some message that only they could hear. The train tracks clicked further…suddenly they all began to move again. "You have been reclassified as *johns*, current customers of ISeeMoHo corporation. Please to note that we are programmed for zero tolerance for deadbeat johns. If you do not allow us to render our services and pay us, it will be necessary to give you a rub down and run you into a ditch."

Maggie and Cobra exchanged looks again. "Maybe if we reason with them?" said Maggie. Cobra nodded knowingly.

"Thank you, Honorable john-sans." The ISeeMoHos rolled forward, this time filing into the corridor singly to avoid getting jammed. "Please to allow us ISeeMoHos to approach and administer our carefully programmed caresses that are unconditionally guaranteed by our friendly global ISeeMoHo Corporation to completely satisfy all reasonable Honorable johns, or your money back." The first robot skated slowly toward Maggie, now about to enter into the first Expo Line carriage as the Warrior chief backed up, also sliding carefully and slowly on her skates.

Passing a subtle gaze at Cobra and another at Pussy and Thrill, who casually took up positions on either side of the entrance, Maggie looked back at the first ISeeMoHo.

"Come right in. No problem."

The first robot propelled forward only to encounter Thrill's leg thrust in front—the ISeeMoHo fell flat on its artificial face. The robots halted while the first slowly struggled back to its permanently wheeled feet, and after a full minute of the tram's ramshackling westward toward the 17th Station, it finally managed to right itself.

Its chin had suffered a dent and one damaged eye was permanently focused on some ethereal object to one side and above the Warriors. "Thank you, Honorable john-san. That was a pleasurable event for your personal ISeeMoHo. Are you ready to experience further unique pleasures with your personal pleasure companion?" The robot posed archly, its eye stuck in Brights position.

They came on again. Pussy thrust her own leg out to trip it again, but the first robot paused and skated around it.

Cobra and Maggie exchanged looks. "They learn quick, don't they."

"Do not flee. Do not be concerned. Please remove all clothing."

Maggie thought again. Her eyes alighted on the leather handholds hanging from the tram's interior for passengers to cling to and prevent falling. "Ok, ISeeMoHo. You persuaded us. We will engage. But here is what we desire: we desire that you first tie your hands above your head using these passenger straps."

The ISeeMoHo halted. "John-san has used the word 'tie' in conjunction with a body part. One moment, please, John-san. We must consult sub-programming unit called Perv—one moment please. . .one moment please. . .running sub-routine Perv. . . Yes, ISeeMoHos have 'tie hands' in our sub-routine Perv *-beep-* now translating Perv to Perl *-beep-* John-san is in luck. Enhanced credit for sub-routine Perv has been approved by third party."

With that, the first two ISeeMoHos stretched their limbs above their robot heads and entangled them in the Expo Line straps, and two other ISeeMoHos provided additional rope for knotting, while Maggie and the rest of the Warriors gazed expectantly out the windows for 17th Street Station.

"Feet too, please," added Maggie. "This John-san desires that ISeeMoHo tie its feet also. John-san will not engage with her personal pleasure companion until two ISeeMoHos have their feet tied to the metal bars of the tram seats."

"One moment please. . .consulting sub-programming Perv routine for 'tie' in conjunction with feet. . . Yes, ISeeMoHos have 'tie feet' in sub-routine Perv. Honorable John-san is in luck. -beep- Third party has approved extended credit for this personal activity as well."

The other robots assisted with more rope and soon both of the lead ISeeMoHos had their hands tied to the overhead straps and their wheeled feet securely tied to the seats' metal bars set in the floor of the carriage.

"Now to remove your clothing, please John-san," recited

the lead robot in its flat voice. "It is required by ISeeMoHo corporate insurance provider that all John-sans who engage in recreational activity with ISeeMoHo personal pleasure companions from our global pleasure-providing ISeeMoHo corporation must remove all clothing and establish physical contact with the appropriate ISeeMoHo unit."

Maggie made as if to remove her pink corset, toying with one lace. "Almost there, ISeeMoHo. Be patient. This John-san is engaging. Not to worry." She looked out the window again.

"Not to worry," repeated the robot.

"Not to worry at all."

"Not to worry. . ."

"Almost there, IseeMoHo. . .hold that position. . ."

"Please accelerate physical contact, Honorable john-san with extended credit. This position is not good for ISeeMoHo's titanium and silicon flesh-imitating limbs. Sensors in limbs are sending messages to ISeeMoHo's central processing unit registering decrease of oil in joints."

The tram hit a bump.

"Oww," intoned the entangled robot. "Bumps in the tram are sending unpleasant signals to this pleasure companion's central processing unit."

The other robot added, "Me too, Honorable john-san. Please hurry to release. Oil getting low. Central processing unit now receiving imminent potential damage signals. Would John-san like more extended credit?"

"Yeah. That would be nice. Now stop complaining."

Another bump hit.

"Oww-oww," spieled both robots together, the other robots that were queued behind them remaining silent and motionless but beginning to exchange concerned robot looks. "Honorable john-san, perhaps this ISeeMoHo has offended kind john-san with inappropriate remark. This ISeeMoHo humbly apologizes. Please to release ISeeMoHo now."

"Don't feel like it."

"Oww. This ISeeMoHo needs relief from tied up position. Not good for IseeMoHo."

Silence followed.

"When will john-san feel like releasing ISeeMoHo?"

"When I'm good and ready. Now shut up or you'll get you-know-what."

The two tied-up robots exchanged worried robot looks. Those queued behind began to skate in agitation.

The tram hit a bigger bump.

"Red," said the first robot.

Maggie looked at it.

"Please to listen to humble ISeeMoHo. This ISeeMoHo says 'red'."

"What was that? Did you hear something?" asked Maggie.

"Not a thing," replied Cobra.

"Red," said the robot with more volume.

"Me too. This robot also says 'Red'."

"Nope, I didn't hear a thing. Just a whiny little robot that isn't worth my time."

Another bump made the carriage jump.

"RED!"

"RED for this unit too!"

"Oh, you're no fun."

Outside, the 17th Street Station came into view and moments later the tram decelerated with a series of sharp severe jerks.

"Oww again. Please to release this ISeeMoHo," blared the first robot.

"Oww for this robot also. Does Honorable john-san feel like releasing this ISeeMoHo unit now? This unit begs Honorable john-san for release," pleaded the second. "This ISeeMoHo will reimburse Honorable john-san."

The doors to the first tram slid open just after 17th Street, and the Warriors hesitated. No roller derby gang occupied the long platform which stretched a considerable distance past 16th Street, but Maggie thought she spied movement up the 16th side street.

A flat tone emanated from the tied-up ISeeMoHos. "Time limit for physical contact exceeded. John-san's personal pleasure unit is activating new sub-routine." With a pop, the ropes snapped and the two lead robots rolled free. They returned their attention to the Warriors and all the robots skated into the first carriage.

"Please to cooperate, Honorable john-sans. Do not be concerned. You must remove all clothing so ISeeMoHos can make physical contact. We are designed to engage with human women as our optional appendages indicate." The robots skated forward, a mix of masculine and feminine body types interspersed with several indeterminate types for occasions such as this, erect humanoid male organs indicating infinite extended credit.

That decided matters.

Knocking on the door of the drivers, Maggie yelled

"Bomb on the track!" With hardly a glance, the Warriors barreled out of the tram and departed the Expo Line, hurtling down Colorado Avenue to outrun the movement from up 16th which increasingly took on the images of yet another derby gang, a score of horny ISeeMoHos exiting the tram in pursuit.

Standing in their midst waving aloha to the Warriors was Vexinator, hand-in-hand with the Japanese schoolgirl pleasure bot, and Bloody Mary, engaging with a hot-bot dressed as a male nurse. Smiling at the Warriors, they shrugged and gave thumbs up. So long as someone else was paying the bill to ISeeMoHo Corp. . .

Behind the tram, another tram appeared, then another, lining up as the first tram automatically froze in place due to mention of the word 'bomb'. One last look from the Warriors as they picked up speed toward Santa Monica revealed a motley herd of angry derby gangs spilling from the queueing trams: puffing red Santas with heavy sacks; spritely tweens with sarcastic come-backs; muscle-women with crew-cuts on newly 'borrowed' mountain bikes; Psycho Teens screaming at whining Krazy Kleptics; frustrated Helles Belles and Bloody Jammers, some taken prisoner by the TakeNoPrisnas, who also spilled out; Fat Whores exchanging fisticuffs with Left Turn Titty Twisters and Big Squeezers, who could not resist getting in some easy practice at the Fat Whores' expense; Ugly Puglies still angry at being tricked into losing their transport; Ballbusters fresh from Griffith Park, mourning the loss of their beloved leader 'old what's her name' and eager to take revenge on anything small and spherical; with several tardy Gocart Furies still upset at missing the action, though now eyeing the ISeeMoHos with interest; not to mention a slew of other roller derby gangs who had arrived too late to join the previous night's pursuit.

Unseen by all, two figures climbed down from the roof of the back carriage, where they had clung since Metro Center, carrying a lengthy tube wrapped in cloth. Adjusting their squirrel hunting caps, the two hurried after the hooting howling mob.

Episode 16

Maggie, Queen Cobra, Pussy Kicker, Thrill Killa, Maiden Hell, Nite Shade, and Suki Vicious rocketed down the platform, picking up speed as they bypassed 16th Street. Barreling south to intercept them along its tree-lined double lane was what first appeared to be a gang of cholos on wheels and boards. As they neared, threatening to collide head-on with the Warriors, rouge lipstick and outsized eyelashes emerged, but clashed confusingly with wide shoulders and massive calves, further mismatched with stretch pullover gowns and gay summer dresses.

Harsh frowns took hold of the cross-dressing Roller Vamps as they sought to cut the Warriors off at 15th Court—an anvil for the hammer of the mass of derby gangs pursuing them angrily on the platform. Bikes, boards, and skates propelled the prissy cross-dressers, ever eager for an opportunity to loose their frustrations on the unsuspecting.

"Come on, Scarlett," shouted the lead-most, flicking her mass of sleek black hair behind a bleached mustache. "I'm sure there's a child labor exploiter somewhere in that group."

"And water-lovers—and environmental polluters. Scratch their eyes out, Loretta," Scarlett shouted back.

Both bared well-polished and dyed nails as they neared their intended victims, the platform narrowing and descending to street level directly on their left as they rolled seaward down Colorado Avenue. Another score of hair-teased wannabes closed in behind, with even more on bikes, certain appendages that were earlier carefully taped escaping their confines to confound and appall passersby who swiftly covered their children's eyes.

And northbound on 15th appeared yet another team, the ever-hopeful Anthrax Pack hoping to finally even their derby score with the Warriors.

The platform's ramp descended and vanished, merging with the street. Vamps and Warriors found themselves cheek by jowl, not to mention their faces, which were suddenly also in close proximity. At a subtle well-practiced signal from Maggie, Maiden Hell took strategic position as Jammer up front while Maggie assumed Pivot, ignoring the rules that called for placing the Pivot start line first.

Taking the lead, Maiden Hell maneuvered next to the Vamps' Jammer. Suki Vicious and Pussy Kicker and Queen Cobra formed a wedge, both teams rocketing southwest down Colorado Avenue, traffic—long alerted by hacker spaces around L.A. to the Roller Derby Ultimathon that had convulsed the City since the prior evening—moving spontaneously aside, and increasingly waved at by growing crowds of spectators lining Colorado, their ears glued to the Live Lips App.

"Listen up derbyers," blared the Lips. "Shirts off to the Warriors on this beautiful weather-perfect morning in the City of Angels. To L.A.'s surprise, the intrepid Warriors, led by growing sensation Maggie P. Squatch, have survived the best that every Roller Derby league could throw at them, the latest to fall beneath their bruiser biceps being the Krazy Kleptics and a battalion of non-kosher IseeMo-Hos, donated by certain third parties eager to squash the Squatch's legend before it grows. The latest to challenge them are the Roller Vamps, talking derby to the Warriors on Colorado Avenue as we speak. Calling Volunteers! Again we say: ain't nobody gonna set up the Warriors' nine-pins once they fall. Calling all derbyers! Calling all roller girls! Ride, rock, or roll to Colorado and Ocean and stop these Rebels before they touch home base and claim Sanctuary. They must cross Tongva Park to get there."

Maiden Hell clashed repeatedly with the Vamps' Jammer, hips blocking, shoulders crunching. More Vamps moved in from the right, while Anthrax teamsters rolled in from the left.

From nowhere. . .to nowhere. . . No sinful water man can touch these little piggy toes. I'll never be room-for-cream'd again. Maggie glanced at Maiden Hell and nodded. Thrusting an elbow into the Vamp Jammer's neck, Maiden sent her sliding under two other Vamps, half of their team rolling into the pile-up like a foggy Vermont freeway at dawn, a vicious slice from Suki in the other direction tumbling a trio of Anthrax members into a separate tangle. Pussy Kicker landed a quick series of merry kicks between the legs of more Vamps, sending the wannabes howling to pitstops to re-tape their non-essentials.

The foremost ISeeMoHos stumbled over the Anthrax pack, laying them flat and out of action, the face-down robot pratfalls freezing their mechanical eyes at quirked angles, so that when they were again upright, they vigorously engaged their optional appendages with the first Santa Claws that skated into view, who swung their brick-filled bags in futile attempts to defend the honor of Christmas. "Do not be alarmed," buzzed robot voices, "you have been selected to experience complimentary pleasure services. . .your feedback is highly valued."

Still on the 16th Street platform, a pair of a different kind of wannabes stood still, one staring through a scope while the other shielded him from prying eyes with camo-linen.

"Ya got her, Ray?" The one holding the camo looked around nervously as more and more trams jerked to a stop to disgorge gangs of vengeful roller derby girls. "Things are gettin' mighty hot around here, if ya know what I mean."

"Etsy can hit a gnat's ass at half a mile. Just hold her steady, Bobby. I want that fifty grand."

Ray stared calmly through the scope as the cross-hairs tracked Maggie's shrinking form down Colorado Avenue, pink corset and blue leather flaps revealing tight buns with every stroke of her sure massive thighs, bottom curled jet-black hair bobbing in perfect time. Slowly, Ray began to pull Etsy's trigger.

Hic.

When he recovered his breath, Ray peered close-up at a shaved face wrapped in a bedsheet, struggling atop a Segway.

"Hot diggedy damn."

"Huh?"

"She's back!" Ray put Etsy down. "She's back, I tell ya. Bedsheet and all."

"Ya don't mean—"

"The hell I do. That Squatch is only one block away—and we've got just enough time to grab her."

"Aliyah?" blurted Bobby. Stars lit his eyes. "Yeah, let's go save. . . I mean, let's go get her."

Two blocks down, the Warriors jostled for position—14th Street rocketed into view—and passed. Spectators waved flags and hooted, chanting "War-ri-ors! War-ri-ors!" From somewhere a self-appointed referee pointed at Maggie from the sidewalk and signaled her to a non-existent penalty box. Maggie laughed and picked up momentum, her skates spraying dust and gravel in his face.

Maggie pulled into the lead, slamming the remaining Anthrax team members into the Vamps, leaving teeth and tears in her wake. The two remaining Vamps, bearing logos that read 'Muslim Local 36', were too distracted hitting each other with halal purses to react when Maggie deftly guided their Segways into a hot dog vendor, bringing their brief pursuit to a red and yellow-drenched—but tasty—end.

Neither did they notice when two yahoos sneaked up behind their erstwhile Sister, whose Segway had stalled and was stuck at 15th Street. Rushing toward her, they slowed to a walk, then tip-toed up her blind side. Just as they prepared to pull her bedsheet over her head—the Segway jumped. Enlivened, it whirred and sped Aliyah away.

A quick disappointed look, and the two yahoos in camo ran in pursuit, joining the ever-growing crowd of roller derby gangs howling and mooing as they poured out of trams and rolled down Colorado Avenue, cell phones channeling Live Lips updates into their ears, minions determined to achieve final victory over the Squatch and her acolytes.

13th Street sped past.

Four more Anthrax rollers and the last two Vamps bumped Cobra and Maiden. Maggie maneuvered in front of the Anthraxes and purposely lagged. With a quick pretend stumble, she arched a skated foot—the lead Anthrax's skate collided with it and tumbled—two more piled on top. "Don't mess with the Squatch," Maggie smirked.

12th Street approached.

Sharp fingernails reached for Pussy's eyes—scraped one shoulder, leaving a trail of blood.

"No. You didn't—" Sliding behind the Vamp, Pussy slipped one hand under the Vamp's dress. Grabbing 'her' tightly taped underwear from behind, she braked. The atomic wedgie sent the Vamp exploding into the sidelines, flattening more wannabe referees, 'her' shaved bony legs and dress up-ended. Their place was taken by several crew-cutted muscle women on their 'borrowed' mountain bikes, mouthing 'I love you', but kicking at the Warriors' shins just the same. Teens wheeled behind, yelling "It's just a lousy hundred. You know I'm good for it." and "Why won't you do my homework for me, like my friend Abby Normal's mother? I hate you."

11th Street loomed, passed by, and shrank.

Maggie squatted as she rolled and she snatched up a metal shiv. Slipping it into a mountain bike's spokes, it came to a sudden stop, flipping the Sergeant Carter over, becoming a stumbling magnet for other bikes and boards.

10th Street came into view on the right. Speeding to intercept were Comet Rippers on boards rigged with sugar fuel rockets, towing hard-faced Angels Without Mercy, their feathered wings fluttering like flags.

The Warriors were too quick. 10th Street came and went and the Angels and Comets merged with the mass of derby-bators flowing down Colorado behind them, the name for once designating a full-flowing river.

At 9th, the Grungematics and Revoltin' Meemies sped from either side—again the Warriors were too fast to be overtaken and passed the intersection before the stench of the former or the revolting appearance of the latter could stop them.

8th Street passed in a blur.

Several Fat Enough 4 U Whores caught up, surprising in view of their girth. Left Turn Titty Twisters were not far behind; and at least two Big Squeezers were catching up, their piston vises snapping on air, and Ballbusters overtaking on either side, pausing only to wallop the remaining Vamps, who decided to finally trade in their tape for crotch-protecting plastic cups.

At 7th, the first Ballbusters caught up with Thrill and Suki. A quick tussle of elbows followed as the Sirius worshipers attempted to guide their nemeses into the gutter. But they failed to account for the unaccountable. Cobra lagged. With a sudden twitch, the metal in her elbows broke two noses, the blood slipping up both Ballbusters, and sending two Fat Whores sliding into a pair of spectator Pastors, who mentally tagged them as the subject of especially exciting Dear Diary entries.

6th Street slipped past.

Up ahead—the end was near.

Maggie laid plans for her next move; the series of moves that she hoped would bring her team home safely to the Holy Rollers' Pollo Ranchero Casino & Bowlarama where the naughty nuns of Opus Dea could stop any attempt by their enemies to molest them.

Sloppy Raggers and Bare Ass Brawlers skated out to challenge them at the next intersection—but once again miscalculated due to the speed of the rivalry—and as 5th Street slid past, merged with the ever-growing crowd in pursuit.

4th Street arrived—giving rise to Manic Mommas and Killa Kommandos, who lost no time in joining the hunt.

At 3rd Street, Maggie made her move—at a subtle signal the Warriors swerved left and sped across the Main Street bridge, arching over the Pacific Coast Highway, the suddenness of their turn sending most of the pursuing horde rocketing past as their momentum took them down Colorado Avenue, only slowing when they realized that the rabbits had flown. By the time the horde stopped to complain of mixed metaphors and began crowding onto Main Street in pursuit, the Warriors were safely inside Tongva Park.

With a jerk, they halted.

Before them was a sight they had never hoped to see. From all directions, covering every open space—and crowding onto Main Street from the direction of Venice, the Burg's skid rows and back alleys were vomiting their worst: Zombiematics, a so-called roller derby club that was in reality no more than failed contenders and stumble-bums who never managed to master the finer techniques of rolling for glory on the rink.

As a result they rolled only slowly, their frustrations given to expression in ever-gnashing jaws that sought toothy revenge on their more successful counterparts who had rejected their applications to join established teams. The disappointment at not being allowed onto any rink by any league, together with multiple injuries from their lack of skating ability, was stamped on their faces, blood and bruises permanently accentuating open jaws.

"Uuuuh," drifted their zombie-like groans.

As their drugged-out eyes slowly sighted the Warriors, their twerk-impaired brains gradually focused. The herd of scavengers converged, dozens more appearing every moment from Ocean Avenue.

Maggie spun on her wheels to look back again over the bridge towards Colorado Avenue. It was too late to retreat. Angry violated Santas, Fat Whores in ripped spandex, ISeeMoHos performing unsolicited optional appendage 'courtesy calls' on indignant roller casualties, Titty Twisters clutching at Helles Belles' bras, Gocart Furies swinging golf clubs at impudent Tweenies and dueling with Big Squeezer pistons, filled the intersection, the rest of L.A.'s derby clubs crowding over the bridge in pursuit.

There was nothing for the Warriors to do but to skate through the growing mob of Zombiematics.

In normal times this would be simple. The Zombies could barely skate. The simplest maneuver sent them stumbling to re-injure themselves. But today was different—they came in their dozens—in their hundreds, as Venice and Santa Monica emptied their skid rows of every female denizen, and any male who felt vaguely feminine, or had feminine sympathies, or fancied himself supportive of such, or had a female relative willing to drop an occasional Lincoln so he could drink or smoke himself to sleep once more—which meant every person in northwest L.A. basin who could sober up long enough to tie a knot on a pilfered pair of skates. The horizon clouded with their numbers as they inched into the fray, moaning for lunch.

With a shock, Maggie noticed her crew was one short. They swiveled. Back across the bridge, Thrill Killa had failed to notice Maggie's subtle message for the Warriors to turn. Now she was cut off, skating backward and pinned against a far wall by angry Santas and Fat Whores who had put aside their own dispute long enough to finish her off. With a look of grim determination mixed with the joy of combat amid a flurry of elbows, Thrill Killa went down—but not without taking a host of enemies with her. Maggie's last glimpse was of Thrill reluctantly accepting a helpful hand from the Pastor hurrying to assist, eager for more than mental notes.

There was nothing Maggie could do. Nothing anyone could do. She bit her tongue—and rolled.

The rollerbators pouring across Main Street sighted the rabbits again. Rollerz flooded into Tongva Park from one side as the Zombies stumbled in from the other—again the hammer and anvil.

From the Park's south side—unexpected sounds, as if in reply.

Hare Krishna
Hare Krishna

Krishna Krishna
Hare hare

The trees lining the Park's south border sprouted a congeries of yellow and orange-clad Hare Krishnas, heads shaved but for tiny ponytails, carrying a platform of a half-human half-elephant godling with huge trunk, flowers and beads around its neck, the god's devotees thumping drums and clinging timbrels as they danced, their parade flooding the Park with another hundred participants.

They glimpsed the Warriors. From behind the Hare Krishnas came a lone voice that echoed across the Park: '*War-ri-ors. Come out to play-yay*," accompanied by a bright clinking of Hindu hand cymbals.

The parade lurched to a halt.

Several devotees stepped aside. Behind them stood a single Hare Krishna devotee in white shirt and yellow robe banging hand timbrels together. He looked at the others—they frowned.

"*Whaat?* Just thought it might be time for a change. I mean the first one thousand 'hare krishnas' weren't too bad—but reciting 100,000 'hare krishnas' is too much for *anyone*."

Another spoke up. "God Almighty. Someone *finally* said it!" The devotee let out a sigh of relief. "If I have to bleat fucking 'hare krishna' one more time I'm gonna go berserk and start killing people! Your new mantra is not bad, Fred. I like the meter. Nice rhyme too. Besides, everyone knows the Warriors are the best derby club around. And they have nice buns."

Together the two tried it out, clinking their little timbrels:

War-ri-ors. Come out to play-yay.
War-ri-ors. Come out to play-yay.

Instantly the rest of the elephant parade took up the phrase, tossing more flower necklaces over their elephant god, thrilled to have something else to chant besides *hare* god damn *krishna*. Passing out colorful invitations to Warriors and Zombies, they beamed smiles and blurted hearty "We love you, brothers. Be happy, sisters. Come out to play-yay." But failed to notice the increasing numbers of Zombies.

"Oww," squealed a Hare Krishna.

A Hare Krishna looked up—his flesh hung from a Zombie's mouth. "Uuuuh," thanked the Zombie, and skated away without leaving any money.

Sarcastically, the Hare Krishna replied, "Oh thank you, Brother. That's really great. Your 'donation' is greatly appreciated." He looked down at the bite on his arm. "Hey. That hurt!"

A second Zombie went in for a taste.

"Hare Krishna—hare krishna—hare-owww!" The Hare Krishna swatted the Zombie away. "That's not cool, dude."

"Uuuoooh. Hungry."

More Zombies went in for the kill, surrounding several Hare Krishnas and biting their necks and arms till they yelled 'Hare Uncle'.

"Ya fuckin' ingrates. Keep your goddam donations. We'll just pick up our stuff after you've ground them into the dirt—*as usual*. Not that you're *being rude* or anything." The Hare Krishna glared at the horde coming closer and muttered to himself. "God-damn prima donnas. Like our message isn't good enough for a bunch of alky derelicts who had to borrow their skates cause they can't even afford a lousy taxi."

The speaker's friend nodded agreement and looked down his nose—the nearest Zombie bit it off. "Fuck, dude. I needed that." Like a capsizing ship, the platform with the elephant god commenced to roll.

It slid and broke.

In the middle of 'play-yay', the elephant crashed and broke.

The Hare Krishnas rolled up their sleeves. "Okay. That's it." The devotees of peace and conscientious objection launched themselves in a rage at the Zombiemanics and proceeded to pound them royally just as the meat-o-matics were trying to taste the Warriors wending their way through the Park.

The resulting tangle of biting Zombies and clawing 'devotees of non-violence' so thoroughly blocked any exit down Main or Ocean Avenue that Maggie and her crew found themselves forced away from Venice and up Ocean Avenue all the way back to Colorado, which virtually all of the pursuing rollerbators luckily had by now vacated in order to cross the bridge over the Pacific Coast Highway and flood Tongva Park, with angry Santas, Fat Whores, and cross-dressers on Segways, all competing with vengeful Krishnas in their efforts to beat off the horde of starving meat-a-tarians.

"Maggie!" called a voice. They looked back. Nite Shade was surrounded by a group of enraged yellow robed Krishnas, their little pigtails swinging in anger. Even as the

Warriors watched, her face took on a hopeless expression as the non-violent angry swarm engulfed her, forcing worthless trash into her hands while leveling harsh looks in fierce expectation of recompense. "I'm done for. You'll have to leave me. I have to take off my skates and pull out my hidden money and give them a donation."

The Squatch set her jaw and turned her head. She gulped. With a harsh look, she signaled the Warriors to resume. Rolling the mean streets of the City of Angels had a steep price. Maybe one day she too would have to pay it—and maybe not far in the future. Retreating back to Colorado Avenue, her crew paused upon hearing a new noise across the crowded Park, from the direction of Venice.

"allAH—allah, allah, allah, allah. . .allAH—allah, allah, allah, allah. . .allAH—"

A green and gold marquee twenty feet wide carried by several green-capped white-robed men burst into Tongva Park from Main Street, English lettering announcing 'Annual Birth of the Prophet Parade', a crowd of men in white robes filling the boulevard behind. Taking one shocked look at the struggling mass of Zombies and *prostitutki*, their jaws dropped.

"Allahu Akbar!" thundered a hundred throats. A moment's delay, and the offended mass flung themselves upon the infidels.

Episode 17

The sign read 'Santa Monica – Yacht Harbor'.

End of the line.

With all other exits blocked and options expired, the only remaining way forward was onto the Santa Monica Pier. As the crowd surged behind them, more and more pursuers spilling onto Colorado Avenue, the remaining Warriors skated onto the Santa Monica boardwalk where roller coaster, tower plunge, ferris wheel, and other circus rides took shape. Maggie counted her soldiers: Suki Vicious, Maiden Hell, Queen Cobra, and Pussy Kicker. The rest had fallen—to be remembered in songs of glory.

Before them something odd obtruded—even more odd than the rest of the night, that is. While Maggie hoped to evade the growing crowd by skating down the Pier and then taking the Ocean Front Walk along the beach all the way home to the naughty nuns' Pollo Ranchero, she discovered that the Walk had vanished under a vast collection of tents and temporary frames.

A circus had come to town.

The Bike Path, however, was still visible and led directly inside. No way around. No way back. Whatever their feelings about red noses and greasepaint, the Warriors had no choice but to patronize this mysterious circus.

A giant white and red sign loomed overhead: 'Cirque de Lumiére'. Maggie narrowed her eyes. The fact that this tent-city was close to sea water made her nervous. The fact that it was frenchified made her annoyed.

"Are you certain there is no way around," panted Maiden Hell, struggling to catch her breath along with the rest of her crew. She stared at the ominous *fleur de lis.* "I mean, what if they force us to take a five-week vacation? Or overdose on cheese?"

Maggie glanced left. The only other possible route was

Appian Way. But a crowd had accumulated there as well, including odd albino-looking policemen who used their batons and whistles to direct traffic into walls or each other, while a steady line of self-driving Uber cars dumped even odder-looking persons wearing floppy French hats. These stumbled about aimlessly, laughing in silence at each accident, joined even as Maggie watched, by a City disability bus that deposited a load of aged, fist-clenching albinos riding sluggish three-wheeled scooters.

There was something about them that triggered a distant memory.

Seemingly of their own accord, as if her legs possessed their own innate motive force, Maggie skated slowly along the concrete bike path into the vast agglomeration of tents and lumber, what was left of her faithful crew reluctantly following.

An entrance had been erected over the path: the neon glowed in its unashamed frenchiness: '*Entrez si vous osez*'. *Enter if you dare*. The liquid font of the glowing characters sank into Maggie's mind; the softness of feminine mystique, of weakness, of deception, of passive aggressive dress styles, of sinful flirtation with latinized *aqua toxa*.

The path led along a narrow passage. No booth appeared to block their *entrée*. No person to demand francs or corrupt Canadian dollars. Just occasional chiaroscuros of unidentified figures in white greasepaint, their unfocused menacing visages gloating as through impossibly narrow windows at victims trapped in a self-serving labyrinth.

The path turned left, then right.

A room opened. Framed by tent canvas, propped on sturdy astroturf, were several tables strewn with a variety of food: dozens of repellent cheeses, with bread long enough to cross rapiers—the Warriors again recoiled at the blatant Frenchiness: spiced mustard; cold cuts; snails; three-bean salad—and four and five-bean besides; cabbage; cauliflower; radishes; and. . . *hot dogs mislabeled as bratwurst*. Maggie curled an upper lip at the base deception. How typically Gallic. The ample pots of vulgar mustard and ketchup deposited on the floor as an afterthought for the primitive locals to put on their 'bratwurst', did not make up for the distaste.

Multiple cross-printed swishes sounded behind and the Warriors briefly turned back—the entrance had vanished. In its place now stood heavy planks hung with mirrors. Not wholesome friendly mirrors such as normal circuses might have, but distorted twisted panels of alien glass shot with schadenfreude, the images the mirrors returned glaring back as if attuned to the emanations of evil twins.

Maggie's svelte proportion, which normally sent admirers into dreamy contemplation at a single glance, now twisted on itself like a banshee, now bloated like a balloon, while the other young women of her crew hesitated, glimpsing their own nightmarish reflections, windows into a horrid future.

"Can they—can these 'things' capture our souls?" muttered Cobra. "New Orleans—where I came from—you can still find the grave of Voodoo Queen Marie Laveau, with dead animals appearing where her followers still do sacrifices."

"Can't do you harm now, Cobra. Just don't drink nothin 'cept what best friends offer."

Maggie nodded her head. "Listen to Maiden Hell, Cobra.

She knows more about death than any old voodoo queens. They're stupid and not fair."

They all nodded.

Spinning on their skates, they returned to the Path, relieved to leave the evil mirrors behind. Skating through the room of deceptive food-laden tables, they came to a smaller room with no exits, a wide expanse of turf laid upon firm wooden floors.

They halted. Sudden. Abrupt.

Clashing static as of a microphone being tested rang through the cloth structure. A moment later came *The Voice*.

"So you did not like ze buffet," squeaked the high voice, echoing through multiple chambers. "I see zat you cannot be bribed mit Amerikanischer hot dogs—even if labeled as goot German *bratvurst*."

Maggie set her jaw. "If you thought that, then you thought wrong thinkin' 'bout how we think."

"We reckon," added Maiden Hell.

Maggie added, "Besides, you're fresh out of nopalitos." She glanced briefly at Maiden but addressed the Voice. "Who are you?"

An evil laugh rebounded. More twisted mirrors suddenly appeared on all sides, the escape route again blocked. "How does ze phrase go? As you goot guys say: *I am legion.*" A pale image appeared in one of the mirrors, a nightmare image of red suspenders over black and white horizontal striped shirt with bright green pants, the face lit with hideous corpse-light as if painted by Death itself, black tattoos framing eyes that mocked, a floppy Gallic hat clinging disgustingly to what passed vaguely for a head.

Worse, however, was the creature that perched on the Evil Mime's forearm, legs dangling, infant arms suspended as held up by wires, its own face as pasty-white as its loathsome host, a tiny blue blazer with white cap lending a nautical air to its puppet body. Green Pants moved an arm in the devil doll's back, and like a Christmasy Gepetto animating a cruel Pinnochio on shore leave from the waters of chaos, the tiny wispy white beard twitched in response. The mechanical chin dropped. For a moment the devilish eyes of Captain French snapped left, right, up, finally to focus on the Warriors who continued to stare with growing horror at the fell image in the glass.

The chin and eyes clicked like castanedas—paused like lemons lining up. "Bevare! *Bevare!* Kapitan French vill be your *Doom!*" Another white face slowly emerged over Green Pants' shoulder. A finger slid under his arm and poked Captain French several times hard in the back.

The puppet jerked and swiveled its head to look behind. "ACH! Vat haf I said about you doink zat, you dumkopf. Vhy do you keep mit ze poking of me in ze backside? Can you not see zat I am tryink to make mit ze scary impression mit zese very bad rollink-arount-on-ze-rink types? Find your own vindow, Ya Egger Hooper—or go back to your FBI!" Stone-faced, Edie's wig-shrouded white-painted face slowly sank below Green Pants' shoulder and disappeared.

The Warriors looked ever more worried upon learning that the number of their tormenters had increased.

Another pane of twisted glass flashed on to reveal a second white-painted devil, with purplish almost black lips, diamond tattoos above and below its harsh glaring eyes, insulting black and white horizontal striped pullover shirt and solid black pants with white on black saddle shoes, accentuated by the usual frenchified floppy black beret draped appallingly on its putrid pale head. The creature made mocking movements as if skating, pointed at the Warriors, and silently laughed behind the glass.

On other walls appeared a third glowing glass pane, displaying a grinning mime entirely in yellow spandex with only a single red star over its heart to relieve the eye, its arrogance and disregard for the feelings of its victims who were trapped inside the Lumiére's circus labyrinth apparent in its monument to poor humor and bad taste: a bowler hat one size too small.

A fourth pane showed yet another mime—its conical clown hat increasing the impression of haughtiness and scorn exponentially, if that were possible. It grinned and raised two fists—one read 'cemetery', the other 'hospital'.

"Ya! Das ist right, little skating arount on ze ground girlie-types. Did you really zink zat you could just roll into our little Cirque. . .Circuu. . .Zircus—oh, zat is hard to say—unt just roll around like zis ist your own little see-boot? Zis Kapitan don zink so! Haa-haa-haaaaa." The wooden chin snapped up and down while the eyes clacked left and right like a slot machine. The mimes in the glass windows pointed at the Warriors and doubled over in laughter.

Another glass pane appeared. Framed in its glowing edges was as frightening an image as the Warriors had yet seen—or could imagine. Under a raggedy mop of blond hair, once fetching but now frayed and worn, was a grease-painted face of whiteness outlined in black, forever scarred by fuschia lipstick, thick artificial eyelashes, and half-plucked eyebrows, its bloated body stuffed into a faded red silk nightgown, red mid-high heels thrust onto blunt appendages that could only be called feet because they were at the end of its legs. Edie had found her *vindow*. A growl like a junk-yard dog erupted: "Turn your head and cough," causing her red ruby earrings to dangle disgustingly.

Maggie turned her head—burped with one hand at her mouth. Suki could not contain herself, but power-hurled. Nothing in the Warriors' experience prepared them for confronting a cross-dressing mime—much less one inspired to survive for decades with an unholy vitality by evil mimes from an alien Frenchified circus.

"Ya, my little ballerinas. Look upon our vonders unt despair. Or hurl! Ze choice is all yours." The castanedas clacked while Captain French grinned.

The next glass pane switched on. In its confines stood an old man in white short-sleeved shirt that was impeccably clean, his wrinkled face displaying a smile perfected from long practice in door-to-door provocation, a Latter-Day Saints Bible held reverently in his hands.

"They tell me that you young ladies have been *very very naughty*. You have been a great inconvenience to our plans for Dryland. . .er, I mean, Earth. The Big-a Big-a Boss is very disappointed. And so is the Big-a Big-a Big-a Boss. Now you must *apologize!*"

The Warriors exchanged concerned looks again. This was bigger than they had realized.

"Apologize! Apologize!" shouted Gary.

They set their jaws, their lips firm. *Apologize? In Hell!*

"Ze Vorshipful Master Gary ist not among ze slow learners, little Miss 'wheels for toes'. You must do exactly as Gary says."

More transparent panes flashed on. In two stood what could have been twins, displaying white short-sleeves on young men in their twenties. Pocket protectors lined with pens graced their chests, their faces freshly scrubbed with soap and a hint of alcohol, their cheeks pulled wide to show a row of unnaturally perfect teeth whose reflection was visible in the shine of new loafers, their thick hair brushed and anointed piously with oil. "Have a cinnamon toothpick," called the first twin, grinning with arrogance. "Do you have time to discuss the Lord?" rejoined the second, with an insulting contemptuous look.

"Yavvol," clacked the evil puppet. "Ve haf a very special quote *just for you!* Haa-haa-haaaaa!"

"Let em have it, Orange Jello and Lemon Jello," called Gary.

The twins opened their Mormon Bibles.

"Let's move, Warriors," yelled Maggie. "I've heard rumors—you don't want to be on the receiving end of a Bible quote from the Jello Brothers." Sighting a flap of canvas that had come loose from its pins, Maggie tore loose an opening large enough to skate through.

One foot snapped a power line—she propelled into darkness.

As the lights died, Suki, Maiden, Cobra, and Pussy froze. Maggie's last words 'Jello Brothers' still echoing about them, the lights flicked back on—no opening remained. Somehow in that split second of time it had been repaired.

Or appeared to be repaired.

The Warriors stood and stared. Skating forward, they fumbled through the canvas, and the curtains revealed a gap. Should they enter? Was this where Maggie went? A sudden sound as of a thundering herd of angry mimes rose from somewhere, and the lights again died.

Without a backward glance, the Warriors dove through.

***

Suki recovered and stood. "Gals, is this the right way?"

No reply.

Pushing cautiously through the blackness, Suki stumbled, recovered, then skated into a chamber.

The lights flicked on. Standing in the middle was another nightmare albino in frenchified costume. Grinning, it pointed at her and pretended to skate in circles, then pirouetted in place. As she neared, it paused. Flapping elbows, it strutted. Stuck out its tongue.

"I got it. You want me to hurl again."

It grinned broader and nodded.

"Well, it won't work. I didn't eat your buffet, so I got nothing left to hurl."

The mime stopped grinning. Two more appeared behind him. They stepped closer, frowning.

With a swift elbow jab, Suki let the first one have it in the ribs—he gasped and fell over.

"So you *can* speak—in a way."

The other mimes turned scarlet with anger and rushed to grab her arms. Not for nothing did the Warriors insert metal sheaves in their elbow pads—with a cross-cut, Suki slammed each mime across the jaw and sent them reeling. A punch to the solar plexus followed, which flattened both.

Into the next chamber she bolted.

The lights grew and she halted in surprise at the sight of a half dozen mimes sitting at a work table. They glanced up without concern, engrossed in sewing pink corsets and blue-black leather flaps, several sets of eight-wheeled skates also on their work-bench.

"What—what are you doing?" A mixture of worry and hope settled on Suki's face.

One held up a new pink corset for show. Suki glanced at her own corset, now torn in a dozen places, the leather cords holding it together popped in three places, leaving her bra-less breasts half-exposed with every skate forward. Another mime held up new blue-black flaps; a third displayed black leather mini-pants. Suki's own were stretched and cuffed. She could not help but stare: the work was flawless.

Unable to stop herself, Suki glanced in a mirror conveniently held up by the fourth mime, and recoiled in shock. Her appearance was a far cry from how she had looked when she had first set out the day before—she no longer even looked like a woman.

The next mime stretched out a hand, offering a selection of makeup and brushes, a bare hint of a smile on his face. The last stood. In his hands was a new pair of skates, stylish, unblemished, and just her size.

She suppressed a sniffle. A tear came to her eye. The others had vanished—how could she know where they were? For all she knew, the other Warriors had already escaped the Cirque de Lumiére and were on their way to Pollo

Ranchero. She had done her duty for the Warriors. It was past time for her to relax.

Accepting the tray of makeup, she sat in front of the mirror and applied it, then accepted the new corset and other clothing. Respectfully turning their heads, the mimes allowed her to put them on, then, as she smiled at her new pretty self in the mirror, they looked back, their jaws dropping in admiration of her beauty, exchanging earnest glances with each other as they nodded respectfully, eyebrows raised.

Finally, the *piéce de resistance*. The last mime offered Suki the new skates. Sitting in a comfortable chair placed there just for her, she took off her old beaten skates and replaced them with the new ones. She spun the wheels—well-greased, they spun perfectly, promised endless months of joyful skating, the rubber brakes new and efficient.

She stood. Rushing to remove the chair, the mimes surrounded her, admiring gazes still on their faces.

She thrust one leg forward—it didn't move. Suki attempted to thrust the other leg—it also refused to budge. Standing in place, she suddenly realized: these skates were not skates at all, but concrete blocks. She would never move from this spot again.

The mimes broke into hideous silent laughter as they pointed at the concrete encasing her feet, and mocked.

The room went dark.

***

Queen Cobra hissed as she skated up a narrow dark alley

between dull green curtains. "Not so fast, Maiden. I can't see you anymore." Pushing forward, she slid into a room, which to her relief, was not entirely dark.

She braked. Maiden Hell was not there; neither were any of the other Warriors. Instead she looked upon a scene from her own Hell: a grave occupied half the room, fresh dirt surrounding a marble slab. On the elaborate headstone was inlaid a picture of a woman wearing a turban. On the grave were dead cats and dogs and chickens, mysterious amulets and bags of dirt beside the carcasses.

Her hands rushed to stifle a gasp.

Slowly she skated around the grave, unable to divert her eyes. Candles lit the room. From somewhere the usual green curtains had been replaced with mahogany wainscoting. Could this be real? How could the grave of Madam Marie Laveau, the most famous voodoo priestess in New Orleans, be here in a circus tent? What magic had these evil mimes used to transport Laveau's sarcophagus and body to Santa Monica?

As she watched, a procession of mimes entered from the other side of the chamber. Ignoring Cobra, they solemnly approached the grave, their chins lowered, their hands folded in respect. At the grave, they formed a semi-circle around it, leaving a gap for Queen Cobra to watch, and mumbled among themselves. From the movements of their silent mouths, Cobra thought she recalled similar rites from her childhood, threats made, vengeance carried out, relatives collected in silent regret over the grave of the victim, followed by treks to Laveau's grave to take unholy revenge.

Who was the victim? Despite the dozen mimes standing

by, she could not resist skating closer to read the name on the headstone.

She froze—the name on the headstone read 'Queen Cobra'.

Before she could react, the mimes grabbed her. More entered bearing enormous loads of dirt, and tossing her on top of the grave, they buried her up to her face, the weight of the dirt preventing her from moving. As she watched, more mimes entered with obscure objects suspended. The objects took shape and form.

She tried to shriek—a mime thrust cloth into her mouth. Her eyes staring in horror, she beheld the mimes deposit a menagerie of dead dogs and cats. Another thrust a chicken over her and removed its head with a knife, the blood drenching her. Through the blood and cloth, she silently screamed.

The mimes pointed at the dirt that covered her body. Doubled over in laughter. Heaving with good humor, they turned off the lights and left.

***

Not far as a pizza delivery drone flies, but eons distant in the private hell of a mind, Maiden Hell burst through what she believed was the path Maggie had taken. At first all seemed well, as poorly lit corridor followed poorly lit corridor, endless curtains of heavy canvas replicating. A room appeared. She gave a quick look: sighted a picture on the wall of a mature man with grey flannel jacket smoking a pipe; another of a smiling woman in pearl necklace and perfect hair.

She rushed on. The noises ahead must be Maggie.

A second room appeared. In it stood mid-century American style furniture including breakfast table, credenza displaying moderately priced Americana dinner plates, with Norman Rockwell pictures on the wall.

A disquieting feeling came over Maiden Hell. Could this really be happening?

Cautiously she entered the next room. A thick door slammed shut behind her—she thumped backward against it, her hand fumbling worriedly for the knob, but stopped struggling when the room's contents took form. At one end was a fireplace warming a man who sat comfortably in an expansive armchair, puffing a pipe—the same man as in the picture, but his face painted white. Her legs shook nervously at his appearance: casual suit, maroon vest, tie, smoking jacket of grey tweed, loafers, his clean-shaven mime face. He winked at her and gestured with his pipe.

"No," spluttered Maiden Hell, one hand clutching her half-shaved head.

At the other end stood a woman bearing a tray of fresh cookies, in a billowy taffeta dress, shiny high heels, her freshly washed and tinted hair drawn up in a half-bun, imitation pearl necklace gracing her modestly semi-exposed chest, the white-greasepaint on her face barely visible. Between the prim husband and wife, playing calmly on the floor were two smiling boys and one girl, each tastefully dressed and scrubbed clean.

"Can't be—" Maiden's other arm clutched her battle-scarred head, flexing the coffin tattoo on her arm with the white skull within.

The mime in the armchair put his hand to his ear like a

phone, little finger by his mouth. He grinned.

Ring-ring.

Something took hold. Unable to resist, Maiden watched in horror as her arm imitated a phone and contacted her own mouth and ear. *Yes?* she silently answered.

She watched the mime's mouth move, and to her surprise—since she was certain that she heard nothing—her mind comprehended his thoughts.

Would you like a cookie? The little wife fixed our family favorite—chocolate chip!

Maiden tried to shake her head. To her surprise, she nodded.

Great! grinned the mime. *Say. . .* He glanced at his perfect mime-wife and well-mannered mime-children. *I've got an idea. How would you like to stay for dinner? Tonight we're having chicken casserole!*

Mmmm came psychic emanations from the white-faced children. *Our favorite!*

They all grinned at Maiden Hell. Standing, they walked slowly to a table that materialized before her eyes—the same table in the same kitchen which she had previously entered.

Despite her desperate efforts to regain control, her feet followed.

She sat. Looked up into the smiling eyes of her new Norman Rockwell patriarch; stared aghast at her new prim Norman Rockwell mother; looked with outrage at the trio of quiet and respectful Norman Rockwell children, who had obediently left behind their gender-appropriate dolls and games in the tastefully decorated living room.

Unable to control herself, her arm reached forward and

took a chocolate chip cookie. She munched it, the taste of tears mingling with the chips.

Donna Reed in white-face leaned over and offered Maiden Hell a tray. *Coffee, tea, or milk?*

Maiden drowned the cookie in milk, let loose a shriek—and the lights went out.

Episode 18

Saint Melia of the Holy Polka of the Galactic Order of tibbets of Opus Dea, and erstwhile photographer of the Marshall Islands, raised the half-drunk bottle in one hand and chugged. Rising to her feet, she paused, suddenly aware that she was no longer on the Santa Monica beach at 4:00 a.m., but inside a congeries of interconnected tents composed of maroon canvas and wood. Slowly her memory returned. The letters 'Cirque de Lumiére' came to mind.

"I'll drink that—I mean *to that*," she mumbled, and emptied the bottle.

Stumbling forward, she became aware of shouts and thumps that roiled within the tents in various locations within the tent city, though she could not fix their precise locales. One commotion in particular sounded like music, though it had a strange beat and lyrics she had never experienced. She shrugged. With a wide swing, the bottle plummeted behind her and crashed. Releasing a burp, she started forward through an ill-lit corridor of canvas toward the strange sounds. True, she had never completed her round-the-Earth trip as planned, but maybe someone in all this stretch of canvas would appreciate what she did accomplish. So few people could claim to have navigated a 1936 Lockheed Electra from the planet Bogland to Earth, with a stopover on Pluto.

***

The Fat Enough 4 U Whore turned and leveled a suspicious glance on the two characters trotting alongside her as she skated from Colorado Avenue onto Main Street. Without losing her stride, she ran her eyes up and down the pair.

Catching her stare, Ray elbowed Bobby and the two of them slowed.

The Fat Whore also slowed. Other Whores did the same, their eyes following the direction of her gaze.

"Who—?"

Before she could say more, Ray sighted an Easter Bunny tween skating down Main and he clutched Etsy, primed and loaded, in triumph. "Hot damn, Bobby. There hops one now. Let's get it." A flip of his eyes toward the Whore to ensure she had heard him, and Ray pretended to aim his ancient hunting relic at the speedy skater in grey bunny costume.

The Whore took in the pair's green and red camo jackets, their soiled green baseball caps, their camo pants, their clodhopper boots, and relaxed. The lack of skates was odd, but clearly the two were performing a public service by hunting down those annoying teeny-boppers. Satisfied the pair were politically correct, and properly 'converged', the Whores skated away.

Sighing with relief, Ray and Bobby resumed their huffing and puffing in pursuit of a certain Segway that dove in and out of the ever-growing crowd entering Tongva Park. At the Main Street entrance, the two hunters paused to catch their breath.

"There," blurted Bobby. "Wait—no, that's not her."

"Over there," Ray said, fixing his stare. "Nope, that's not her either. Almost makes me wanna cry, seein our fifty grand get lost in the shuffle like this."

"We'll get her, Bobby. Just keep lookin."

Walking down the entrance, they halted—a Segway backed out of a frantic contretemps between a pack of shouting Muslims and angry Hare Krishnas who were both at odds with the Big Squeezers. On board the Segway was a dark figure in white shroud, its back turned to them.

The hunters tiptoed.

Screeeech.

Barely missing the two, a white car bypassed them and hit the Segway, crushing one of its wheels and sending its rider tumbling into the front passenger seat of the white Model Tesla X, its driver's side twisting into a pretzel and sending its motor into a death spiral. As the motor ground to a halt, the former Segway driver peered upside down at the Tesla's driver, taking in the stylish wide-brim white hat, tailored silk dress provocatively open down the back, open even more provocatively down the front, to reveal furry cleavage, the driver's entire face closely shaved. Two furry hands clutched the now useless Tesla steering wheel.

"Kind lady, you would not happen to be a U.S. citizen, would you?" Having lost her Segway, Aliyah smiled an upside-down smile at Gilda from the passenger seat of Gilda's Tesla.

Gilda shook her head. "Sorry. Lookin' for the same myself."

The cross-dressing Muslim snapped her fingers for better-luck-next-time.

Came a deeper voice: "*I'm* a citizen. We both are."

For the first time, Aliyah and Gilda noticed the Fudd twins standing beside the Tesla.

Ray's jaw was open. He followed Bobby's lovesick stare to Aliyah—who returned Bobby's stare with star-struck eyes. Ray's gaze wandered to Gilda.

"Bobby…"

"Yeah, Ray?" Bobby could not take his eyes off Aliyah as the Muslim cross-dresser righted herself, still swathed in an unlikely cross-patterned bedsheet.

"It *shaves*. . .ya know what that means?" Ray asked.

"It means she's *real*. We were wrong, Ray. It ain't no ape-suit after all!"

"*Ape suit!*" said Gilda gaily. "Don't tell me y'all fell for that li'l ol trick that my li'l ol' mammy and pappy back on the farm in Washington State liked to pull on strangers who got fresh with li'l ol' me? Why, I can tell y'all is *way* too clever and good-lookin' a man to fall for tha-yat." Gilda batted her Sasquatch eyes at Ray.

Aliyah batted her eyes at Bobby and drawled, "Why, y'all never did mention that li'l thing to me, you country peach." A Southern accent, apparently contagious, had taken hold of Aliyah's speech as well.

Ray stood hesitantly, confused. His eyes fell on Gilda's furry cleavage, her trendy clothes, her seven-foot three-hundred pounds of muscled body, her hairy hands and feet, and above all her closely shaved forehead, face, and neck.

With a confident smile, Gilda opened her purse and took

out a powder puff, exposing a treasure trove of large denomination bills fresh from her popular Sasquatch sitcom while she powdered her shaven nose. "Why, y'all is as handsome a model of a man that this li'l ol' belle ever did see." Gilda demurely covered her closely-shaved face while managing to show even more furry cleavage.

The blood drained from Ray's brain. A big smile settled on his face. He pushed out his chest and said, "Actually, other ladies have also said that about me—"

Gilda fluttered a fan. "Fancy all of us meetin' heah like this. Why I have the most mahvelous idea. Why don't we get away from all this bad ol' noise and go someplace quiet where we can get to know each other betta." Her Sasquatch eyes batted again at Ray.

Bemused by the simultaneous display of cleavage and currency, Ray stood and swayed as if punch-drunk. A purse with a hundred grand was only five feet away. Ray gulped.

"Hey-ell!" he said. "I cain't think of a goddamn reason why not." Ray broke out in a smile as he offered a forearm to Gilda; smiled even broader as she elegantly stood and took his arm, neither being nonplussed by the fact that she towered a foot and a half over Ray and could have shot-putted him across the Park.

Aliyah similarly draped a willing hand over Bobby's forearm and beamed happily at her new beau.

"Yo! Taxi!" shouted Ray at a city disability bus rolling nearby.

A black face hung out the window. "Who dat?"

Gilda flashed some Benjamins.

"Dat muh favorite color—and Uncle Ben, muh favorite

face." Clarence jammed on the brakes and Bobby and Ray assisted Aliyah and Gilda on board the empty van.

Ray thrust two of Gilda's bills into Clarence's shirt pocket. "How fast can you-all get us rednecks outta here?"

"As fast as dis nigga can put pedal to da metal." The engine gunned, and with a jerk, the van barreled through the Park, red Santas, Fat Whores, Comet Rippers, Krazy Kleptics, and every other roller-obsessed gang who happened to be in the way forced to skate to one side or be introduced to eternity, while outraged Hare Krishnas—now rechristened (or 're-krishnaed') "Come-Out-To-Play-ays"—and irate Muslims banged on the side of the bus with flags and sticks.

Ocean Avenue arrived; the road was packed with frozen cars and buses. A series of wooden barricades loomed.

"Try the next street," said Ray while Bobby whispered sweet nothings in Aliyah's hadith-filled ear. The van rumbled forward, laying two wooden barricades flat. Where Seaside Terrace turned into Appian Way, an odd white-faced stranger in horizontal black and white striped pullover shirt and blue policeman's cap directed Clarence to steer the bus rightward, sending it into a dense blockade of angry bus and truck drivers, their vehicles hopelessly snarled. The mime pointed at the resulting tangle and guffawed.

"What the hell?" scolded Ray. He stared out the window at Appian Way, which was thick with more of the white-faced strangers in horizontal black and white striped pullover shirts busily misdirecting traffic. "Who the heyll are these clods? And how dare they appear in public dressed like that?"

"And misdirectin traffic—"

"Yeah. That too."

Ray looked back towards Pico. "There's nothin' that way except more of these ugly whatcha-mimes."

Clarence looked. Sure enough, Appian Way was crowded with aged mimes in scooters, waving canes and laughing at innocent pedestrians, egging on the police-mimes who were making the traffic jam worse with every moment, their own assault on good taste and civilization evoking more silent mocking laughter from the pasty-faces. Their number increased each moment as more marched out four abreast from a giant tangle of tents covering Santa Monica beach next door, and still more from convoys of self-driving Uber cars arriving from who-knew-where.

"Can you back this thing up?"

Clarence shoved the bus into gear. "Read 'bout it in tomorrow's papers."

Jerking into gear, the wide van crept backward, beeping like a nuclear plant gone schizo, its decibels echoing off every building in Santa Monica. "Hope yo got yo hearin' aids fixed, white Massas, cause dis heah van is in service!"

A bevy of mimes looked up from their scooters, mocking grins pasted on their faces like an extra layer of paint. As the van neared, the grins changed to anger, then concern as it was almost on top—then to fear—just in time for the first scooters to disappear under its wide wheels.

The other mimes stared open-mouthed as they sped up their scooters to escape. Desperately they cranked up their motors to a full three miles an hour, rubber-necking at the van as it barreled upon them, its horn blaring like a shofar of doom.

Too slow—more went under the van's wheels, their canes feebly smacking the back doors, their faces angrily protesting in silence to the end. A police-mime stood and pretended to direct the van backward, laughing only harder at the pasty-faced bodies of its brother mimes as they fell under the van. He continued to double over with mirth until too late for himself to escape—alternately laughing and protesting, he also went under.

From the Park stumbled a batch of Zombiemanics attracted by the prospect of fresh meat and by the loud beeping—they too fell under the van's wheels, skating too slow to evade.

"Yahoo! Get em all!" shouted happy pedestrians from the sidewalks.

Cross-dressing Roller Vamps appeared with Domina-Trixies at their side. Joined by Angels Without Mercy and Sloppy Raggers, they pounded the sides of the van. The crowd grew thicker, more and more mimes arrived, pressing angry white faces silently on the glass windows of the van's sides, breaking into maniacal silent laughter at inappropriate times, upsetting the passengers by their eeriness. The van slowed under the pressure.

"What do we do?" Clarence blurted, the van straining under the impact of the growing crowd.

"I don't know," Ray shot back in desperation. "*I don't know.*"

Bracing themselves, Ray and Gilda together with Bobby and Aliyah watched as the doors on one side of the van began to give way under the pressure of an immense Fat Enough 4 U Whore fresh from her troll cave, and on the other side, by the biggest Bare Ass Brawler they had ever seen, her enormous bare ass sending the last remaining pedestrians fleeing in panic, the remnants of a recently consumed Tweeny on her signature bib.

Episode 19

The lights flickered back on. Maggie rubbed her eyes.

"Could it be, Miss Sqvuatch, zat you still do not realize vhere you are?"

Maggie regained her feet. She passed a quick glance around her. Only Pussy had made it through. Instinctively she felt behind her to ascertain whether the entrance was still there, was still available in case she and Pussy had to beat a quick retreat.

"Unt don't bother feeling for a qvick retreat either."

Her hand found not canvas or wood, but cold concrete. Whatever these things were, their cosmic kung fu was the best. Maggie's lips twitched; again the ancient memories. . .

"Ya. Now you know who it is zat you are dealing mit. Unt *who* iz ze fool."

Maggie took in the Captain French doll's perpetually grinning mechanical face, its lurching Pinnochio arms, its dangling twig-feet as it sat on Green Pants' arm. No argument there.

More alarming was the fact that there was no longer any glass separating Green Pants and his doll from Maggie, and Green Pants stood before her in his full Christmasy colors. The grinning Evil Mime in green pants and red suspenders held Captain French in its grasp, one arm animating the devil doll from behind.

From behind them appeared Gary with the Jello Brothers at one elbow, at the other the mime dressed in single Yellow Spandex with bowler hat, and the horrifying blond-wigged Ya Egger Hooper bringing up the rear.

The aged Gary shook his finger. “We warned you Little Miss Thing—we warned all of you pathetic Roller Bowlers to stay out of our business. To stop interfering with the Big Green G’s plans for Planet Earth. Did you really think that you could stop our global warming—excuse me, I mean ‘climate change’? Don’t you watch the news? In only two hundred years we have already raised the sea level by a whole foot and global temperatures by a whole degree—and in another century or so, we will raise it another foot and another degree—or even higher!” Gary grinned wildly at their plan’s immense success, crossing his hands Hitler-like demurely across his chest.

A fierce expression settled on Maggie’s face. Insulting Santa Lucia of the Holy Bowlers was one thing—drowning the world in poison from ‘climate change’, was another.

“That’s not fair. That’s stupid.”

Captain French and Gary exchanged skeptical looks.

“Fair ist as fair does. Unt ve don’t like any of ze bodies zat likes zose evil *tibbets*.”

Now Maggie looked puzzled. “Tib-bets?” Her mouth stumbled over the unfamiliar phrase.

“Don’t play the Not-Fair-That’s-Stupid with us, Squatch-squaw,” Gary said. “We know how to resist the lamentations of you and your other little skating-around types—and your little wannabe *cross-dressers from Pluto*!" Gary smirked. "And now—you must pay for your naughtiness."

"Haa-haa-haaaaa," agreed Captain French.

Before the mimes could react, Maggie leaped entirely over the concrete wall at their back, taking Pussy with her. She hoped they would land back in the same room as the rest of her crew—instead they were again surrounded by total darkness.

"Where are we, Maggie? I can't see a thing."

Maggie scanned the dark nook. "This way, Pussy. Stick close to me. I don't want to lose you."

Together they scrambled over parts of a three-ring circus, trapezes and nets scattered about in a temporary storage area and emerged in a better lit corridor of canvas. The corridor twisted and turned. It gave into a small room, then narrowed again.

Maggie stood straight. Alert. Scanned the lofty ceiling of maroon canvas suspended by wires and lit by ever-present florescent bulbs. "Do you—?"

"Yeah. I do. They're watching us."

Into the next room.

They again paused.

"Where does all this lead? There's got to be an exit somewhere."

"Yeah. If all this is real—and if we're still on Earth."

Maggie and Pussy looked at each other. For the first time, Pussy looked worried, intimidated.

"I don't know, Maggie. Maybe we should try working with them."

The Warrior Queen turned a surprised look on Pussy.

"What are you saying?"

"I'm just sayin. . . we've been chased, proposed to, fondled, admired all night. Now it's these *things*. And, after all, they're not really that bad looking. Who knows what assets they may have underneath. . . Maybe—maybe they're not so bad. . ."

"You can't mean it, Pussy!" said Maggie in shock. "After all we've been through. You're one of my crew, my soldiers. You're mine, after all. You're *my* Pussy. Don't give up now!"

Pussy grew silent, and they again skated forward.

In the next room, Maggie halted. Another glass mirror had appeared. As she stared, she gradually became aware of someone's back showing through the glass.

"Give it up," croaked a deep voice.

Maggie stepped back, stared hard.

"Give up your Pussy," the voice repeated.

"What?" Maggie blurted.

"We want your Pussy. Give it up."

Pussy looked scared. "What could these things possibly want with *me*?"

"Who can figure them out?" said Maggie. "They're Stupid and Not Fair."

"Pussy wants us too," the deep voice added. "Let your Pussy go," it croaked.

"Ha," yelled Maggie. "What would you sinful evil mimes know about my Pussy?"

"Your Pussy wants us." The back in the mirror turned—stared at Maggie.

Momentarily, Maggie covered her face with her hands as the shock of what she saw overcame her. She opened her eyes. The big green toad still filled the glass, chameleon eyes swiveling constantly but always looking at her, huge floppy feet and prehensile hands manipulating complex devices as it watched her. What shocked the most: two huge penises that thrust hard and erect in full view, almost plunging 3D into the tent's compartment.

"Come home, Maggie," croaked the froggy voice. "You're one of us. Our orgies are eternal, your pleasures will know no bounds. Listen to your Pussy, Maggie. Let your Pussy go—and come home!"

Again Maggie's hands covered her eyes. "No. I remember you now. . . you're evil. . . you're sinful. . . you're the evil sinful water men who kidnapped my parents and turned them into—tools."

"Willing tools, Maggie. Your parents volunteered! They have tasted the eternal pleasures of Bogland and happily served the interests of Great Gork, the Big Green G. Won't you join them? Listen to your Pussy, Maggie. Your Pussy wants to join us—has joined us."

From somewhere a frightened cry echoed. Looking behind her, Maggie stood, again stunned—Pussy was gone.

Maggie turned back to the glass. "Bring her back, Gork, you monster! What makes you think you can just take people and change their desires? Don't you know that people are born a certain way and that nothing can be done to change it?"

The Big Green G shrugged. "Nonsense. People's nature changes all the time. Just read your newspapers."

"I can't—that is, I have a crew that does my reading for me."

"Okay by me. But what we ribbets do, we do for the Universe—all must be like me, like us, merging into the galactic ribbet consciousness, splashing ribbet to ribbet in the sacred eternal orgy. All forms of life must swim in sacred water, all land everywhere throughout the Galaxy must be covered by water and procreate without limit."

She covered her eyes with her hands. "No. That cannot be. Water is evil! Water is sinful! It must be banned. Water can never touch my Pussy!"

Gork sniffed. "Boy did those cross-dressing tibbets from Pluto *fuck you up*," he calmly observed, one webbed hand wandering in Sigmund Freud fashion to where a human chin would be, had frog-like ribbets possessed chins.

Maggie covered her ears with her hands and closed her eyes. She broke out in song:

Sweet pokelicious
Likes her nopalitos
No sinful water man
Will touch her little piggy toes

Gork shrugged. "Have it your way." The Big Green G disappeared.

Moments later, Pussy's voice erupted. Maggie opened her eyes and ears—Pussy was in the mirror. Lost, confused, looking this way and that, but unable to see Maggie through the glass.

"Pussy. My Pussy. Don't be lost. Look at me!" With an elbow Maggie smashed the mirror, thrust forward—but there was nothing at all behind the glass.

Lifting the canvas revealed only solid masonry, which could not have existed prior to the Cirque coming to town, since she knew the tents of the Cirque de Lumiére were pitched on the sands of Santa Monica beach—more miraculous ribbet science.

She skated up the next tangled alleyway of canvas into an area where the neglected florescent lights flickered, casting eerie flashes in the darkness, avenues and offshoots confusing Maggie even more.

After a time she was forced to conclude that not only was she lost, but that the mimes had also lost her, and she paused to rest beside a large pole, four-feet thick and stolid enough to hold up the entire complex of Cirque de Lumiére tents.

Unknown and out of her sight, a mime approached the same pole from the opposite direction. Diamond tattoos framing his eyes, floppy hat on his head, and purple almost black lipstick on his lips, he pranced up to the main tent pole where a second mime, in yellow spandex, joined him. They paused, their backs to the pole, while the two mimes communicated together in silence via an elaborate code learned from Clarence and Rodney, which was based on shaking hands, slapping palms and snapping fingers accompanied by winks and swaggers.

At the same moment, yet another figure approached from a third direction, apparently as lost as Maggie, stumbling forward, red-rimmed eyes focused on the floor. Arriving at the pole, Amelia Earhart turned her back to the same four-foot wide obelisk.

A minute passed with Maggie, Purple Lips, and Amelia all standing, each with his or her back to the same pole, each thinking in silence, none noticing the others. Purple Lips ceased communicating with Yellow Spandex, and for a moment, he too was lost in thought—or what passed for thought in a mime's head.

As one, the three stopped moving: Purple Lips, Amelia, and Maggie. All three stared upward with mouths open as if to receive a sudden revelation from above.

Nothing came.

No angel appeared bearing messages from the divine. No devil danced on their shoulders.

All three shrugged and wandered back the way they had come.

Angry and hurt at the loss of her Pussy, Maggie skated forward into yet another tangle of maroon corridors and quasi-storage rooms. Her eyes peered left and right in the semi-gloam, determined not to be trapped as before when she had blundered forward, then attempted too late to retreat.

Carefully she skated into what was the widest room yet that she had entered. She braked to a halt.

A noise from behind informed her that her tardy attempt to retreat had again been blocked as another concrete wall materialized behind the canvas.

"Damn," she muttered.

When she turned, still another shock presented itself—the chamber had suddenly transformed into a replica of a Lodge of the Latter-Day Masons of Lower Middle Utah and Fish Fry. Even now the aroma of red snappers rose from a cooker in the corner.

On one wall was a panorama of past Worshipful Masters, including every past and sitting President of the United States, not to mention every crime kingpin ever to grace a post office bulletin board, and every robber baron ever to crash a stock market.

Over all was suspended the glowing sign of the Big Green G. Underneath the 'G' stood Gary, Western hat on head, Mormon Bible in hand.

"Have a seat, won't you please, *'Professor Squatch'*," he mocked, grinning. He pointed to an antique wooden folding chair that stood before his squat wooden lectern.

Maggie's eyes narrowed, but needing time to think of a stratagem, she complied with Gary's instructions, skating around the central altar with the unholy Mormon Bible outstretched on top, and she sat complacently in the folding chair. For Gary was not alone—but was flanked by the Jello Brothers, with their Bibles open to the most lethal passages in their whispered fearful cultic book, while aged mimes crowded into the chamber on three-wheeled scooters, their elderly faces alternating between angry protests while they clattered canes and indulged in mocking pantomimes of Maggie.

And more—Yellow Spandex appeared, with the puppet Captain French still on his arm; Ya Egger Hooper of the FBI, strangely also wearing the Western hat of a Worshipful Master despite 'her' blond wig and fuschia dress; and a growing number of mimes, these not in scooters, but in their prime, flexing muscles, prancing arrogantly, and drawing meaningless boxes in the air before stumbling through them onto the floor to each other's silent guffaws.

All went silent. More silent, that is.

The lights dimmed and a soothing sound as of wind blowing through meadows of giant sunflowers swirled about Maggie, lightly upending her jet-black hair, quieting her ever-restless mind. Mimes lit incense in large copper burners, and the aroma circled in the lodge chamber forming entrancing geometric patterns in the air, leading Maggie's eye ever deeper into unknown mysteries. "My thighs know the way," she mumbled. The bright florescents lowered, their light replaced by subdued circus displays and glittering incandescent LEDs like gently falling snow. Her eyes struggled to remain open. "Mmmomma. . . Mmmomma Maxie. . ." she mouthed.

Her eyes closed.

Putting his Western hat to one side on the lectern, Gary walked toward Maggie with the sternness of a traffic cop. Approaching her, he took another folding chair offered by Lemon Jello.

Gary sat. He leaned forward and paused, his face close to hers.

"How are we feeling today, Maggie?" came the aged Gary's still-adolescent high voice.

Her head nodded. "Enough."

"Good? Bad?"

"Good enough to be bad."

One of Gary's eyebrows arched. Then lowered.

The mimes drifted closer, forming a circle around both. Maggie's eyes remained closed.

"You will repeat after me, Maggie. Do you understand?"

Eyes closed, Maggie looked perplexed.

"You will repeat everything I say."

Her eyes shut, Maggie briefly nodded.

"Father knows best," Gary said.

In a soft voice, Maggie repeated: "Father knows breasts."

"Best," Gary corrected.

"Breasts."

"Father knows best," said Gary, frowning.

"Father knows breasts best."

Gary looked annoyed. He continued: "The Earth is our playground."

"The crotch is our foreground."

Again Gary looked worried, but carried on: "The more children, the better."

"Small children are bed-wetters."

"More children—"

"Small children—"

"The more children—"

"Smell children—"

"The more children, the better."

"Smelly children are bed-wetters."

Hearing enough, Captain French yelled at Maggie: "Nein, you dumkopf! Vat ist ze matter mit you?" His little legs straightened as he stood on Yellow Spandex's fore-arm. "Don' you unnerstan ze good English?"

"Sssssh" hushed Gary as tension suddenly crossed Maggie's face. "Repeat after me," Gary said softly. "Thank you for smoking."

"Thank you for fucking."

"Smoking."

"Foking."

"*Smoking.*"

"Fucking."

"Thank you for smoking."

"Thank you for sucking."

Gary thought a moment, then slyly said, "Thank you for smuking."

"Fuck you for smoking."

Gary pulled an open palm down his face in exasperation. Took a breath. "Raping the Earth is fun and profitable."

"Not giving birth is fun and prof—pruf—praf—"

"Profitable."

"Probable."

"Prof-a-ble."

"Pok-a-ble."

"Raping the Earth is fun and games."

"Rolling with girls is my middle name."

Gary shook his head. "Global warming is good for you."

"Global warming is doom for you."

"Good for you—"

"Drowning you—"

"Warming's good—"

"Women's boobs—"

"Warming's best."

"Women's breasts."

"Global warming's good for you!"

"Women's thighs are right for you."

Again Gary passed his palm down his face. Gave it one last try. "Water is Nature's medicine. . ."

Tension seized Maggie's face. She said nothing in response, but bit her lip.

Louder repeated Gary, "Repeat after me, Maggie! Water is Nature's medicine!" He threw concerned glances at Captain French, Lemon Jello, and Orange Jello. For emphasis, Gary reached below and pulled out a plastic bottle of water. He unscrewed the top and let its vapor waft under Maggie's nose. . .

Episode 20

For a long moment nothing happened. Slowly the mist drifted out of the bottle and lodged, molecule by molecule, on minuscule airborne detectors in Maggie's sinus. Inch by inch the poison moved; micron by micron.

Maggie's eyes jerked open.

One rippling bicep snagged Gary by his replica Navajo black tie—Maggie was not happy.

"Water is the curse of evil sinful water men!"

A finger slid forward—caught Gary in his eye. With a yelp, he fell backward.

Grabbing his folding chair, Maggie tore it in pieces, and clutching one rod like a club, proceeded to smash everything in the Lodge, the altar shattering like cheap highway furniture, the spectator chairs ripping up and flying through the air as so much confetti.

Captain French's mechanical jaw dropped. Beside the altar was a small wooden bridge used by initiates in imitation of crossing over to 'new life' in the Lodge. Alive with an unholy life force, the abominable puppet clambered down from Yellow Spandex's forearm and scrambled under the bridge where it hid behind a dust cover.

His mime eyebrows crawling up his pasty white face, Yellow Spandex jerked backwards in surprise as flotsam and detritus flew about the Lodge room, splinters of seats and lecterns reverberating after sticking in the ceiling like knives. The walls came down next. Caught in Maggie's tornado, pictures of Presidents flew about, smashing into angry mimes. Maroon canvas was suddenly exposed and Maggie's preternatural musculature ripped them to shreds as well, transforming the Lodge room into just another space inside a big tent.

"Orange! Lemon!" yelled Gary, reeling under the impact of a smiling picture of Barack Obama. "Take her down—*take her down!*"

The Big Green G's hitmen removed the safeties from the Bible holsters on their thick leather belts. Hard looks took hold. Of all the emergencies which they had handled for the Latter-Day Lodge, this was the worst, their eyes glancing up where even the largest tent poles holding up the entire collection of canvas of the Cirque de Lumiére were beginning to shake. Their target this time was no innocent homeowner naively allowing them to enter and deliver their deadly message. This was the Queen of the roller derby Warriors. Who knew what the results might be?

Orange whipped out his Mormon Bible. Quickly, but without haste, he flipped it open—already primed with perhaps the most lethal quote lurking within its gruesome fonts. It had felled many an unsuspecting victim in the decades that had elapsed. He caught his breath. Could he live with himself after this? His eyes narrowed. He had long since stifled his conscience, drowned any feelings he may once have had for the recipients of his brutal work. This passage was designed to bring down not young women—but elephants.

Selecting a cinnamon toothpick from a small box permanently resting in his shirt pocket, he cleared his throat. "And the Lord God did cause a skin of blackness to come upon them. Saith the Lord God: I will cause that they shall be loathsome unto thy people. And cursed shall be the seed of him that mixeth with their seed; for they shall be cursed even with the same cursing. And because of their cursing which was upon them they did become an idle people, full of mischief and subtlety."

Lemon Jello let loose the other barrel: "Wherefore, it must needs be expedient that Christ should come among the Jews, among those who are the more wicked part of the world; and they shall crucify him, and there is none other nation on earth that would crucify their God. For should the mighty miracles be wrought among other nations, they would repent and know that He be their God."

Maggie paused as these sounds came over her and their meanings penetrated her being. For a moment she stood quite still, her gaze directed at the fluttering stretches of canvas above, her pouting lips open. Pleasant memories of motzah balls on Bogland surfaced.

With a swift movement she dropped to her knees. Lowering her head and folding her hands, she intoned: "The Embodiment is in hand, God prepared Mary to have the Last Word, jail full of Grease, the Lord is with thee, Mary is wonderful, fear not for you shall conceive and give birth to Jessie whom no sinful water man shall touch by the power of Jessie Christina the Holy Spirit, and She shall be called the Lamb-Rack of God, behold the lap dance of the Lord, the Word is lusty and dwells among us."

Stunned, Orange and Lemon Jello stumbled. Falling upon their backs, they stared up at the main tent's poles as they shook, the fluttering canvas overhead tearing to reveal the rays of a bright afternoon sun.

"I never knew the sky could be so blue," wheezed Orange, a sprinkle of cinnamon toothpicks thrust like needles into his chest. Gary stared in shock at Bible pages that had settled on his former hitman, ripped loose by the ferocity of Maggie's riposte, water from Gary's plastic bottle leeching dark ink on Orange Jello's suit. Even Yellow Spandex and Green Pants stared with horror, for once unwilling to turn a tragedy into a mockery.

Lemon Jello lay beside his brother. His Bible also lay face-down, more pages ripped and shredded. He murmured, "I was primed and loaded, Orange. What happened?"

"We got whipped, Lemon. Her scripture kung fu was better."

Lemon stared at the sky. "I hear tell the weather's nice in Arizona. Ain't no Latter-Day Lodges there, or JWs with long memories."

"But there will be roller derby clubs. I hear tell the weather's even better in Brazil."

"Brazil it is, Orange."

Rage swept over Gary. Turning about, he swung his arms wide, and from all around irate mimes swarmed, eager to lay their pasty hands on the one who had disturbed their tent-city, like bloated termites erupting from their nest.

"KILL HER," he suggested.

Their jaws gnashed in fury—though of course promptly transformed into ridicule and pantomimes, as many paused to stick out a leg and trip their comrades then double over with silent laughter.

As the ant-army of mimes closed about Maggie in their inefficient stumbling way, a sudden barrage of amplified noise rolled over them. Behind the horde, Maggie's eyes glimpsed two familiar figures—like cave-mimes, since they were larger and more vicious than the rest, if that were possible.

The pair jumped onto the Worshipful Master's dais, their white-mime faces distinguished further by grinning clown lips arching high to their temples. Shoving the lectern aside, the pair whipped out microphones and the former Insane Clown Pasta broke into a backbeat rap tune, having exchanged their pizza makeup for mime paint and bulging doppelgangered assets, fresh from a quick trip to Bogland, both clowns coincidentally being named Joseph:

They left the gate up, so I rolled
It's been six months since I skate in the Derby bowl
Bitches all said I weigh too much
So I stole a pair of skates and said: Ho's, I don't give a fuck!
But I ain't naggin braggin
Here come my Mimes—I can hear their twin pokes draggin
Pussy gave it up with a faint
One look at my pokes and she's lickin' my greasepaint
Who would you guess is givin strokes?
My first day back, and I caught my pokes.
*My first day back, and I caught my pokes.**

(*To the tune of First Day Out by ICP.)

No sooner did the lyrics finish, than Maggie spun like a top—and launched. Kicking doppelgangers here, poking painted eyes there, the bodies soon piled up. She closed with a mime and took him down in a leg-lock, flipping him aside.

Another mime took his place.

On her back, she thigh-wrestled him and with a twist sent him tumbling, floppy head over saddle-shoe heels, out of the ring.

But more crowded in, pausing only to point and mock at their fallen brothers by limping and holding a palm over one eye. Then they too retreated, poked and flipped in turn.

She became aware of a yellow blur flying through the air—Yellow Spandex had had enough, elevating in the air with toad kung fu. As Spandex raised an arm and aimed it at Maggie, she grabbed the nearest mime—distracted by his elaborate mocking pantomime of angry and jabbering Captain French hiding beneath his little bridge—and she propped the mime in front of her. Yellow Spandex's invisible force almost stunned her, but her unfortunate 'mime-shield' absorbed most of the blow. The mime's floppy French cap burst into flames and the mime lurched in circles while the other mimes pointed and laughed, running behind him on exaggeratedly bent legs, their open mouths mocking his silent cries.

Again Spandex unleashed his power—point-blank. Again Maggie shielded herself with the body of one of her enemies, sending the second mime running about with his hair in flames.

A third and a fourth assault accomplished nothing except to ignite the tent's maroon canvas, Purple Lips and Green Pants rushing to put out the flames while the rest of the mimes pointed at the pair and laughed, and losing no opportunity to trip them. The Cirque's fire-fighting procedures thus found somewhat wanting, Purple Lips and Green Pants gave up, and while Yellow Spandex continued his efforts to zap Maggie—which only succeeded in starting more fires—the former two Mimes-in-Chief looked at each other with serious expressions and nodded.

It was time for The Nuclear Option.

Turning to the mime in the white conical hat, Purple Lips and Green Pants aimed their arms and unleashed their best toad kung fu in double dose. As Maggie watched, deflecting punches and delivering her own thrusts into the ever-growing crush of run-of-the-mill mimes, the Fleur de lis imprinted on the conical hat grew exponentially, and with a shock, Maggie became aware that the conical hat mime's size was rapidly increasing. In less than half a minute, the mime's head brushed the tent tops.

The other mimes paused to watch, their mouths dropping open.

Higher and higher grew the pinhead mime until his head and shoulders penetrated the tears in the canvas ceiling and with a silent roar the mime ripped the hole wider to stare down at Maggie without obstacles. Its chest grew thicker and stronger, its legs massive as columns.

On Appian Way, the tangle of police and scooter mimes paused in their harassing of innocent pedestrians to stand and stare at the Cirque de Lumiére tent, even the roiling crowd of roller derby fans in Tongva Park finally suspending their mutual molestations to do the same.

Conical Hat stretched his gigantic arms skyward. His monstrous mouth writhed with anger at the puny human who dared defy the mime plan for this minor primitive planet called Earth, dared to defy the mimes' Overlords, the Galactic Empire of Ribbets and their Leader, the Big Green G.

Lifting one huge leg, he positioned it over Maggie. She jumped to one side just as he slammed his foot, crushing several puny mimes too slow or too preoccupied with mocking their fellow white-faces to evade. Again he sought to step on Maggie, kicking a tent pole and yards of canvas aside; again she managed to bounce, leaving only luckless mimes to be crushed by the Attack of the Fifty-Foot Mime.

Leaning over, the giant mime displayed two gargantuan fists. One was tattooed 'Cemetery', the other 'Hospital'. With a gigantic heave, 'Cemetery' slammed into the floor of the tent—but again missed Maggie, succeeding only in sending several mimes to the hospital. A second punch, from 'Hospital', sent more mimes to the cemetery.

Conical Hat leaned further. The crowd of mimes was continuing to grow around Maggie, their vicious mocking faces squashing her soul, as the wheels of mime scooters attempted to squash her toes.

The end was coming.

The giant mime's hands and feet finally cornered Maggie, a solid wall of angry and mocking pasty faces blocking the other exits.

"Apologize!" yelled Gary, ecstatic to finally have success in subduing Maggie. "Apologize! Make time to discuss the Lord!"

Maggie went down.

Gripped in half-a-hundred mole-like termite arms that had never known the sun, she could no longer resist, and while a length of tent-rope was wound about her fulsome chest, she glared hatred at her captors as they tied the rope to one of the few remaining tent-poles in the Cirque's main ring.

While the mimes paused to catch their breath, and Conical Hat began to shrink back down to his normal size—the effort seemingly having drained Purple Lips and Green Pants of their kung fu powers, both of whom now lying flat on the ground half-conscious—Maggie saw something glint through a small opening in the canvas forming the far wall, in an area free of mimes. The opening was not far. The mimes seemed not to notice, and Maggie calculated that if her bonds were freed, she could bound through the small opening before any could stop her.

The glint emerged from the opening. It took form.

Maggie stared in shock.

The diminutive globular overseer and Mother Superior of the naughty nuns' Pollo Ranchero Casino & Bowlarama of Opus Dea for Upper West Los Angeles – Precinct 9, stared with a cautious expression at Maggie, the ends of her wide mouth twitching.

"Momma G-Spot," called Maggie. "By Jessie Christina and the Holy Saints Lucia and Melia, you have come. We must be quick. Look, the leader mimes are down for the count. Get me loose and we can escape before the evil sinful ones recover."

The malformed little spindly legs and round body, which were symptomatic of alien tibbets stationed on planets where poisonous water was plentiful, carried Madam G-Spot forward until she stood in the midst of the mime army. Uncomprehendingly, they seemed not to be alarmed and made no move to interfere or apprehend their ancient tibbet arch-enemy.

"Momma G-Spot. . .what does this mean? Why are

you—? Why are they not—?"

A strange look came over Madam G-Spot. She took out a glass bottle labeled Thunderbird.

"Perfect—that's perfect, Momma G-Spot. I need a charge. Give me a drink and cut these ropes, and I'll show them what for."

Grasping the bottle with one hand, G-Spot's other hand pulled the label off the bottle. Visible through the transparent glass was transparent liquid. G-Spot revealed a cruel look.

"Momma G-Spot—what's in the bottle? You can't—you don't mean. . ."

G-Spot's lips compressed. "I can—and I do."

The mimes stared at the two, finally unable to come up with a pantomime to reflect such treachery.

"And do you know why?" Madam G-Spot, the little ball of alien toad that was representative of the far-spread Galactic Empire of water-hating *tibbets* to upper west Los Angeles on this minor water-infested planet Earth, focused her widely separated eyes on Pollo Ranchero's latest addition to its roster of naughty nuns.

"*Do you want to know why?!*" Without waiting for an answer, G-Spot shouted, "Because you're the worst Opus Dea nun we've ever had! Because you start fires and smash things everywhere you go! Because not a day goes by without someone complaining or suing the Ranch because of things that you did. And because—" a sad look came over Madam G-Spot, "mostly because. . .despite all that, the nuns all *love* you and *adore* you." She sniveled a breath. "It's not fair! You were made a Professor even though you can't read or write. They gave you a Nobel

Peace Prize although you start fights everyplace you go. They even gave you a Pulitzer Prize just for scribbling your stupid little nopalito song on a bathroom wall. It's not fair, I tell you!" She stamped her little stick-foot.

Maggie stared back. "Who cares? They're stupid."

"No, Maggie. They should know better—*you're* the one who's stupid."

The Queen of Squatch returned a puzzled look. "Stupid is as stupid does. Untie me now so we can get the hell out of here."

A look of incredulity came over Madam G-Spot. She slapped a little hand to her broad tibbet forehead. "Can it be that you still don't you get it? Don't you ever understand anything? I'm not going to untie you—I've been trying to *kill* you all week. How could you not realize that? I hired hitmen to shoot you. I gave your picture to the mimes so they would hunt you down. I even approved payment to a hundred ISeeMoHos to find and eliminate you. And still," the sad eyes returned, "still everyone adores you." She sniffed back a dry tibbet tear.

A harder look took hold of G-Spot. "But it's not over. They all failed, but there's still time for me to finish the job." G-Spot raised the bottle again, with the mysterious transparent liquid. "Do you know what this is?"

Fear registered on Maggie's face.

"Yes. That's right. It's nature's poison—H2O." Maggie tried to get away, wrenched back, stretching the ropes. "Whatever it touches is never the same again. Ribbets love it—but we tibbets can't stand its touch. With enough exposure, it is lethal to us. Turns our beautiful fat toad bodies into—" She looked at herself, "—this."

Maggie looked away. Unable to free herself; unwilling to listen to one who had turned on her—especially not from the leader of the very same Naughty Ranches that were supposed to protect her.

"Now, 'Professor' Magdalene Pokelicious Squatch. Have a little of what you have given to others for so many years. *Drown in your sinful poison!*" Popping off the top, G-Spot drenched Maggie's neck and breasts with water, the foul liquid foaming and dripping like acid, spare drops flicking on G-Spot's own skin where they instantly flared like acid. "Maybe after this, your soul will finally be *clean.*"

"Aaaaa," moaned Maggie, wrenching against the ropes. "The sinful liquid. No one can be so cruel." With a jerk, she fainted. Maggie's eyes closed.

Watching from behind G-Spot, Gary motioned to Edie and the cross-dressing mime strode forward. Edie frowned—more than usual. "Turn your head and—oh, never mind." Edie groped between Maggie's legs. A growing look of surprise transformed Edie's face. Feeling further, Edie finally stood straight and stared at Gary, 'her' brows crawling up to the blond wig that served as hairline. "Worshipful Master, Gary. This *shuman* does not have one penis and two vaginas like *tibbets*. And she does not have two penises and one vagina like *ribbets*. This shuman is unique—*she has one of each!*"

Gary looked at the Chief Mimes, who shrugged their shoulders. He looked back at Edie. Something about Edie's stance, standing next to Maggie, attracted his eye.

Without warning, Edie whipped out a pistol. "FREEZE GOOFBALLS! You're all under arrest by the FBI."

Through the rips in the tent's canvas ceiling dropped a dozen black-clothed agents in body armor, wielding guns and showing badges, arms clinging to swing-ropes, helicopters overhead suddenly buffeting the interior of the tent with currents of air. Warning shots rang out.

The mimes stared calmly at the invaders. Gary and the Chief Mimes looked at each other, their eyebrows arched as if merely surprised by unexpected callers.

"Maggie. Wake up. This is Edie—I mean, Ya Egger Hooper of the Fuck in the Backside. . . Oh, I mean, J. Edgar Hoover of the Federal Bureau of Investigation. I infiltrated the mime organization decades ago just so I could finally expose them and save the U.S. of A. from their vile plans. Now's your chance to escape."

No response.

Edie put her ear to Maggie's ample chest. Edie took a deep breath and looked sad. "I'm too late. Her heart has stopped." He sniffed a tear. "She's gone."

The FBI agents finished dropping from the sky and produced many handcuffs. They started moving through the crowd of mimes, who stood silently giving no indication of resistance, or, weirdly for them, not even engaging in mocking pantomimes.

Gary yawned. Stifled it with the back of his hand. "Okay, that's enough." Nodding to Purple Lips, the latter took out a shiny device and aimed it at the FBI agents. He pressed a button. The FBI agents froze in place. "Even though we would love to harass and ridicule you, right now we have no time for gate-crashers."

Gary turned to Edie, who was more surprised than anyone. "Gee, like we didn't see this coming." Gary chuckled.

"We've been expecting this from you since the very beginning. Once FBI—always FBI. Your little white-face and blond wig never deceived us for a moment. We knew you would do this. After all, you are not a real mime or even a real woman, just a wannabe-both, who still can't coordinate eye shadow with accessories."

Edie bit her knuckle. Tears flowed.

"No cross-dresser could ever be a *real* Worshipful Master—or a real mime. We only humored you so we could use you."

Bursting into tears, Edie, formerly J. Edgar Hoover, Director of the FBI, sat next to Maggie and cried 'her' heart out.

Yellow Spandex looked at Purple Lips and took on a mocking pose as if Yellow Spandex were the one holding the freeze gun. Purple Lips responded with feigned anger, silently mouthing a reproach.

"That's enough of that, now," said Gary to Yellow Spandex. "We're workin' here."

Not satisfied, Yellow Spandex pranced in front of Purple Lips while Green Pants dropped on all fours behind him. With a sudden shove, Spandex sent Purple Lips reeling backward over Green Pants.

"I said: that's enough. No messin' around, you clowns." Gary frowned.

Spandex and Green Pants looked at Purple Lips lying on his derriere and pointed and laughed in silence.

Something shiny landed in front of Edie. Before anyone noticed, Edie picked it up and pressed a button.

Instantly the FBI agents came unfrozen. "Freeze goofballs!" they yelled. As Edie watched in relief through filmy tears, the FBI agents unloaded bullets non-stop into the surrounding mimes, sending a dozen plummeting forward, clutching their chests. Other mimes pressed forward in outrage. Their mouths twisted in rage as they swarmed, only to trip over the outstretched legs of their colleagues—including those lying with bullet wounds—who could not resist pointing and laughing at their stumbling and injured comrades even as they took their last breaths.

One silent mime slipped from the crowd and approached Edie. Standing directly in front of her, the mime briefly stared down at Edie—then turned to Maggie. Before Edie could interfere, the mime took out a knife.

The ropes imprisoning Maggie parted.

As they fell to the ground, the mime caught Maggie in his arms. He shook her.

"Maggie—Maggie. Look at me, Maggie! Don't you know me?"

Taking out a flask from his pocket, he poured its contents over Maggie. An aroma of Thunderbird Wine wafted through the chaotic tent. Slowly her eyes opened. Looking into his, she saw white greasepaint and recoiled. Quickly he rubbed it off—her eyes shined with relief and renewed hope.

Her lips slowly moved. "Hey You."

"Yes, my dear. It's Richard. . .now *Professor* Pierson. My Maggie, my beautiful lovely Magdalene. My virgin love who brings light and warmth to the world. I'm here to bring you back."

"But—my heart."

He smiled. "Only one heart stopped. You have two, in case you didn't know."

"Hey You. I can't hear. There's too much noise."

Looking up, Pierson let loose a shout. "HEY JOE!" Instantly, every mime in the tent, each one of whom was named Joseph in their former pre-mime life, froze and looked at Pierson.

Pierson looked back at Maggie, cradling her in his arms. "Two," he repeated.

"Two?" she smiled hesitantly.

He nodded. "You have two hearts. Relax. The Thunderbird got the first one started again. You're back to normal now."

"Normal?" her eyes briefly shut. "What's normal?"

"That's what I've been trying to tell you, Maggie. The secret that you hold. I've waited seventy years to see you again, to tell you what I've learned since that day on Mount Stirling in Nevada in 1951 when you befriended a lonely boy and gave him a reason to live."

Her eyes opened again. "Secret?"

Nodding, he resumed. "Edie was right." They glanced at J. Edgar Hoover, who sat beside them, one hand propping up his sad, mascaraed with traces of mime, face. "You are the perfect balance, Maggie. Your father was human. And your mother was human. But you are also part ribbet—and part tibbet. You're not all male, or all female, and neither ribbet nor tibbet—you're a hibbet! A hermaphrodite, the most lovely and exquisite form worshiped by the ancients. The great Unifier. When you were conceived, Gork—the Big Green G—mixed ribbet and tibbet genes with your parents' DNA, so you have all of them within you. Which means. . ."

She looked puzzled—and worried.

"Water doesn't harm you. Unlike real tibbets, you are not allergic to water."

For a moment she closed her eyes again, the mimes and the FBI agents still staring and listening. "You spent seventy years exploring the Universe with your astronomy to learn this?" Maggie muttered.

Pierson nodded. "And trying to get the Academy to call Pluto a planet again. Can you imagine them kicking my favorite planet out of the Solar System like that?" He looked put out and frustrated. "Their only reply is to talk about 'Universal Laws'."

She looked up, inquiringly.

Pierson ranted. "They don't have to tell me about Universal Laws. I can tell them about Universal Laws. Like the First Universal Law: attempts to communicate peak the moment one steps into a shower. And the Second Universal Law: candy corn can only be sold legally in October. And now the Third Universal Law: Pluto is a planetoid, not a planet." The hard look returned. "It also means you are immune to the mimes' Whammy."

"To what?"

"Their little shiny devices—their little tricks. Because you're part ribbet, their Whammy doesn't work on you. Ever."

A smile of relief—and renewed energy—crossed Maggie's face. She stood up and stretched her biceps. "Pop the Thunderbird, and strap on your Pro-Designed's. It's time we taught these clowns the *Fourth* Universal Law: *You Don't Mess With the Squatch.*"

Episode 21

"They must think they're playing with children." Turning to the nearest mime, Maggie said, "Watch out—I skate like a girl," and ran over its toes, elating at the look of surprise and pain that seized the mime's face. "Oops. Sorry, Edie," she said. "Friendly fire," Maggie muttered and wheeled away.

Rushing upon the next nearest figures with pasty white faces, Maggie propelled full-speed at them.

Pierson's heart skipped a love beat as he watched The Juggernaut slam into mimes and knock them down—bounced mimes heads over heels—kicked doppelgangers till the tent seemed strewn with squids. Without looking back at Pierson, who whipped out a cell phone and jabbered, Maggie rolled down a line of mimes, deftly poking every other eye, then rolled back crushing every other foot. Those mimes would not challenge her again. Thigh flips disposed of some; diagonal hand chops more; her open arm clothes-lined those who still dared to stand.

But the odds were against her.

More mimes flooded in from adjoining tents, unconcerned at their losses, their faces registering either mock anger or mock ridicule of both Maggie and their own fallen comrades.

From seemingly nowhere the Insane Clown Pasta re-appeared, unleashing more barrages of their insane clownish lyrics into microphones from another stage behind the mimes, while Gary and the Chief Mimes directed the action in between, sending their cohorts against the FBI agents, who ran out of ammo and fell before the mimes' superior numbers, and sending more mimes against Maggie, pausing only to trip and shove each other while pointing and laughing at each other, and at Gary's increasingly exasperated expressions.

Through the wide tears in the canvas overhead suddenly appeared a squadron of mini air drones. Dropping loads of pizza and bottled water, the drones exited while Pierson punched payment into his phone. He lost no time in unscrewing the first bottle.

Maggie paused from repeatedly punching the formerly white but now bloody face of a small relatively helpless mime to stare at Pierson quizzically. "But that only works on tibbets," she suggested.

"Watch," he assured her.

Approaching the nearest mime, he drenched the mime in the life-destroying poison. To the shock of everyone, the mime shuddered and a hideous whine escaped his throat belying the notion that they had no vocal chords. The whiteness disappeared and the mime's body began to change.

"What is it?" asked Maggie, in disgust.

"Our true enemy! Gork's serum turned people into mimes—but that was only the first stage of their transformation. After global warming raises water levels on the Earth, the mimes will be drenched in water and change into ribbets. That was how Gork planned to change Earth into a copy of Bogland. Why not frustrate Gork's plan by drenching them now?"

True enough, while Maggie watched—and to the surprise of the other mimes in the tent, who had not known of the final transformation that Gork had planned for them—the mime turned into a fat olive-green toad, its stalk-eyes glowering. Before Maggie could slap it silly, it hopped away.

"What's happening?" called a familiar voice. Maggie turned—Suki stood at a gap in the canvas behind her. "One moment I was surrounded by mimes. And suddenly they had all come into this tent. I could walk again, so I followed."

Pierson tossed her a bottle of water. "Start drenching pale-faces."

Shrugging, Suki popped a cap and joined in. In seconds, another mime turned into a toad and hopped away.

However reluctant Maggie was to risk touching the evil liquid encased in clear plastic bottles, as more mimes came near with arms outstretched to grab her, she swallowed her disgust and carefully unscrewed the top off one. A mime neared and she poured its contents on his vile frenchified head. With a painful shudder and high-pitched scream, the mime collapsed to reemerge as a squat green toad. It too bounded clear.

This was fun!

Queen Cobra appeared at the threshold rubbing her eyes. "Where'd everybody go?" Handed a bottle of water, Cobra soon was drenching mimes with as much enthusiasm as Maggie and Suki and Pierson.

As the toads' numbers grew, and the number of mimes diminished, the Pasta Duo disappeared and the arrogant lyrics which they had been belching ceased. Still more mimes continued to crowd in—Pierson accepted another air drone delivery of pizzas and bottled water, and the Warriors were back in business, eating pepperoni while kicking ass—or whipping it, as several mimes laughingly offered bared bums before submitting to the baptismal font and transforming into frogs.

Gary stood with his jaw gradually dropping as mime after mime converted to froggery and gave up the fight. With a look of consternation as his boggy retirement went up in mist so to speak, he locked his eyes on the Chief Mimes, who finally paused from their mutual tripping and mocking and eye-poking, and motioned them to advance on the enemy. "Stop it, you clowns. And stop her."

With feigned outrage, Purple Lips rushed forward, using his Whammy powers to skate without skates. Yellow Spandex followed behind. As they neared Maggie and her Warriors, Purple Lips paused to dance his usual arrogant jig while directing a look of triumph at his imminent victim.

"Wha—?" Someone snatched a bottle from Pierson's hand. Looking up, Pierson saw Green Pants sailing through the air using his own Whammy powers.

"Look out!" Pierson shouted to Maggie as Green Pants flew near, carrying the bottle.

For a second, Maggie halted, arms raised, face wrenched in anticipation. But to everyone's astonishment, instead of attempting to drench Maggie—which would have inflicted no harm on her but could have severe consequences for everyone within her batting range—Green Pants alighted next to Purple Lips. Nudging Yellow Spandex, Green Pants pointed at Purple Lips and smirked.

Spandex nodded in agreement, alerted to the hilarity of the plan.

Still dancing his jig, Purple Lips paused as he sighted the

open bottle of water poised over him, held by Green Pants. His Purple face wrenched in outrage. He swung his arms. *How dare you endanger our entire Earth operation by threatening to pour water on your Chief Mime and turn me into a toad*, Purple Lips mouthed. But his outrage was only feigned and then he too doubled over in laughter at the absurdity of the idea.

Yellow Spandex too doubled over, holding his stomach, and elbowed Green Pants. What else could add to the hilarity? Spandex stuck out a leg and tripped the Christmasy mime.

The bottle fell.

Lipstick melted down Purple Lips' chin. . .

With a hiss, the Chief Mime—in charge of all Dryland operations for most of the past century and looking forward soon to his own well-deserved retirement with green balloons in endless swampy bogs—shriveled like twin pokes on Planet Iceland, steamy mist filling the tent, until nothing remained of Purple Lips, the smirking supercilious grease-painted fiend with the floppy frenchy beret and diamond tattoos and silly striped shirt. . .except another squat fat toad.

One look, and Green Pants and Yellow Spandex laughed so hard that they rolled over each other in paroxysms. A single step with another up-ended bottle by Maggie finished the pair. In moments, two toads had taken their places and hopped away, leaving their vile mime clothing of green pants and yellow spandex on the ground, a too-small hat resting beside.

Maiden Hell appeared. In no time she too was drenching mimes both-handed.

Maggie stared with relief as the last Warrior re-joined. “I have my Pussy back,” she crowed, jumping back into the fray, Pussy Kicker landing grand-slams on mime doppel-squids with a grin.

Meantime, a certain olive-green toad, who had watched the entire fiasco from a secluded room, which from the electronic equipment installed about him evidently served as the Cirque’s communications base with Bogland, booted up his link with HQ. A familiar face appeared on the giant plasma screen.

“Your news, Xplak? What is your news?” Joseph Smith of the 333rd Degree of the Chartreuse Lodge of the Latter-Day Masons of Upper Middle Utah and Fish Fry leveled his toad face barely concealed by the shuman mask at Ribbet Agent Xplak, who noticed that the top of Joseph Smith’s head had finally healed from its encounter with Melia's bottle of Johnnie Walker.

Xplak shook his head. He spoke directly; there was no time for politeness or niceties. “I’m broadcasting direct from the war front. The casualties are mounting, O Elder Smith of the Eternal Plasma Screen. Gork’s intervention—has *failed*.”

Smith dropped his shuman-face-on-a-stick and looked directly at Xplak *sans* white-face, pure toad. “So I heard. But the enemy should be defeated by now anyway, with no issues.”

“Despite our numbers, the Squatch broke through. I regret to report, O Great Smith, that the Great Plan is in deep trouble. It is, how do these *shumans* say: up a creek without paddling.”

Worry turned to consternation on the Joseph Smith’s

face. He put on an English hat, stuck a cigar in his frog mouth, and assumed a bulldog stance. "General, we have no more mimes to send you. Where are your strategic reserves?"

"Mon dieu! We have none."

"Not even Sardauker?"

"They have all retired and are enjoying green balloons on their own globally warmed and flooded planet by now."

"Hmmm," said Smith. He threw away the cigar and hat. "This will be very bad news for the Great Green Gork. What sort of casualties do you have?"

"Turns out Gork's serum had a defect. The mimes are all turning into ribbets prematurely. They are all turning into—pardon my saying it, O Elder Smith—big fat toads like you."

"Thank you for your compliment, Xplak. So there is no hope?"

"I'm afraid not, O Elder Smith. You know as well as I do what is sure to happen when untrained croaks hop around on planet Dryland without Gork's injection of serum to turn them into silent mimes."

"Then we must evacuate the lot—and quickly." Smith turned and punched some buttons, then returned. "Transports are on the way via the usual wormholes. Make ready to board. You, Xplak, are to stay however to coordinate a future invasion. Do you have a suitable disguise that will not arouse the Drylanders' suspicion? The U.S. army soldier disguise that you and that AWOL deserter Korplash adopted before is no longer appropriate."

"Yes, O Smith. I have a new disguise that Earthlings assure me is completely impenetrable and will keep me safe in all circumstances."

"Good, Xplak. Now go knock em dead."

The plasma screen flicked off.

Clicking his shiny device, Xplak was immediately transformed into his new disguise. Putting on a blue cap and propping a mailman's delivery bag over one shoulder, he stepped out.

Attracted by an unholy racket that nevertheless had an interesting beat, Saint Melia Earhart of the Holy Polka—like so many prophets, scorned in the land of her birth—disconsolately made her way through the labyrinth of canvas of the Cirque de Lumiére. Turning a corner, she paused.

Before her, at an angle that allowed her to see only a side-view, her eyes took in a stage, or dais, on which two men stood. Looking upon some scene hidden from her, they were too engrossed in their lively artistic performance to notice her. She, on the other hand, was immediately entranced by certain unexpected qualities of the performers: her eyes zeroed in on their gorgeous white face-paint, followed the fine form of the pair's athletic bodies, and ran down their fronts until her pupils bulls-eyed on tell-tale *twin* bulges on their crotches.

Bingo.

Forget that white-tease Professor.

Fuck that lying clown, Blinky.

This was the Real Thing—the Diet Koch Conspiracy—the Mimeograph Meat Machine. No way could these Monsters on Campus, these Katzen-jammer-doppel-gangsters, be mistaken for anything but the Pelvi from Toadland she craved.

Twin Pokes—here I come!

Cackling with joy, Melia dashed behind the Insane Clown Pasta. She yanked them backwards off the stage. Before either Joseph realized what was happening, she had pulled the pants off both and tossed her own clothes aside and proceeded to bounce from one poke to the next with the agility of one of the Cirque's trapezists, howling at the moon as their Monster Trucks came to uber-life with minds of their own.

"Who's this bitch, with an ass like a truck?" asked U.

"Long as she don't stop, who gives a fuck?" answered B, astonished but smiling.

A few minutes later, with Melia showing no sign of slowing down in her long-denied passion, B. noticed that the sounds in the main tent on the other side of the stage were diminishing. Lying invisible behind the stage, it seemed a good time to exit.

"Slow down, honey. We like bi-atches as much as the next rap star, but you gotta pace yourself." B and U leashed their animals and harnessed their pants. "I'm Big B and that's Two U. "What's your tattoo, Little B? You don't mind if we call you that—for Little Bi-atch?"

Melia grinned and attacked his belt again.

"Hold off, Little B! You can have all you want later. We gotta zip outta here first."

Arms protecting their newest prize groupie, and triumphant yells from the Warriors in the main tent indicating their imminent victory over the mimes, Big B and Two U hurried down a corridor of canvas.

They halted.

Before them stood a diminutive sphere with spindly legs and wide-set eyes, that despite their clearly alien origin, glared hatred.

"How dare you?" it hissed, barely audible in its anger. "How *dare* you?"

Big B and Two U looked at each other, then at their hot Little Bi-atch. Just who had dared what?

Her eyes focusing on Big B and Two U, the odd-looking creature with the skinny legs and arms spouted, "You two are *mere men*. I understand that you have no control over yourselves. And you have the added disability of having spent time on Bogland and were injected by Gork's serum for people named Joseph, so you cannot be held responsible for what you do."

She turned to Melia. "But *you*. How dare you pretend to be a Saint of the Holy Orders approved by Central Tibbet HQ, and even after bringing new sacred rites that have already been adopted by tibbets throughout the galaxy. Look at yourself!"

Despite the gravity of the situation, Melia still could not resist yanking at her companions' belts and stroking the beasts that strove to escape their cages. She let loose a giggle.

"Stop what you're doing at once! Saint Melia is a nun of the Holy Order of Opus Dea. Teacher of our new rite of the Drunken Holy Polka. You are not allowed to have sex with anyone unless they dance the holy polka or roll strikes in our bowling lanes, and then only for the purpose of persuading them to enter our sacred Back-To-Nature-Wigwam to further the spread of the Galactic Tibbet Empire by transforming them into water-hating cross-dressers."

Madam G-Spot's little arms waved furiously in the air.

Melia paused and looked at G-Spot. "Sorry. But I got a ass like a truck—so who gives a fuck."

Madam G-Spot's triangular alien mouth dropped open. Behind G-Spot, a troop of new mimes entered the corridor and pointed angrily at the Duo, who had been IDed as mime deserters. The mimes approached at a run, for a change not pausing to trip each other.

It was Melia's turn to get angry. "Now I've had enough of *you*. Speaking as Saint Melia of the Holy Polka . . . Madam G-Spot of Pollo Ranchero: *You're fired!* I'm appointing Maggie as the new Mother Superior of Pollo Ranchero—after I exile *you* to Planet Junglerot!"

G-Spot's mouth dropped open even wider. Before she could recover, Big B ripped G-Spot's ill-fitting clothes off and turned her upside down. "You know what?" calmly observed Big B. "That Professor guy was right. Tibbets *do* have two vaginas." Inserting thumb and forefinger into G-Spot's twin orifices, Big B turned to the onrushing mimes and swung his makeshift bowling ball behind his back. While G-Spot defensively sucked her spindly limbs into her round body just in time to form a perfect sphere, he let loose with a swoosh down the corridor.

The white-faces fell like mime-pins.

"We're outta here," yelled Two U. Melia briefly paused. Turning to the sphere that had come to rest dizzily down the corridor, she yelled at Madam G-Spot, "And, oh, I forgot to tell you—I really *hate* bowling."

In another moment, they were free of the devilish Cirque de Lumiére and its frenchified whiteness and were racing down Appian Way.

A City wheelchair bus backed into view, crushing mimes and Zombie skaters, then ran into trouble. Ambushed by a Fat Enough 4 U Whore and a Bare Ass Brawler, it could make no headway and was being rocked by a crowd of skater gangs and figurative and literal hangers-on.

As Big B approached, the Bare Ass Brawler released the bus and turned toward him. Ripping off her enormous bib with snack remnants of Tweenies on it, she threw it aside and assumed a wrestling stance. Big B smirked as he accepted the challenge.

They grappled—twisted—flipped each other—but in the end Big B wiped the Bare Ass Brawler's tearful face with her own bib and sent her scurrying.

Meanwhile Two U confronted the Fat Whore. For half a minute they circled each other, looking for an opening. The Whore delivered a kick below the belt—she wailed in pain. His doppelgangers were as tough as they were large. She paused and began to smile instead, batting eyes at his bulges. Without pausing, however, Two U delivered his own kick to her backside and sent the Fat Whore running after the Brawler.

Cowed, the other roller derby types fled.

The Bus' entry doors swung open and a smiling face thrust out. "That was sho nuff righteous. This Sasquatch Special is Texas-bound. Ya'll need a ride?"

They bounded on board, Melia right behind. "Sho nuff," she grinned.

With a jerk, the bus crushed the few mimes remaining on Appian Way, to the accompaniment of beeps and whistles and clapping pedestrians, and headed for Ocean Freeway.

Inside the main tent, meanwhile, his mime squads reeling from the assaults of The Warriors led by Maggie, and the growing number of ribbet frogs bounding every which way, including his erstwhile Chief Mimes, and the defections of every other ally, even Conical Hat having hopped away, Worshipful Master Gary held his breath in fear of what he knew must follow. A century of infiltration by ribbets of this minor planet Dryland, called Earth by the locals, not to mention others in this part of the galaxy, had always met with the same result. Knowing what was coming next, Gary closed his eyes. . .

Croooooak.

Across the ridges and mountains of canvas surmounting the tents of Cirque de Lumiére, crashing burps like a fleet of Mississippi steamboats escaped the throats of the scores of ribbets from their various hidey-holes, their natural urge to court others of their kind by uttering deep guttural calls impossible to suppress any longer.

"There goes the neighborhood," muttered Gary, and kicked the now empty stage.

Sure enough, precisely on cue, several pie-shaped alien spacecraft dropped through the tears in the canvas tent's ceiling to hover neatly just above the ground while multiple snouts thrust out of superstructure windows, wet pink tongues lolling happily in the wind.

"Woof, woof, woo-woo-woo, arf-arf-arf!"

Bigtooth alternately snapped his jaws and grinned out of one craft with his crew of siridogs beside him including Thumper, Noseupass, and even Windinface who was finally back in Bigtooth's graces, while Spike and his

Dobermans leered from a second craft—and a fat man with the military cap and chest salad of an American General thrust his cigar-accented mouth out of the superstructure of a third.

All three alien ships landed inside what remained of the Cirque's main tent, amid a horde of hopping toads, which froze in stark terror upon sighting their mortal *enemies—siridogs*.

"Bigtooth. Is this the puny planet where that Croak tricked you into losing your spacecraft?" bellowed Field Marshal Ramey, adjusting his vast array of decorations which he had awarded himself as the new Most High Pack Leader on Planet Sirius.

With a whimper, Bigtooth nodded. "Yes, O Big Cigar Bill."

"And forced you to return to Sirius in his damned Croak dumpster stinking of more Croak?"

"Yes, Big Cigar Bill." Bigtooth looked cowed, while Spike grinned at him in triumph, enjoying his rival's embarrassment.

"Well, we've been after these Croaks for years—now is the time for you to take your revenge. Go for it!"

Bigtooth lit with joy. Here was his chance to recover his reputation, and have fun doing so.

"But don't take too long—we're scheduled to pillage Planet Katz by midnight. That's where the real action is." Ramey took a big puff on his cigar and Bigtooth and his crew of barking siridogs jumped from their craft, Spike and his Dobermans right behind.

With a barrage of frantic croaking, the ribbets panicked and scattered in every direction, hopping madly to escape the crushing and snapping snouts of the merciless siridogs, who could not hide their glee at the prospect of finally catching a few of the wily frogs, the joy of the hunt quickly causing them to revert from their usual two doglegs to all fours.

Behind the tent they caught some—crunching and growling erupted. Behind the stage, more Croaks went down amid wild barks of joy and rapid gulping of Croak-flesh.

Returning to his spacecraft and inspecting the huge fake testicles attached to one end, Bigtooth sighed a deep sigh of satisfaction, rubbing his tummy. "I've had frog legs—but these are FROG LEGS! Damn tastiest I ever did eat." Bending over, he retrieved a toothpick off the ground and picked freshly killed ribbet from his teeth. "Mmmm. Cinnamon."

Spike walked back on his crooked hind legs. "Big Cigah Bill. Dem Croak transports is landin' all round and most o dem croaks is gettin' 'way." He peered sideways at General Ramey, one eye wide.

Ramey looked up to where large sheets of canvas were ripping from the ceiling and collapsing around them. The tent had become more an open-air stadium with portable bleachers than a covered pavilion. North and south of the Cirque, huge semi-visible transports were dropping soundlessly out of the sky to land on Santa Monica beach, and as access doors plopped open onto sand, masses of ribbets hopped swiftly on board, joined by the mimes whom the Warriors had not yet managed to drench with water, not even baying packs of Dobermans preventing the mimes from occasionally delaying their evacuation by tripping each other amid expressions of hilarity.

From one end of the bleachers, the Warriors watched. Maggie found her eye drawn to a lone figure that seemed to stare forlornly at the ribbet transports as they finished collecting their passengers and finally launch upward into shimmering invisibility, heading back to Bogland.

Standing on the bicycle path to Venice Beach, which was now clearly visible beyond the ruined tents of the Cirque de Lumiére, the forlorn figure adjusted his letter carrier's delivery bag as if unused to its feel. He removed the cap from his head and replaced it—and froze stiff.

Across the Cirque, now nothing more than a pile of collapsed canvas, stood Bigtooth and a dozen siridogs staring fixedly at him. Sheer joy was on their faces—what more could a siridog ask for this side of Heaven? First Croak legs, now a certified uniformed U.S. mail carrier—complete with mailbag stuffed with letters.

The bag hit the ground.

Baying with all their might, the siridogs launched after Xplak, who took a few steps, then promptly abandoned his disguise and with a single prodigious hop landed on Appian Way. Another bound and the ribbet frog banged into a City Wheelchair van, where flat on his back on the ground, he read a sign in the door: 'Texas or Bust'.

The bus door jerkily opened. As the baying behind him grew, indicating a quick arrival of the siridogs, Xplak whipped out a portable communications device and shouted "Elder Smith! Tell the Big Green G: 'You all can all go to hell—I'm going to Texas!'" Tossing his device in a trashcan, Xplak hopped into the bus.

Minutes later, Ray and Bobby with their Sasquatch brides, the Insane Clown Pasta with their doppelganger pokes, Saint Melia of the Holy Order of Inebriated Dance and Intergalactic Flight, and the new convert to non-violence—Xplak the reformed ribbet—were rolling on their way to a certain town in central Texas that was rumored to have an opening for a Saintly Instructor in the Holy Polka.

Before the bus left the Los Angeles city limits, Melia was already teaching Big B and Two U the finer arts of polka dancing, which they promptly supplied with more forceful lyrics, and Clarence and Rodney, in their capacity as captains of the bus, which was finally rolling forward instead of backward, pronounced marriage rites between Ray and Gilda on the one hand, and between Bobby and Aliyah on the other, in exchange for two bottles of Johnnie Walker and a fat stack of Benjamins.

Before the month was out, more rumors had it that Xplak was reunited with his old ribbet comrade Korplash, now spoiled rotten by his new wife, a certain moo-moo-wearing Brunhilda, who was ecstatically happy with her new doppelganger husband and kept both him and his equally entrancing new ribbet pal well-supplied with dunkel-brau and hot dogs, while Korplash and Xplak avoided croaking by taking up country singing, and avoided homesickness for Bogland by frequenting the local water parks. And that a certain pair of Germans of mysterious provenance had returned to the area in retirement with tall tales about how bratwurst and the Holy Polka had saved the Earth from annihilation, with occasional input from a pair of card sharps in Rio who sent regular postcards supplemented by inappropriate Latter-Day Saints Bible quotes.

***

Leaving her Warriors, who were now reunited and busting lips and shins again at the Holy Rollers Derby Club, Maggie skated up the on-ramp to Madam G-Spot's Pollo Ranchero Casino & Bowlarama of Opus Dea for Upper West Los Angeles – Precinct 9, and noticed with surprise that several nuns on ladders were removing 'Madam G-Spot' from the neon sign. As she watched with raised brow, they put 'Madam Maggie P. Squatch' in its place.

At Maggie's ear was her phone with the latest seductive Live Lips broadcast:

"Good news, derbybators. The big alert has been called off. It turns out the early reports were wrong. Now for that group out there that had such a hard time getting home—*sorry about that*. I guess the only thing we can do is play you a song."

Maggie skated into the Casino to the tune of 'Texas Roller Derby Girls' by Boom. Immediately she was surrounded by the establishment's staff of nuns in both the fully clothed and skimpily covered variety. Passing her gaze over the Casino's interior, she noted that both bowling and polka dancing were being properly administered by the nuns, and that a steady stream of new human clients continued to enter.

But there was something awry. The nuns looked at each other with worry and Maggie realized the problem—there were no more cross-dressers emerging from the Pollo Ranchero's Back-to-Nature-Wigwam.

The nuns pointed to the back.

Maggie accompanied them.

In the Bowlarama's private apartments, her escorts paused before a certain door. The sign above said 'Nun Much'. Below the sign was the sacred doorknob that would release its lock only to those with special bones in their wrist—bones that tibbets possessed but that Earthling nuns and cross-dressers lacked. Now that Madam G-Spot was gone, none of the nuns at Pollo Ranchero could enter. Their supply of purple mannequins for their Back-To-Nature-Wigwam had run out.

They stared at Maggie. They said nothing, but she perceived that their hearts were in their throats.

Grasping the knob, she paused. For a moment, she stood and thought about the consequences. If she turned the knob, the Pollo Ranchero would be back in business and the nuns would resume their substituting of robot mannequins from Pluto for body-snatched humans and restart their assembly line of politically correct, brainwashed Cross-Dressers from Pluto, and—far from merely opposing the ribbets' plan for global warming using an army of josephs converted to evil mimes by Gork's injections—the tibbets' own Plan for the exact opposite would resume, reducing global ocean levels by global *cooling* and by eliminating water entirely from the world as far as possible, the mannequins being their equivalent version of Gork's injections.

With a shrug, Maggie turned the knob and opened the door. "No sinful water will ever touch *these* little piggy toes. I like global cooling. I'm always over-heated anyway."

Joyfully, the nuns rushed to escort to the Wigwam the latest winners of the Ranchero's Special Reward to the best polka dancers and bowlers, leaving Maggie to loiter in the supply room. Her attention was soon drawn past the mechanical contrivance—the function of which seemed to be to set up white bowling pins, but strangely was never used for that purpose—to a plasma TV screen at the back. Even as she watched, it flicked on, apparently auto-alerted to her presence.

A round patch flickered in the center, gathered color, and after half a minute finally coalesced into a familiar face. More than familiar. . .

"My leetle dung beetle! You have finally accompleeshed what I had in mind for you from thee veery beginning. How happy I am to see your beautiful beautiful face once more."

Jaw slack, Maggie stood and stared. Finally she spoke: "Mmmomma Maxie. Mmmomma Maxie Climax." Maggie lay a calming hand on her pounding hearts. Both of them.

"Yes, my sweet leetle Magdalene. I am not dead after all, as you see. The nuns found and rescued me and I was brought back to Pluto where they put me back together again. Just so I could keep helping my lovely leetle Maggie. Leesten well, my dung beetle. I knew you could stop that Gork and his mimes because of your *specialness*. Your radiation capsule gave you special powers: you will age only slowly compared to Earthlings. Now you must use your powers to help us tibbets reverse the evil ribbets' global warming projects on other planets throughout the galaxy. You have powers we tibbets do not have. The ribbets cannot defeat you."

A knock on the door sounded behind Maggie.

She turned and saw Professor Richard Pierson standing in the doorway alongside someone who also looked strangely familiar. In another moment, she exclaimed, "Sonny!"

"Yes," said Richard. "This is my Uncle Sonny. Better known as Howard Hughes."

"The silver suit. That old beat-up Ford truck. The radiation capsule." Maggie looked Hughes up and down in more surprise. "But you—you must be over 100 years old!"

Uncle Sonny smiled. "Surely you don't think that the radiation-curing capsule in which I put you in 1951 was my *only capsule*?"

Richard chuckled. "Uncle Sonny kept a second capsule on Mount Stirling. He went in immediately after you. And he just came out." Then Richard turned serious. "But we're here on business, Maggie." Looking behind her to the plasma screen, Richard exchanged nods with Maxie Climax. "There are evil mimes everywhere, Maggie, including reports of frenchified floppy caps and saddle shoes on Planet Flux. Like Maxie Climax said, we desperately need your help to stop the ribbet invasion of planets throughout the galaxy. Will you help us?"

Still and thoughtful, Maggie stood in silence. At length she took out some preserved nopalitos and took a bite, then chased it with a slug of red Thunderbird Wine.

"Not today. I'm going to the Bowlarama weight room to flirt with big titty women."

***

"Fuck this," muttered Edie staring into a compact mirror, trying to remove the greasepaint from her face. Losing hope, she tossed the mirror and towel aside. "Oh well. In fact, I kind of like it." Edie turned and again enjoyed the panoramic view offered from Stirling Peak and 'her' eyes settled on the steel-grey capsule that lay horizontal before her. Smiling at the secrets that only a former Director of the Fuck in the Backside Institute could know, she nodded.

With some effort, Edie climbed over the edge and jostled her jelly-like body inside. "I'm sure the future will be a better place than here and now for cross-dressing mimes." Edie grinned evilly. "Especially fifty-foot ones." Pocketing a shiny device that she had picked up from underneath tent canvas, the former Ya Egger Hooper closed her eyes and took a deep breath, enjoying her last few moments in early 21st century California.

She closed the panel—paused as its edge caught on something. Opening it wide, she again attempted to shut the panel. This time it closed. On the outside of the capsule, dials and lights flashed, and finally settled as Edie passed into a deep sleep. Just before slipping into the abyss of nothingness, she thought she glimpsed a pair of mechanical eyes staring up from her feet, also inside the capsule. But that was clearly impossible. Then she was gone.

"Haa-haa-haaaa," came a whisper.

***

Meanwhile, uncountable light years away on the other side of the galaxy, the Big-a Big-a Big-a Boss Elder Joseph Smith of the 333rd Degree shuffled into the office of the Biggest Boss of all—the Great Green G.

Briefly, Smith fumbled his fingers. Finally he spat out,

"I have something to report, Great Gork . . ." He fumbled again. "It appears that Xplak has gone AWOL—just like Korplash."

The big green toad Gork paused from his studying of vast swaths of galactic geography in his 3D visual edition of the Encyclopedia Toadica and swiveled his chameleon eye-stalks toward his first failed experiment—Joseph Smith, who had 'volunteered' from a place called Nauvoo, Illinois, in 1844, after glancing at a picture of Whistler's Mother.

"And what about our Chief Mime 'Purple Lips'—that is, Judge Joseph Crater—whom Korplash and Xplak snatched from 44th Street in that place the Drylanders call New York City, on August 4th, 1930? Joseph Crater, whose love affair with Amelia Earhart here on Bogland produced their child Maggie? Did Crater survive the debacle on planet Dryland?"

Smith nodded. "Yes, Great Gork. But his condition is . . . as irreversible as mine."

"This fellow Crater seems to have had as much bad luck with the number 44 as you. What have we done for him?"

"As reward for his services, I have given him a job as a judge in one of Bogland's more crowded districts—and a new family. Just to make sure he does not become lonely on Bogland."

"Good thinking, Smith. I approve. We will return to Earth in time and here are some books you can distribute to prepare our way." Gork pointed to several works on a bookshelf: *Road To Serfdom, Atlas Shrugged, The Creature From Jekyll Island, The Bell Curve, The White Nationalist Manifesto, The Death of the West*, and of course.

. . *Mein Kampf*. "Now I am done with the matter. I have other projects that require my attention." With that, Gork turned back to his Toadica projection that mapped future galactic invasions, while Joseph Smith waddled out of the room, his arms full of books.

Not far away, a squat bulbous frog flopped its huge webbed feet tiredly inside a building with a wide low entrance. Ignoring the happy croaking, crunching, and buzzing by other ribbets in the Bar, he waddled to a low empty table inside a long shallow pool and waved to the help.

A young ribbet waddle to his side and paused, pencil in hand.

"Bowl of jacks and green goo."

"Welcome back, Judge Crater." The ribbet waddled away and soon returned with a tall glass of green liquid and a bucket of insects. Crater handed the young server some metal bits.

"Straw!"

The server halted in mid hop, threw down a straw, then leaped away before Crater could demand more service.

Attempting to put his chin in the palm of one floppy webbed hand, he again failed since frogs don't have chins, and let loose another depressed sigh. Wistfully he stared at the many attractive young ribbets splashing with each other around him and wondered if any were named Sally. Selecting a wingless dragonfly, he opened his wide toothless mouth . . .

"J-O-S-E-P-H! JO-*SEPH? JO*-SEPH!"

Dropping the insect, Joseph Crater looked up in terror. "Bond-ribbet find Crater!" With a prodigious hop, he bounded to the door.

Seconds passed.

Crater reappeared, backing up before a huge green ribbet twice his size, pink curlers on its head and a rolling pin raised threateningly in one giant webbed hand. "Have you been splashing and drinking green goo? Tell the truth now or you know what will happen."

"No, my sweet lily pad. I swear it!"

The rolling pin struck Crater's head a glancing blow.

"Joseph LIE!" The giant ribbet's other hand grabbed Crater by one vestigial ear. "Joseph no drink green goo! No eat jacks! No splash with other ribbets! Joseph come home now. Joseph's four hundred and thirty-seven little ones need changing and putting to bed."

A sigh answered. "Yes, my warty lotus." Judge Joseph Force Crater, former New York Supreme Court Justice and undercover operative for the Federal Bureau of Investigation, dragged his floppy feet out the door, and to the accompaniment of a chorus of tiny croaks, dwindled in the distance.

ADVENTURES OF MAGGIE,

THE RADIATED LESBIAN NUN

END?

If you enjoyed THE WARRIORS, please post a review on your favorite website:

www.amazon.com
www.authorsden.com
www.siriusreviews.com
www.goodreads.com

And consider becoming a supporter at:

www.subscribestar.com/books-for-men

Also sign up for the free newsletters at:

www.EquusPublishing.com

Other titles by
Glenn Lazar Roberts

FICTION:

Maalstrom
The Selk King
Frenzy
Quantum Marlowe
Judge Crater Takes A Powder
Cross-Dressers From Pluto
The Warriors
The Glow
Jihad Bubba

FACTION:

Sharia Law & The Arab Oil Bust
Islamic Human Rights & International Law
Commissar & Mullah:
Soviet-Muslim Policy From 1917-1924
SJWs and the PC Cult

Translation Error.

Dr. Glenn Lazar Roberts is an attorney and writer of sci-fi, horror, satire, and adventure fantasy novels. Glenn has taught college, professionally translated Arabic and Russian, hosts a writing critique circle, and has edited the work of many aspiring writers. He credits an eclectic group of famous authors for inspiring him to write, including Jack Vance, Robert E. Howard, Edgar Rice Burroughs, Mervyn Peake, H.P. Lovecraft, Arthur C. Clarke, and H.G. Wells, among many other Masters of the Art. "I love language. I am perpetually afloat on a sea of script."

www.ingramcontent.com/pod-product-compliance
Lightning Source LLC
Chambersburg PA
CBHW070111120726
47909CB00002B/563

* 9 7 8 0 9 6 7 5 8 0 9 7 5 *